I0565806

The Emancipation of Emily Rosenbloom

a novel by Elinor Gale

BLUE LIGHT PRESS ◆ 1ST WORLD PUBLISHING

SAN FRANCISCO ◆ FAIRFIELD ◆ DELHI

The Emancipation of Emily Rosenbloom

Copyright ©2019 by Elinor Gale

1st World Library
PO Box 2211
Fairfield, IA 52556
www.1stworldpublishing.com

Blue Light Press
www.bluelightpress.com
bluelightpress@aol.com

Book & Cover Art & Design
Melanie Gendron
melaniegendron999@gmail.com

Author Photo
Mark Reverdy

First Edition

Library of Congress Control Number: 2019948130

ISBN: 9781421836386

For Helen and Kent,
my cheering squad,
with love and thanks

The Emancipation of
Emily Rosenbloom

CHAPTER 1

—

EARLY SIGNS

On WBCN in Boston this morning, the Cosmic Muffin announced that Mercury is in retrograde, which means it appears to be moving backwards, messing up communication and clear thinking. I wish I believed in astrology or had at least paid attention to the warning.

My colleague, Shelley, and I have just arrived at the annual company holiday party at the Cambridge Hyatt. We're wearing our smart, black wool dresses and are on a mission to find me a man. I've even had my hair done in an attempt to tame my wayward curls and cowlicks. I'm in my mid 50s, claiming to be 5'4" and weight proportionate, a bit of a stretch, but I still look good enough, I think, despite my aging body and wardrobe.

I've been going part-time to graduate school and have just a couple of courses left. I've also been looking for a position in my new field, workplace adult education, while I continue the marketing job I've had forever. You'd think that would be enough to keep me busy, but I also want love in my life. It's been a while, so I've enlisted Shelley's help in the manhunt. She's a tall, attractive, optimistic woman who still turns heads with her dark, shoulder-length hair, graceful body, and mischievous grin, although she's been happily married for 23 years. She's savvy about relationships and must know something I don't. I've been divorced and single for a decade and a half, raising my boys alone and bumbling in and out of disappointing entanglements with unsuitable men.

The large ballroom is noisy and crowded. In one corner, a geriatric band, whose drummer appears to be dozing, plays "Fly Me to the Moon" at a volume that possibly reaches the moon. In the center of the ballroom, red and green lights on a tall Christmas tree blink on and off, the corporate version of strobe lighting.

Shelley and I navigate to the bar, where other suits and smart, black dresses stand three-deep, waiting to order drinks. Eventually, we get our Chardonnay and work our way to a relatively unpopulated spot away from the bar.

We begin to scan the merrymakers. Almost immediately I notice a tall, rakish looking man in a navy pinstriped suit who stands in a group to my right. "What about him?"

"Him?" Shelley looks in the direction of my nod. "That's Chet Peterson. He's a womanizer, married at least three times and still plays around. Forget him." She looks away, searching for better prospects.

I glance one last time in Chet's direction. Too bad, Chet. It could have been fun.

"That guy, that guy over there," Shelley nudges me. "You can tell he's a good guy. He has kind eyes. You can tell a lot by the eyes."

"Him? He looks like my cousin, Eli, the Orthodox rabbi," I reply dismissively, "definitely not my type."

"Forget the beard. Look at the eyes. He's looking this way. Smile."

She's right. Big, soulful, brown eyes are looking our way. Dutifully, I smile my flirtiest, attempting to ignore the black, bushy beard that shrouds everything but the eyes. I remember my father's admonition, "Never trust a man with a beard. He's hiding something." But my father wasn't astute about men either. He had liked and trusted my ex-husband.

Encouraged by our smiles, the rabbi is crossing the room in our direction. He's about 5'8", slim, and walks like a duck. Dressed in preppy navy blazer and gray slacks, he looks like an Ivy League-rabbi-duck. Not that I'm judgmental.

"Hello, I'm Will Slipway," he says extending his hand first to Shelley and then to me. "I couldn't resist your warm smiles."

"It's nice to meet you," Shelley says. "I'm Shelley Sullivan and this is my friend Emily Rosenbloom. We're in the wooden toy marketing department. I don't think I've seen you before. Where do you work?"

"I'm in research and development, up on the hill."

We continue to chat awkwardly for a minute or two, and I am about to back away when Will says, "Would you like to dance?"

He's looking at me.

"Who, me?"

"Yes, you."

"Okay, I guess. I'm a little rusty."

"That's okay. I am, too. Shelley, if you'll excuse us? It was so nice to meet you."

As Will leads me to the dance floor, I thaw slightly. How thoughtful of him to acknowledge Shelley that way.

We're clumsy together at first and his hand is damp. "Oops, sorry," he says as our toes bump.

"That's okay," I reply, stifling an ouch. "I don't know about you, but I haven't danced for a long time. I guess it takes a while to get back in the groove."

He squeezes my hand gratefully and we both relax, enjoying a few more dances until the band takes a break. We find an empty table away from the dance floor. Will brings drinks from the bar and we talk, exchanging information about our work, our kids, and interests.

I've decided that with a trimmed beard, he might be attractive and am just warming to the idea when he asks, "How long have you been divorced?"

"Almost 14 years."

"Really? I'm surprised you haven't remarried."

"I was busy raising my sons," I hesitate, "and never found the right guy, I guess. How about you?"

"How about me?"

"Yes, how long have you been divorced?"

He hesitates, pushes the melting ice cubes around in his glass and replies, "I'm not exactly divorced."

Somewhere just below the belt, I feel a thump and let out a deep sigh. "You're not divorced. You're married. You live with your wife?"

"Sort of."

Oh, geez. "Sort of?"

"I live in the same house but mostly in the basement."

"Finished basement, I hope?" I cannot resist.

Ignoring my wisecrack, he looks doleful as he elaborates, "My wife and I married when we were kids. We've been married for 26 years but haven't really lived together, I mean slept together, for the last six years. I'm just staying until my kids finish high school."

I look away. "That's different, then. I thought you were single. I'm not interested in getting involved with a married man."

"Who said anything about getting involved?" he asks indignantly. "I thought we were just having a nice evening, enjoying each other's company. I didn't intend anything more than that."

Am I turning purple with embarrassment? How presumptuous of me!

"Oh, I'm so sorry. I just assumed... I assumed the wrong thing. I am sorry and I've enjoyed this, too. I think I should go now."

"No, no need to hurry off."

"I think it's best. Besides, tomorrow is a workday. Up and at 'em." I fumble with my coat and purse.

He takes my coat and holds it as I slide it on, saying over my shoulder, "It's been a pleasure, and remember, I don't live too far from you, so if you ever need a ride to work or anything like that, I'm happy to help."

"Yes, thanks." I'm anxious to get out of there, and I leave him at the table without looking back.

Me and my assumptions, making an ass of me again.

The next day, a large bouquet of red, gold, and orange winter blooms arrives at my desk. The card reads, "Thanks for the wonderful evening. Will."

Who's the ass? Who sends flowers to acknowledge a "nice conversation and a few dances?" I'm tempted to dump the flowers into the wastebasket but take them instead to the receptionist's desk. "These will look better out here," I say as I place them on the counter.

"Really? Are you sure?"

"Very sure," I say as I walk back to my cubicle.

CHAPTER 2

—

WHERE THERE'S A WILL, HE HAS A WAY

D o I thank him for the flowers or tell him off? Why would I want any contact with him at all? I should dig deeper into that question. Instead, I decide to send him an email, acknowledging the flowers and telling him off. An email will be easier than a phone call. I'm much more adept at blasting people in writing than nose to nose—not enough breathing space.

Will,
I received the flowers this morning. And, while they are beautiful, I do not appreciate your sending them. They suggest more than just a pleasant evening's encounter.
Thank you.
Emily

When I return from lunch in the cafeteria, I check my message box and find one slip of paper.

A Will Slipway called and left his ext. number: 2376. Is he the guy who sent the flowers? —Carol

Fine. The receptionist has probably told the whole office about the flowers. I should have dumped them in the basket. That will teach me to share. I do not return Will's call and am relieved when I finish my day's work without hearing from him. I hope that's the end of this brief misadventure.

The next morning, I have one arm out of my coat when my desk phone rings.

"Hello, Emily Rosenbloom, Wooden Toy Marketing. How can I help you?"

I hear a chuckle. "You can help me by not always taking things the wrong way," a tenor voice says. It's Slipway. I put down the phone, take off my coat, and hang it on the peg near my desk.

"Hello? Are you still there?"

I pick up the phone and reply, "Yes, I'm here. As I said in my email, the flowers were nice, but they send the wrong message."

"Were nice?"

"Are nice… but they're no longer on my desk. I put them in the reception area."

"You really misunderstand me. I just wanted to thank you for an enjoyable evening. That's all."

This time I'm not falling back on the defensive so easily. "If that's all you intended, thank you. I appreciate the gesture and hope you have a good day." I hang up the phone and wait to see if it rings again. Quiet. I sigh. Why can't I get flowers from a nice, available, single guy? Where are they? Have they all gone back to their mothers?

I walk across the hall to Shelley's cubicle and knock on her wall. "Shelley, have you got a minute?"

Shelley looks up from the papers on her desk. "For you, of course. Besides, I can't make heads or tails of Michaela's edits on this ad. Do you think she knows what she's doing?" She motions for me to come closer. "Honestly, I don't think the woman can breathe and think at the same time."

"You're talking about our esteemed new manager," I say. "I don't want to talk about that jerk. I want to talk about another jerk."

"Uh oh, you have that look."

"What look?"

"The 'I've got to find someone to blame' look."

"Bingo! You know the guy with the kind eyes, our friend, Will Slipway, the one I favored with my charms at your recommendation?"

"The one who sent you the gorgeous bouquet of mums?"

"Yes, that one, the one who's married!"

"Married? Mr. Good-Guy is married? Who says so?"

"He says so."

"Must be so, but at least he told you," she says, trying to repolish his tarnished image.

"Reluctantly," I counter, "and then after insisting the evening was an innocent nothing, he sends flowers!"

"He does have old-world manners."

"Hmph!"

"Sorry."

"Not your fault," I concede.

"Now she tells me," Shelley smiles. "Listen, Steve's got a Lions Club meeting tonight. Do you want to go for a drink after work and really dish this guy?"

"Sure, why not?" I return to my cubicle, grateful for my friend, despite her bad judgment in men.

•••

Slipway seems to have burrowed underground. The phone sits silent except for occasional calls from a client or my mother, who's growing increasingly lonely since my father's death six months earlier. It doesn't help that at 88, she has either outlived her friends in Florida or has watched them move away to be nearer to their children. Recently, she's begun hinting about moving back north or a much less attractive alternative.

"Mum, you'd hate the weather. Remember the winter storms— the ice and freezing temperatures?"

"I know. I know," she pauses.

I wait.

"Have you ever thought about moving here?" she asks.

The truth is I did think about moving to West Palm Beach to be near my parents when my kids were young and I was raising them on my own. It was tempting, but that was years ago.

"Not really. My life is here. I have my friends, my job… my network."

"Your what?"

"Network, Mum, all the people who support me emotionally."

"I can do that," she humphs.

"That shouldn't be your job at this point," I protest.

"We'll see," she says ominously.

When we hang up, I vow to be in a meeting the next time she calls. That won't be a problem since Michaela, the manager who learned her management skills from Dilbert, summons us to brainstorming meetings at the drop of a hat. Typically, we sit around a mahogany table in an overheated conference room, waiting for Michaela, who is predictably late. Finally, she flings open the door and totters in on stiletto heels, grabbing a marker, sniffing it, and wrinkling her nose. In her early 40s, Michaela is a bottle-ash-blonde MBA who dresses like an expensive bimbo. Her designer knits cling too lovingly to her plentiful curves. She's top-heavy, always threatening to fall over. I watch her warily.

When she reaches the white board, we spring to attention, trying to follow her as she flits from one topic to another like a skittish butterfly, unable to light on a single flower. She talks, expands, and explores her ideas, rarely letting any of us utter a complete sentence. Then, just as quickly as she has begun her brain dump, she ends it midflight, saying in a breathy soprano, "Whoops, gotta go. I'm late for another meeting!"

She leaves us shaking our heads. What was decided? What are we supposed to do? We anxiously try to decode Michaela's ramblings, desperate to figure out what she wants because her slap-dash assignments of flyers, emails, and other marketing material often include urgent deadlines. We do the best we can, cornering Michaela to ask clarifying questions and putting in extra hours to deliver our assignments on time.

Frequently, as vital papers mount in piles on her desk, long enough for spiders to weave cobwebs around them, we realize the deadlines are urgent only to Michaela, who has the impulse control of a two-year-old.

I sigh, lamenting my incompetent manager on a late February afternoon when the sky is already dark and the chill of winter seeps through the industrial-strength windows. When the phone rings, I welcome the cheerful sound, interrupting the gloom.

"Emily Rosenbloom, Wooden Toy Marketing."

The chuckle. It's Slipway. "How nice to hear your voice on this winter afternoon."

"Hello."

"Do you know who this is?"

"I know it's you, Will. What can I do for you?" I attempt a professional approach.

"And how are you?" he asks, implying I have forgotten the amenities.

"Fine, thanks. And you?" My tone chills the air.

"I'm going to be in your building tomorrow morning and wondered if you'd like to get a cup of coffee?"

"The coffee's terrible here," I say.

"The coffee's irrelevant," he replies.

"Then why bother?"

"Wow. Can we start again? Emily, would you like to join me for a cup of coffee, tea, glass of juice, or any other beverage of your choice tomorrow morning around 11?"

I giggle, despite my resolve. "I suppose a cup of tea wouldn't kill me, although I don't see the point."

"I just wanted to say hello…and since I'm going to be in your building, what better time? So can we agree to meet in the café at 11 tomorrow morning for a pointless cup of coffee or tea?"

"No hidden agenda?"

"Are you always this cautious?"

"Only when there's good reason. I'll see you tomorrow. Bye."

What will I wear? Does it matter? I chastise myself. He's married—unavailable. I decide on my long-sleeve, silky red blouse and black wool skirt, the one that shows off my legs. Might as well look nice. No point in being a frump. I think about telling Shelley about the coffee date but decide against it. It's no big deal and certainly doesn't require a consultation.

As though I've rubbed on a magic bottle summoning a genie, the adenoidal voice of Dr. Rothman, my former therapist, glides over my shoulder. What the hell? This has happened once before. I hear his voice and feel his presence as if he's in the room. Help!

"So, Emily, what do you have in mind?"

"Nothing," I snap. "Can't a girl have a cup of coffee?"

"The coffee's terrible, you said."

"A cup of tea then. Must you be so literal?"

"This isn't about me, is it?"

"I don't need your advice. I'm just getting an innocent cup of tea with an acquaintance."

"Innocent? Interesting word choice."

"For heaven's sakes!" I say. "I didn't mean anything by that. Don't put words in my mouth."

"I didn't."

"Go away, you chubby busybody!" Did I say that aloud? I sit at my desk, shaking my head. Great, the phantom of my former therapist is messing with me!

CHAPTER 3

—

RED FLAGS FLAPPING

Dressed in the red silk blouse that drapes my middle-aged body in a flattering flow over my black wool skirt, I take the elevator down to the café at 10:45, determined to arrive before Slipway. At this hour, the café is nearly empty and quiet, permeated only by the aroma of burnt coffee and stale coffee grounds.

He is already seated at a corner table, wearing a sly grin—or is it sheepish? It's hard to tell with his mouth still wreathed by beard. But, wait! The bush has been trimmed to half its original breadth and length, a definite improvement. I notice he's wearing a smart-looking blue and gray tweed sports coat with gray slacks. Not bad. He dressed for the occasion, too.

He rises to greet me, bumping into the table as he extends his hand, which is slightly clammy.

"Great to see you. You look terrific!"

"Thanks. I like your new look."

"New look?"

"The tamed lion's mane."

He chuckles, "Part of my spring wardrobe."

"Out of hibernation?" Why do I think of this as jousting?

"What distasteful beverage would you like?" he asks, gesturing toward the café counter.

"Not the coffee. That's for sure. I'll have a cup of Earl Grey tea, please."

"Caffeinated or not?"

He's been well trained. I must find out more about his marriage. "Caffeinated. I can use the caffeine."

He carries our cups to the table, his left hand shaking slightly. Nerves? Alcohol withdrawal? One can never be too suspicious.

"So, what kind of meeting brought you down the hill today?"

He sighs, "A budget-planning session for the next quarter. Not one of my passions."

"What are your passions?"

He looks at me quizzically. "Is that a trick question?"

"Why would you think that?" I ask, feigning innocence.

"Something in your tone."

Now it's my turn to chuckle. "You're probably right. Let's talk about something else. Tell me about your work."

"That's one of my passions," he grins.

"Really?"

"Yes, I love what I do. I'm a model maker. I get to build the prototypes for the toys the engineers design. It's like building really complex, intricate airplane models. I even get to sniff glue—just kidding."

His boyish enthusiasm is disarming.

"That does sound like fun. Play at work!"

"Right, exactly."

"How long have you been playing here?"

"Almost 23 years, since I got my degree. If you're trying to do the math, I'm not that young. I served in the Navy for four years after high school."

College degree, 23 years on the job. The guy has a brain and is steady, too. Good signs.

"Now, what about you?" he asks, leaning toward me. His hand isn't shaking now.

"I don't love my work. I write marketing copy, maybe for some of your toys. At this point, it's just a stopgap. I'm still in graduate school and want a job in adult education, teaching reading and writing to adults. It won't pay that well, but it's satisfying. I also like to write fiction when I have time."

"Sounds like an interesting combination."

"Yes," I agree, suddenly feeling self-conscious.

"So, Emily, do you have a steady beau?"

Steady beau? How quaint, I think. "A what?"

"A boyfriend? Do you have one?"

"Why are you asking that?"

"You're so beautiful." His tone is almost reverent.

I lurch backward in my chair, which screeches in protest. "Is this why you wanted to see me?"

"I haven't been able to stop thinking about you," he stumbles over the words. "I had to see you again."

"That's flattering, but it was a mistake."

I pull my protesting chair away from the table, grab my bag and turn toward the door.

"Hey, wait!"

"Wait? Are you still married? Are you still living at home? Are you free to say such things to me?"

He is silent.

"I thought not. I told you before I do not want to get involved with a married man. Been there. Done that. Not what I'm looking for. Look, you're a nice guy, I'm sure. You mean well, but please don't call me again!"

Not waiting for a response, I huff across the café and out the door, mumbling under my breath, "Wait? Wait? You wait, you two-timing Romeo!"

I hear Dr. Rothman asking, "Well, Bambi, what did you expect?"

CHAPTER 4
—
TIMING IS EVERYTHING

It would be easy to forget Slipway if I could bury myself in work, but my work has gone the way of the dodo bird and the three-dollar bill! As the principal writer in my marketing group, I should be too busy to take bathroom breaks, but I suspect I could take that break, a spa treatment, and complete makeover, and not fall behind.

Reluctantly I approach Michaela, my manager, and peek into her office.

"Hello, Michaela, can we talk for a moment?"

She looks at her watch. "Okay, but I've got a meeting at 10 so I can't give you much time."

I sit on the chair in front of her desk before she can change her mind. Have you noticed that managers sit behind desks, facing the door, so no one can surprise them, while we peons are forced to sit in cubicles facing the wall, our back to the entrance, so anyone can carry out a stealth attack?

Teetering stacks of papers hide Michaela from view. It looks like she's building card towers, trying to keep the piles erect, until finally, one false move topples the entire structure. Just a breath would do it, I muse.

"I can see you're busy, so I'll make this quick. The problem is that I don't have enough work. I know we've spoken about this before, but I'm still not seeing projects come my way, so I thought I'd mention it again."

I wait for her response, wanting to bellow that my brain is dying of oxygen deprivation, waiting for work in my shoddy, little cubicle.

Michaela peers at me from above her black, sequined drugstore glasses.

"Stuff is coming. It's just a matter of time. I'm pretty sure you'll look back at this period and not believe that it was ever so quiet. I promise you'll be busy soon. Meanwhile, maybe you should take advantage of the downtime and do whatever. Just enjoy the lull."

"Enjoy the lull?"

"Yes, that's what I said. I've got to go to a meeting in five minutes. Bye."

Is this code? What's she telling me?

I sit in my cubicle, trying to read *The Curious Incident of the Dog in the Night*, but I can't concentrate. I can hear Liddy's shrill voice penetrating the cubicle walls as she explains to Jeanne that she hasn't posted a photo on E-Harmony because she doesn't want to be chosen for her looks. No danger there, I think. I can hear Franny laughing at the joke Ernie's telling her and Conrad mumbling endearments to a young woman he met in a strip club in the North End. This isn't working, I think, picking up my novel and taking myself to the nearest empty conference room, where I sit in a corner with my book, trying to ignore my bizarre circumstances and enjoy the story.

Not yet totally immersed in the novel, I notice Michaela's manager walk by and look into the conference room. I don't think too much about it. After all, I could be doing research for a project, right?

Six and a half minutes later, Michaela's reddened face appears in the doorway. "Emily, can I see you in my office… now!"

Oops.

She slams the door shut and turns on me. "What were you thinking? Sitting in a conference room reading a book?" Her voice shakes. "Randall saw you and came storming into my office to complain! Emily, I thought you were more mature than this," she scolds, leaning toward me, boobs first, as always.

"But you know I have no work!"

"I don't care. You can't sit in a conference room, reading a book."

"But…"

"Listen, I don't want to talk about it any more. Just stay out of trouble, okay?"

"Okay."

Oh brother! Stay out of trouble. More code words. I attend to my email, mostly personal, shop online, read theater and book reviews, do homework for my feng shui class, edit interviews for my freelance work, and browse job postings. I fantasize about dancing a sultry tango on the roof of the building with Clive Owen, who can't keep his hands off me. "Clive, please, the dance!" I try to ignore my nagging feeling of worthlessness. When I weary of my cubicle, I sneak into conference rooms on the floor below mine to call friends on my cellphone. "Hello, Katie, I'm calling you from jail."

With so much time on my hands, I begin taking walks around the perimeter of the campus, driving to the Lakewood Shopping Center or walking over to Starbucks for an iced coffee. I bring a pillow to work, which I keep in my car for afternoon naps. I begin with 20-minute power naps and gradually work up to 40 minutes, discovering I can set my internal clock and rely on it to awaken me at the appointed time. But still I'm tired of having nothing to do. This management-induced "lull" threatens to render me comatose—a 21st century Ripella Van Winkle.

The minute I hear the first whisper of layoffs, restructuring, and downsizing, I begin chanting my mantra. "*Lay* me off, lay *me* off, *lay me off!* Morning, noon, and night if you listen closely, you can hear me chanting. And if you look closely, you might notice articles disappearing from my cubicle shelves and drawers as I begin a stealth packing campaign just in case.

I bring two cardboard boxes into my cubicle, stuffing them under my desk behind my feet, and begin quietly, surreptitiously dropping in a photo of my sons, a placard honoring five years of perfect attendance, job search files, pens and push pins, careful always not to bury anything I might need in my almost negligible work. These boxes became my "just-in-case" containers—"*Lay* me off, lay *me* off, lay me *off*."

I breathe deeply, paying attention to each breath just to calm down.

Don't hope for too much, but be prepared, I tell myself.

When the first wave of layoffs hits the shore, my department is left intact. Since my colleagues are relieved, I keep my disappointment to myself. I resign myself to spending 7.5 hours, five days a week, rubbing water bottles, wishing for a genie to scoop me up and away on his magic carpet. By the end of each week, I feel so weary and drained I can barely stay awake on my 20-minute drive home. Some Saturdays, I struggle to get out of bed. On a gray, rainy Saturday morning in June, the phone rings me awake, and I answer mid-yawn.

"Emily, it's Will. My wife has just said she wants a divorce. Will you go clothes shopping with me?"

"Will I what?" This man is crazy.

"Go clothes shopping with me. Andrea said she wants a divorce and I'm working to oblige her as fast as I can. I feel like celebrating and I need new clothes."

Why would I want to help this strange man buy clothes just because his wife has finally cried uncle or seen the error of his ways? Who could live with him? I'm about to refuse but, instead, hear myself saying, "I'll go with you on one condition."

"Great! What's that?"

"It has to be during the week, on a workday, preferably not during lunch."

I hear silence, a cough, and then, "That's not easy for me, but if those are your terms, so be it."

"Those are my terms."

"I'm sure you have a reason."

"I do."

"Okay, how about next Friday at 2?"

"I'll meet you in the lobby of my building." I hang up the phone and roll over. If I'm lucky, I may be able to get back to sleep. I wait for drowsiness to overcome me. Instead of my gentle snoring, I hear Dr. Rothman's voice, his nasal tones infiltrating my weary brain.

"What are you thinking?"

"What's the problem?"

"You know this guy has a screw loose. Why would you want to encourage him?"

"Screw loose—is that your professional diagnosis?"

"Wait a second! This is your unconscious speaking, not mine."

"Maybe he's just an impulsive romantic or just a little quirky! What's so bad about that?"

"Romantic—who knows? Impulsive—for sure. He's still married. Just because his wife said she wants a divorce doesn't make it a done deal. Their relationship isn't over yet. Come on, Bambi, you know better."

CHAPTER 5

—

MIXED BAG AT BLOOMINGDALE'S

In the men's department of Bloomingdale's, Slipway tries on at least 20 pairs of slacks, 30 long-and short-sleeved shirts, 40 sweaters, and 50 neckties, I swear, while I make appropriate noises of approval or revulsion. After 40 minutes of playing the surrogate wife, I begin to shift restlessly from one foot to the other, finally excusing myself for a trip to the ladies room. I'm not a shopper, and I'm uncomfortable in the wifey role. Mercifully, by the time I make my way back the half-mile from the bathroom, Slipway has made his purchases and seems satisfied: two pairs of summer slacks, gray and tan, a navy cotton crewneck sweater, and a couple of Tattersall sports shirts, very preppy.

Relieved the expedition has ended, I lead the way to the escalator. Midway between floors, I hear his voice behind me. "Let's stop in the women's department before we leave."

Great, now he wants to pick something up for his wife. I whip around to face him, expecting to see Dr. Rothman grinning like a Cheshire cat over his shoulder. "Why do you want to stop in the women's department?"

"You'll see."

Curious, I get off the escalator and find myself in the midst of Halston, Calvin Klein, Anne Klein, and Diane von Furstenberg, heady company. I'm about to suggest we take the A train out of this neighborhood when I spot a divine, teal cashmere jacket draped over the shoulders of a wire mannequin. I move closer to caress the lush wool and sigh.

"Like it?"

"It's gorgeous!"

"Try it on."

"What?"

"I'll buy it for you."

I swear I hear Dr. Rothman gagging, but I'm tempted. "That's terribly generous of you, but my mother told me never to take candy from strangers."

"Oops."

"I think we should go now."

As I grip the escalator again, I suddenly remember the last time I was in Bloomingdale's.

Twenty-four years ago in Manhattan, pregnant with Gabe, I am riding up the escalator, in the queasy first trimester of my pregnancy, sensitive to tastes, odors, and dizzying heights. It's winter and I'm wearing a heavy wool coat, perfect for the 20 degrees on Manhattan streets, but overdressed for this too-warm department store. I can feel sweat trickling down my back but don't remove my coat. That would mean loosening my hand from its death-like grasp on the escalator railing. I once stumbled a third of the way down an escalator in the Port Authority building before a kind stranger grabbed me from behind, so I'm hyper-cautious on these moving stairs.

I look down at the black-and-white checked floor and the glitzy jewelry displays. I hear the din of shoppers moving along the aisles below, misted by a noxious potpourri of Chanel No.5, Shalimar, and Charlie. Rising above Lexington Avenue, I become dizzy, nauseous, and stumble off the moving stairs and hurtle into the ladies room. Minutes later, I leave the store without making a single purchase.

Now, this suburban Bloomingdale's is more sedate and I am not pregnant, but it's still too rich for my taste and wallet.

"Can I at least buy you a meal?" Slipway asks as he backs out of the parking space, interrupted by the frantic honk of a car horn. He is not a good driver, I decide, based on inadequate evidence.

"Okay, I wouldn't mind a cold drink and something to eat."

"What kind of something would you like to eat?"

"I don't care."

"Really? You have definite opinions on clothing, coffee, tea, and courtship. Don't tell me you're indifferent about what you eat."

I look at him, sideways, reappraising. "Okay, I'd really like a burger."

We sit in a back booth in the Beacon Street Creamery, a 50s-style diner with jukeboxes and soda jerks. Johnny Mathis croons, "Chances Are," and a waiter carries a tray of shakes and fries to the table next to us.

We order burgers and fries.

"So, tell me about your family," I say. "How old are your kids?"

"Hallie and Hunter are twins. They're 17 and are graduating from high school in a week. We'll have two in college next year."

Dr. Rothman nudges me. "Did you hear that 'we'?"

"How long have you been married?"

"Twenty-seven years. We met in high school. Not exactly high school, because she was a townie and I boarded at Concord Academy. We met at a party at the lake. A bunch of us had been drinking and were jumping off a raft. I landed on her and knocked her out. Then I had to haul her in to the shore. Scared the shit out of me."

"Twenty-seven years is a long time together. It must be hard to end a relationship after that long."

"Actually, I think it's a relief for both of us. I've just hung in the last few years because of the kids. I didn't want to leave them alone with Andrea. Now, they'll be out of the house, so the timing's good."

Dr. Rothman nudges me again. "Ask him why he didn't want to leave them with their mother. What's that about?"

"I'm curious," I pause. "Why didn't you want to leave them alone with their mother?"

He hesitates as though this is painful for him to disclose. "She has a mean temper and can be abusive, especially when she's had a few drinks."

I should ask more, I know, but my stomach is beginning to churn.

CHAPTER 6

—

IN THE NICK OF TIME

I don't have time to obsess about the dysfunctional Slipway family because my 88-year-old mother arrives for a 10-day visit from Florida the day after the Bloomingdale's debacle. Unable to find a kennel cozy and indulgent enough for Raspberry, her cockapoo, she descends the airport escalator balancing the trembling pooch in her arms. Despite her strawberry blonde hair and sporty denim dress, Mum looks frail and older than she did only six months ago.

"I hope you're glad to see us. Raspberry and I have just endured a five-hour ordeal."

"Of course I'm glad to see you." I kiss my mother's cheek and scratch Raspberry behind the ears. Raspberry licks my hand gratefully. "Was the trip that rocky?"

"Who said anything about rocky? The cabin was too cold. I couldn't stop shivering and Raspberry had to stay in his carrier under my seat where it was even colder. He cried the whole time."

That must have been pleasant for the other passengers, I think, noticing a whistling sound escaping from my mother's chest as we walk to the baggage claim area. "Are you okay? You're wheezing."

"Wheezing? I don't hear any wheezing."

I haul two large bags off the luggage carousel and heft them onto a carrier. "What have you got in here—the family silver?"

"Books, my crossword puzzles and double acrostics, knitting, Raspberry's toys and food, his bed, his medications, homemade spaghetti sauce. I couldn't come without a jar or two of your favorite food. I also threw in a few mangoes and avocados from my yard…"

"Raspberry's food? Couldn't we get that here?"

"Not this brand. I get it from the vet. It's got twice the protein of most other brands."

My mother, the spokesperson for Special D dog food!

"You know, Mum, you fuss more about that dog than you ever did about Alan and me."

"That's because he doesn't give me any trouble."

My mother nuzzles Raspberry as she climbs into the car. She seems unsteady as she tries to settle the dog on her lap.

"Are you okay?" I ask as I fasten her seat belt, trying not to decapitate the dog. My mother looks so tired and her face is thin.

"I'm fine, just a little weary after that trip. We're not used to traveling, are we, Sweetie?" She kisses Raspberry on the nose and is rewarded with a wet tongue across her cheek.

Since my father's death, Raspberry has become my mother's closest friend and confidante, for which I'm grateful—just as long as the dog doesn't get more dessert.

My mother, Raspberry, and I spend the next few days checking out the local dog parks, grocery shopping, cooking Raspberry's favorites—hamburger, chicken livers, and boiled chicken, and some of mine—potato kugel, Hershey's cocoa fudge, and Sarah Rubin's chocolate-chip, chocolate Bundt cake. I think I get the better of the deal.

I persuade my mother to leave Raspberry for a few hours so we can go to see *Back to the Future* and dine at a Thai restaurant near the movie theater.

When we're seated at our table, my mother takes her cigarettes and lighter out of her handbag. She doesn't smoke in my apartment in deference to me, so I almost feel bad when I have to say, "Mum, you can't smoke in the restaurant."

"Why not?"

"They don't allow it any more."

"I never heard of such a foolish thing." She stuffs the cigarette back into her pack. "I thought this was a free country."

"It's annoying to other diners and, besides, secondary smoke is harmful to people around you," I say, mounting my soapbox.

"Your father said there was no such thing, and he was a physician. He should know."

I don't remind her that my father finally quit smoking after his third heart attack and could not be considered a reliable judge.

"So," she asks, unfolding her napkin and placing it on her lap, "anyone new in your life?"

"Anyone new? I have a new neighbor—a college kid who's really noisy."

"That's not what I mean." She pours tea into our small, ceramic cups. "What about men—any nice, new men in your life? You know how your father worried about you."

"I certainly do. He wanted me to marry again because he was sure I couldn't take care of myself."

"No, he just wanted you to be happy."

"And he thought I needed to have a man to make me happy. It sounds as though you feel the same way."

"Wouldn't you be happy to have a man in your life?"

"I'm not in a hurry to get married again."

"Who said anything about marriage?"

I look at my mother in surprise as she opens her menu. "What's good here? I'd like a curry dish."

"I like the prawns with yellow curry and vegetables. It's not too spicy but has a kick."

What is my mother saying? Man without marriage? Sex without a contract?

We order our food and I attempt to return to the topic, casually, I hope.

"So, you don't think marriage is necessary?"

"Not for everyone. Not at your age. You've had your children, so what do you need it for?"

"Security?"

"With a gambler and an alcoholic who can't pay the bills?"

"Every man is not a gambler or alcoholic. Look at Dad."

"Your dad was as straight as they come, honest, responsible…"

"I know. I should have looked for a guy more like him, but I took honesty and decency for granted. I just wanted a guy who wasn't a worrier and had more sense of adventure. I was looking for someone who wasn't like Dad. I got that in spades."

My mother nods as the waiter approaches with a tray of steaming Thai food. I decide not to mention Slipway.

CHAPTER 7

—

WHO'S WILL?

Juggling bags of groceries, I manage to insert my key into the lock and use my shoulder to push the door open to my garden apartment, euphemism for basement. I live in an elegant, older building in a residential neighborhood of Boston. The "garden apartment" with a view of pedestrian legs and feet is the best I can manage on my salary, but it's home—adjacent to the laundry room and furnace—but home. I sigh, ready to relax into my quiet solitude. I have forgotten I have company.

Raspberry, feet flying, gallops toward me, yipping, tail wagging wildly, rejoicing at my return. I struggle to hold my balance as he leaps at me.

"Hold on, nutso! Let me get these groceries to the kitchen."

In contrast, my mother grunts at me suspiciously from the navy corduroy couch in the living room, her knitting on her lap, the phone at her side.

"Hi, Mom, I got salmon and fresh asparagus for dinner. Are you hungry?"

"Not particularly. I had a snack."

"What did you find to snack on? Not much in the refrigerator, but I've got lots of good stuff now. I bought you creamed herring, hummus, and Saltines."

"I found some old cheddar cheese and sliced away the mold."

Raspberry yips at me, jumping at the groceries.

"Yep, I bought you chewies, too," I reassure him as I carry the bags into the small, windowless kitchen just beyond the living room.

"You just missed a phone call… a young man, who mumbled in a high-pitched voice—not very patient when I asked him to repeat himself. I don't know why people can't slow down on the phone. What's the big hurry?"

"A young man? I don't know any young men except your grandsons."

"And a mumbler. I had no idea what he was saying, but I think his name was Will."

Will—a young man? I suppose so, relative to her 88 years. Why is he calling me at home?

"Will? Will… let me think." I pause, pulling an avocado, lettuce, tomatoes, and onions out of the bags and placing them on the counter. "I bought Vidalia onions. Those are the ones you love, right?"

"What? I can't hear you. You know you can't talk to me from another room. Come in here if you want to talk to me. So, who is this Will? Anyone I should know about?"

I poke my head into the living room. "Why don't you come sit in the kitchen while I unpack the groceries and make dinner."

"Only if you let me help."

"You can make a salad," I reply, hoping she's forgotten about Will. I wouldn't call his voice high-pitched. It's more tenor-ish.

"Whoever this Will is, I told him you were out and he's going to call later."

Oy. Between the two of them, I haven't got a chance. "He's a colleague, that's all," I say, immediately realizing I've said too much.

"If he's a colleague, why's he calling you at home?" Miss Marple sniffs for clues.

"Colleagues can call each other at home," I reply defensively. "Sometimes there are questions about work."

I wash the lettuce, tomatoes, and onion and hand them and the avocado to my mother, who has come to stand beside me at the sink, paring knife at the ready. I notice her hand trembling slightly.

"Mom, if you're tired, I'll make the salad."

"No, I'm fine. I'll just sit at the table if it's okay with you. Sometimes I get a little dizzy if I stand up too quickly."

"Have you mentioned that to Dr. Arnone?"

"He says it's nothing to worry about. Maybe my blood pressure is a little low."

According to my mother, there's never anything to worry about, but that's her secret. She smokes, salts her food before tasting it, eats processed meats, cheese, and chocolate like it's health food, and my father had the high blood pressure.

"When you can, will you put a hamburger patty in the skillet?"

"Hamburger? We're going to have salmon."

"It's not for me. It's for Raspberry."

"That's not good for the dog," I protest.

"It's low fat."

As I place the lovingly prepared little meat patty in the skillet, Raspberry trots to my side, tail wagging, and body shaking with excitement.

"Okay, you spoiled creature, how do you like it—rare or medium rare?"

We are clearing the dishes from the table when the phone rings.

"That's probably young Will," my mother says. "You'd better answer it."

Young Will? Now he sounds like a character from Robin Hood. Young Will, troubadour of Sherwood Forest.

"I'll get it in my room," I say, trotting down the hall and out of earshot. My mother wouldn't pick up the living room extension, would she?

I close my door, pick up the phone, and sit at the edge of my bed, noticing Raspberry's chewy rabbit peeking out from under the edge of the spread.

"Hello?"

"Hi, is this Emily? It's Will," he shouts.

"Hi, yes, it's me and you don't have to yell."

"I called earlier and spoke to someone, maybe your mother, and I had to shout to be heard."

"That was my mother, and according to her, you mumbled." I don't add "in a high-pitched voice," thinking that would be too cruel.

"Mumbled? Does she wear hearing aids? She should. I had to repeat everything at least twice."

"She wears two and said you seemed impatient about having to repeat yourself. Why are you calling me at home anyway?"

"Why not? I really enjoyed our shopping expedition and wanted to thank you again. I also wondered if you'd like to meet for a drink one evening this week."

I can hear my mother clattering dishes in the kitchen and Raspberry scratching at my door. I sigh.

"Will, are you still living in your basement or have you moved out and gotten a quickie divorce in the last two weeks? I really meant it. I don't date married men."

"I told you my wife has finally decided she wants a divorce."

"That's what you said, but is anyone suing anyone for that divorce, or is it just a wish that may never be fulfilled?"

I can hear Dr. Rothman's voice now. "Tell him to call you back when he's divorced."

Geez, another country heard from. They're coming at me from all directions, these busybodies. But I know he's right.

I realize Will's been talking and I haven't heard a word. "Sorry, Will, I was distracted. My mother's dog needs to go out, so I'll have to hang up in a minute. What were you saying?"

Dr. Rothman harrumphs. "Don't ask him what he's saying. You don't want to hear anything from this guy until he's divorced."

"I was saying, Emily, that Andrea and I are getting a divorce, but it takes time. It doesn't happen overnight."

"Okay, fair enough. Call me when it has happened. I'm hanging up now."

I hear Dr. Rothman saying, "Good girl."

Raspberry is still scratching at the door and whimpering now.

"Shut up, all of you," I say as I open the door to the wagging tail. "Where's your leash? Go get your leash and I'll take you out."

I watch Raspberry scamper up the hall toward my mother, who calls to me, "So, did you get your business straightened out?"

"Yes, Mum, all straightened out. If you put on Raspberry's leash, I'll take him for a walk."

CHAPTER 8

—

BACK TO THE DRAWING BOARD

I wait until I see Shelley settled at her desk, sipping her coffee. The office is quiet. I've arrived earlier than my usual 8:30 to catch her before the morning madness begins.

I knock on her cubicle wall. "Hi, Shel, have you got a minute?"

She turns toward me, her warm smile lighting her face. "Sure, what's up? Good morning, by the way. How's your visit going with your mom?"

"As well as can be expected… no, that's not fair. It's fine. We've actually had a good time, and I think she's happy to be here. I know she's been lonely since my dad died. Now, she's putting all her emotional energy into that silly dog, talking to him constantly, and I swear he understands what she's saying," I chuckle.

"It must be nice for you to have company for a change. How much longer are they here?"

"They leave on Thursday. My mother has to get back for a duplicate bridge tournament."

"Wow, she's still sharp, isn't she?"

"Actually, I wanted to get your expert advice about something else."

"Like the sterling advice I gave you on that guy who turned out to be married and a stalker?"

"Not really a stalker, just lonely and persistent. He's supposedly getting a divorce and still calls me, but I don't want to see him again. It makes me uneasy that he's still living in the same house as his wife."

"And that he's still married. I know. Our pastor once counseled a friend who got involved with a married guy. He said that one relationship begun before ending another, cannot thrive."

"Pretty heavy, but I get it."

"Yeah, there's still a connection, unresolved stuff going on."

"That's what I'm afraid of," I agree.

"How can I help you?" Shelley asks, sipping on her coffee.

"Same old story. How can I meet a man who's eligible, available, and unmarried?"

Shelley sits back in her chair and stares at the ceiling. "Hmm. Okay, don't think I'm nuts, but what about trying the personals?"

"Personals? You mean those ads in the *Globe*?"

"Girl, you are behind the times. Have you ever heard of the internet—the magic of instant communication?"

"You're kidding, right?"

"Wrong. I have girlfriends who've met great guys that way. Have you ever heard of Match.com or SinglesMeet or Dateme. com? One of my friends met a guy on Dateme and they've been going out for months. Looks like they're getting serious."

"How old is she—22? She's certainly not in her 50s. Did I tell you about the time I tried to sign up for Lunch Out when I'd just turned 40? The owner, no less, called me after reviewing my application to tell me I was too old—couching his words carefully to avoid a lawsuit, of course. I still get angry when I think about it."

"That was then. This is now. Lots of men your age are on these dating sites."

"And they're all looking for younger women."

"Not necessarily. Some may be looking for... "maturity, wisdom, adult experience."

"All right. I get it, but I still don't like the idea."

"Why not? What have you got to lose?" she grins. "I'll help you write the ad."

Shelley turns to her keyboard and stares at me expectantly.

"I have no idea where to begin," I whine.

"Of course, you don't. You just make your living writing and putting words together." Noting my forlorn expression, Shelley relents. "Okay, I understand. This isn't easy. Let's see. Hmm. How about this:

Warm, witty, 50s female…

"Whoa! Doesn't witty sound too smart, like it will scare men off?"

"You're right," she agrees.

Warm but humorless, compliant female…

"That's not what I mean! And, 50s female sounds as though I'm stuck in the 50s."

"Do you want to write this yourself?"

"No."

"I thought not. Why don't you let me take a crack at it and then you can edit to your heart's content? Okay?"

"Okay, do your worst!"

For days we go back and forth until finally one chilly morning when the frost is on the pumpkin, Shelley summons me to her cubicle.

I am a warm, witty, liberal writer, lover of the arts: literature, theater, movies, museums, classical music, and some jazz. Lively conversation, good friends, and mutually giving relationships are important to me, as are my family. I'm affectionate and empathetic. I love to read, write, and learn about new ideas, cultures, and people. You can often find me in a class of one kind or another. I like to play, waste time, and eat junk food once in a while. Although I'm not a bungee-jumping, hang-gliding kind of woman, I love spontaneous getaways, adventures, and finding joy in what life offers.

I'm looking for an open-hearted, honest, affectionate, and optimistic man who wants to share life's possibilities. It would be great if he has a sense of humor, a sense of adventure, and shares some of the interests I enjoy. I'd like a long-term relationship.

"So what do you think, kiddo?" Shelly grins.

"It's good. It sounds like me. I'd even be interested. But do you think we should add just a little bit about my kids?"

"Enough already. Men don't want to hear about your kids, even if they're out of the house. It's time to launch, my dear."

"I'm not sure. I don't know where I want to put this."

"If it were up to you, it would probably go in your bottom desk drawer. You let me take care of placing it. I'll let you know when I've posted it… and where."

"I can't let you do that!"

"Trust me!" Shelley wears her wounded child look, still surprisingly effective.

"Okay, but wait until after this weekend."

"What's this weekend?"

"I did something impulsive. I committed to going to my 40th high school reunion. Let's wait until after that."

CHAPTER 9

—

40TH REUNION

Two weeks after my 40th high school reunion, sounds and images still echo, waking me in the middle of the night. Last night I grabbed the pen and notepad on my night table and scribbled these words:

> Mixed bag, bittersweet morsels
> triumph and tragedy—agoraphobia, addiction
> scholarship, heroism
> financial success, ruin
> balding, thickening, softening, mellowing
> deepening, desiccating
> marriage, monogamy, divorce, depression
> delight, romance, rage, age
> wrinkles, facelifts
> wizening, wisening
> reuniting, reckoning.

In the morning, munching my Cheerios, I ponder my list and chuckle, thinking about how much time and energy I spent obsessing—should I go or not go? What will I wear? Who will be there? Will they all be happier, more successful, thinner than I am?

My childhood pal, Lucy Kramer, finally persuaded me to go with her. "Don't you want to see what's happened to everyone? Come on, we can hang out together and dish the dirt."

I go on a crash diet of vegetables, fruit, and tea to shed five pounds of flab. I buy a sophisticated emerald green sheath in anticipation of my weight loss and schedule an appointment to get my hair straightened a week before the reunion. That should allow enough time for the smell of rotten eggs to dissipate.

By the night of the reunion, I've lost three and a half pounds and can squeeze into my new green sheath if I don't breathe too deeply. However, a nasty front of damp, humid air has coiled my straightened, sleek hair back into a nest of curls and frizz.

Lucy and I meet in the ladies room at the appointed hour, exclaim in delight at our dressed-up transformation and buoy each other for our entrance, feeling like teenagers at a sock hop. We've kept in touch despite our busy lives and are always happy to see each other. Lucy, a cardiologist, looks half her age. She's petite, maybe five feet tall, has managed to maintain a near approximation of her high school figure, and still has her sweet, pretty face—not a sag or pouch in sight. Her hair is still light brown—thanks to Clairol Cream in Your Coffee—and quietly frames her heart-shaped face. I fight against feeling like a big, gray-haired balloon.

We enter the gym, which is decked out in our school colors, everything black and orange—streamers, lanterns, strings of light, and table centerpieces, making me wonder if I should be carrying a trick-or-treat bag. My stomach does a slight downward flip as Dennis Hanks, class sophisticate and man about campus, and I've heard—recovering alcoholic—approaches us. Within seconds, I realize he's still pining for Lucy, whom he'd pursued senior year. Their relationship had suffered a sudden death after Dennis, correctly identifying Lucy's breasts as virgin territory, had mistakenly attempted to explore them. In the 50s, good girls went no farther than first base.

As he turns his charm on Lucy, I inch away and look for a friendly face. Maggie Casey grins at me. I've always admired

Maggie for her brains and sense of humor. She'd joined the Peace Corps after Radcliffe and now is heading a community healthcare agency. Recently married for the first time, she radiates warmth. Standing next to her, Jenny Alter, another of my favorite class-mates, beckons me over. I've heard she's a professor of linguistics at the University of Michigan. We chat enthusiastically, trying to catch up with each other in just a few sentences. We giggle, reminiscing about our ski trip sophomore year when I, a novice skier, landed headfirst in bushes at the bottom of the slope because I didn't know how to put on the brakes.

"Whoops, don't look now, but Ian Ramsay is heading in our direction, approaching your left shoulder," Jenny warns me.

When I feel a tap on my shoulder, I spin around, dropping my glass of Chablis at my feet. Fortunately, the glass is plastic and doesn't shatter. Instead, it bounces toward an unsuspecting couple engrossed in conversation. Without missing a beat, Ian bounds after the glass, grabbing it before it reaches target. I applaud as I wipe the spilled wine off the floor.

"Oh, god, thanks for coming to my rescue!"

"It's okay," he says. "I'm just surprised I can still move that fast."

He greets Maggie and Jenny, giving me a chance to regain my composure. I look up at him. Still tall, I think with relief. He's grinning that same sweet smile. Hair graying, slightly receding, still the same freckles and blue eyes, behind aviator glasses too big for his face. What do I look like to him? At least 20 pounds heavier, distributed unkindly around my face, neck, and waist. Wrinkles and worry lines with no freckles to hide behind. Too late for a makeover now!

"Emily! It's great to see you." Ian pulls me close in a friendly hug. He still smells of fresh soap.

"You, too. How are you? You still have your freckles!" Geez, could I sound any clumsier?

"You still have your curls," he replies, grinning. "Let's find somewhere to sit so we can catch up." Nodding toward Maggie and Jenny, he takes my elbow and steers me toward an empty table.

I don't remember much of what I told Ian, the usual about my marriage, children, jobs, and life in Boston. I do, however, remember what he told me. He's living in Seattle where he's sales manager for a large, multinational electronics company. He's lived in Europe and Asia and just recently returned to the States. Widowed for a few years, he has two daughters in their 20s. Although he dates, he's not looking for a long-term relationship. Unlike some widowers who were happily married and looking to repeat the experience, Ian describes his marriage as lukewarm toward the end, long before his wife's illness. Not really hostile, but their 20-year marriage had lost momentum and eventually stalled. He described himself as satisfied and busy with work, golf, travel, and his daughters' lives, when they let him in.

No big drama it seems. I wish I could say the same. I wish I could say the same about our relationship in high school. We met in algebra class where he was a star while I was a poet who didn't understand math. I never did get word problems. We fell madly in love, necked ourselves silly, and swore eternal allegiance. I remember a New Year's Eve party in Jenny Alter's basement where Ian and I glommed onto each other on a long, wooden bench and stayed glued together, fully clothed, for as long as the party lasted. I couldn't have told you who was at the party, who got sick on spiked punch, who had to leave for a midnight curfew.

When Ian and I were together, the world disappeared. Not for long enough. My parents and his didn't like the match, worried that we'd interfere with each other's studies, jeopardize each other's college prospects, and end up in dead-end jobs at the local supermarket. At least, that's what they said. Ian was a churchgoing Presbyterian and I was a Jew. In those days, that kind of mix was forbidden. I suspect that my parents also worried that I could become pregnant despite my being a devoted virgin, remaining fully clothed while we necked.

Our virginity was probably another factor. Sex confused and intimidated me. While I loved the feelings that stirred in my body when we necked, those feelings scared me. A good girl of the 50s,

I didn't quite trust my urges and where they could lead.

Finally, on trumped-up charges, I accused Ian of two-timing me with Sandy Silvia, the class slut. Someone had told someone who'd told me she'd seen them necking in the library stacks. I chose to believe this fabrication, even though I knew Sandy had no idea what or where the library stacks were. I blindsided Ian with my suspicion and accusations. He was straightforward and honest, an Eagle Scout whose feelings seemed less complicated than mine. Puzzled and hurt, he cried uncle and walked away three weeks before graduation. We hadn't been in touch since then. Over the years, I'd thought about him and wondered what life would have been like if we'd stayed together. Sometimes that "what if" saddened me.

I did apologize that evening at the reunion, trying to explain my adolescent behavior without justifying it. I ended my confession with, "I'm really sorry for behaving like such an idiot."

"I wondered what was going on and was pretty broken up for a while," Ian conceded, "but having raised two daughters, nothing surprises me anymore."

"Touché, I deserve that."

"Just teasing. You're forgiven, and to show there are no hard feelings, let's stay in touch."

"I'd really like that," I said, wondering just how long he'd felt "broken up."

Sitting here two weeks later, sipping my coffee and watching legs and feet stroll by outside my kitchen window, I smile, remembering how much I'd worried that he'd be at the reunion, at the same time wishing he'd be there. How much time had I spent over the years wondering what had become of him, wondering what if?

I refill my coffee cup, and I'm about to open the newspaper when I hear the mail tumble through the slot in my front door. Tucked in among bills and grocery ads is a letter from Ian.

• • •

Wednesday, June 5

Hi, Emily,

It was so good to see you at the 40th and catch up. Can you believe we've been out of high school that long? Did I tell you I really admire your going back to school now? I was going to say so late in life, but that's not what I mean. I'm glad you're going after what you want and that you still enjoy school. I liked it, too, but it was always hard work for me, especially in the engineering program. I've thought of going back but never followed through. Anyway, I'm glad for you.

Unlike you, I've managed to lose touch with too many friends from the past. Maybe that's partly due to traveling so much and living outside the country. I was happy to reconnect with some old friends at our reunion, and I mean old in the kindest sense of the word. I'm going to stay in touch with Paul Petrov and Jim Goldsmith, who were both Eagle Scouts and on the wrestling team with me. I'd also like to stay in touch with you. You remember what Ms. Carroll, our sophomore English teacher used to quote: "Make new friends but keep the old." Now, where did that come from? I haven't thought about that in close to 40 years.

Anyway, Emily, at the risk of being repetitive, I want to say I was happy to see you and would like to stay in touch. I'd like to know how you're doing and what's happening in your life. If you feel the same way, write back when you have a chance.

Best wishes,
Ian

• • •

Tuesday, June 20

Hi Ian,

How nice to hear from you! Wasn't the reunion fun? Not the snooze I expected. No doddering, decrepit curmudgeons yet. I was happy to see my friends are all still sharp. I hope we can be friends now that I've apologized for my abhorrent behavior 40 years ago. I hope you've forgiven me. I've almost forgiven myself.

How are you and what are you up to in Seattle? You said you like it there, but I don't remember the details. Do you live near the water? I confess I don't know much about the Pacific Northwest. My impressions come from the film, Sleepless in Seattle, and the houseboat where Tom Hanks and his son lived.

Confession time—You said you admired me for being in grad school. The truth is that I am and I am not. I'm stuck. I have only one course left and an internship commitment to fulfill. The course is statistics—a snaggle-toothed hyena, hungry for human flesh. It's been sitting on its haunches for almost a year, glowering and daring me to try it. Now, before you rush to say, "What are you waiting for," I'm going to remind you of the trig exam we took in Algebra 2. Do you remember when Mr. Drohan handed back the test papers and announced, "Miss Rosenbloom was the only student who managed to make her mineshaft rise into the air." Mortification! My body heat could have burned a hole in the creaky, wood floor beneath my desk, and I would have happily crawled into it. Here I am, 40-plus years later, still haunted by the humiliation!

The internship presents a different kind of problem. The placements are during working hours. That's when I'm at my job in my claustrophobic cubicle 8 to 5, Monday through Friday. Without a clone, I don't see how I can be in two places at once. But enough of my self-pity. I just wanted to set the record straight about my triumphant stint in graduate school.

Otherwise, life is good. My friends and I love low-risk adventures and have good times. This coming weekend, a few of us are going up to the Maine Blues Festival near Portland. I love Maine. It's my getaway place. Love the rocky coast and small, back-road towns, even the attitude. If you've lived in Maine for 50 years but weren't born there, you're "from away."

I'm rambling now and am reluctantly going to close this letter and return to the tasks of the day. Again, so nice to hear from you.

Best,
Emily

• • •

Monday, June 26

Hi Emily,

Your letter sounds just like you. You write the way you speak. That's good because I feel like you're talking to me. I can see how you'd be good at writing marketing copy. You haven't said much about your work, but I got the feeling when you mentioned it that you don't like it much. Is that why you're in grad school? I think you said you were taking courses in adult ed and counseling. Quite different from what you're doing now. I'd love to hear more about that.

While we're on the subject, let's talk about grad school. You're only one course and a few hours away from getting your degree? You can't quit now! I know you said you were stuck, but the problems you mentioned have solutions. You know me—Eagle Scout and engineer, inveterate problem solver.

I know you can do the statistics. It's more about confidence than anything else. How about hiring a tutor? It would be worth the cost, wouldn't it? Besides, if you find a graduate student, they probably wouldn't charge that much.

I agree that finding the time for the internship is a bit stickier. Have you talked to anyone at your job about it? Maybe they'd agree to your taking off a few hours a week or maybe you can make up the time somehow. If you haven't asked, you don't know what's possible. It's worth trying, isn't it? You're so close you can't give up now.

End of lecture. But, seriously, I know you want to finish, so think about what I'm saying please. Remember, the worst they can do is say no.

To answer your question, I do live near the water but not in Tom Hanks's neighborhood. It's hard not to live near the water in Seattle. I own a house in West Seattle, a nice, older area with lots of homes built in the '40s with pretty parks, close enough to more urban areas where the action is.

This weekend, while you're listening to the Blues, I'm going to be experiencing my own kind of blues. I'm golfing in a foursome in a small, local tournament. Given how little I've been playing or practicing, I'm not sure this is the best way to relax or win friends. My uneasy joints may rebel!

Tonight, my younger daughter, Nancy, is coming over to try out a new recipe on me before she serves it to her boyfriend. Lucky me! She's a good cook and enjoys experimenting, which is fine as long as the ingredients aren't too exotic. I'm really not up for deep-fried spiders or fertilized duck eggs!

Now I'm getting carried away. It's your influence, I suspect.

I'm enjoying our conversation, Emily, and hope we can continue it. I'll stay tuned for the next segment.

Best,

Ian

• • •

Friday, July 14

Hi Ian,

Sorry it's taken me a while to get back to you. I thought about your suggestion that I ask at work about taking time off for my internship. I went back and forth, trying to find the courage. Finally, I decided to do it. As you said, what did I have to lose?

Last Tuesday, I approached Michaela, my manager. Have I told you about Michaela? She's a poster child for "Inappropriate Dress in the Workplace," wearing sweater dresses that cling like Saran Wrap to her abundant curves and tottering around on stiletto heels. She speaks with a nasal lisp. Catty, aren't I? More important, she's an inefficient workaholic, who can't organize or delegate. She's buried under piles of papers that she shuffles around her desk, hoping some slide off into the wastebasket. As far as we know, she has no life outside work. The rest of us suffer because she can't imagine anyone having a life beyond the office and doesn't understand concepts like holidays and vacations.

I'm telling you this so you have an idea of what I was facing. When I told her about the graduate program and internship, her first response was, "Why would you want to get a degree in adult education? What kind of jobs can you get with that? How much can it pay?"

When I mentioned spending a few hours a week at an internship, she surprised me and didn't say a flat "no." Instead, she frowned and asked, "When would you do your work?"

I refrained from saying, "What work?" She and I have danced around that subject for months. Taking your good advice, I said I'd come in early or stay late to make up the time. Again, she didn't immediately say "no." I was shocked to hear her say she'd talk to Randall, her manager, and get back to me.

Her response gave me hope. For once, maybe the glass was half full.

Ha! This morning she called me into her office to tell me that she'd asked Randall, who wasn't enthusiastic but agreed to check with the Human Resources Department. HR told him that my graduate program had nothing to do with my job, so it wasn't possible to grant my request. They also asked him if I'd been getting the company to pay for any of my courses, because that wasn't allowed either since the courses had no relevance to my work. Furthermore, if the company had paid for any of my courses, I would have to pay the money back!

Never mind glass half empty. It's been drained! Those turkeys! Once I lift my sagging spirits off the floor, I've got to ramp up my job search and send out more resumes.

I wish I had better news. Hope you're well and enjoying good news of some sort.

Best,
Emily

• • •

Saturday, July 22

Hi Emily,

So sorry to hear about your company's ridiculous response to your request. That attitude is shortsighted and petty! I know you're disappointed, but at least you tried. That's got to make you feel good about yourself.

At the risk of being a pain in the ass, I'm wondering if you've done anything about the statistics course. Have you thought about signing up and hiring a tutor? In the meantime, you can look for another way to do the internship. You're clever and creative. You'll come up with something. I'll keep thinking about it, too.

Nothing much new with me except a business trip to Japan next week. I know I shouldn't sound so blasé. I like Japan and doing business there. The culture is fascinating. The trouble with business trips is that I spend most of my time in meetings and don't get to see much else—not always, though. Since this is my first trip to Kyoto, I'm going to take a couple of extra days to see some of the famous temples and shrines. Looking forward to that.

I feel weird talking about my trip and sightseeing when you're not having such a good time. I know you have good friends, and you mentioned a couple of adventures. That's great! I hope you keep having fun in spite of the curveballs being thrown at you. Speaking of curveballs, are you still a Red Sox fan? I go to Seattle Mariners games, but my heart is still with the Sox. Back to fun—I have to work on having more of that. Sometimes, I get too wrapped up in work. Don't want to end up like your manager. I've known people like her. No thanks!

I wish I could be more helpful and will keep trying to come up with solutions. It feels good that we're back in touch so keep your letters coming. Let me know what you come up with next. I'm rooting for you.

Best,
Ian

CHAPTER 10

—

LOOKING FOR LOVE IN ALL THE WRONG PLACES

Delighted to be writing back and forth to Ian, I'm also inspired to find someone closer to home, so I tell Shelley, "Time to post it, pal."

I wish I could say the responses from eager suitors flood my email. It's more like trickles or drips from a faucet that needs a new washer. And most of the guys are in their 70s or 30s. I'm 50ish and apparently too old for men my age and just old enough for men who miss their mamas. And then there are the fetishists and philanderers.

I get a ding on my email from Cupid's Arrow.com.

You've got a flirt from footlvr!

Footlover?

Should I get a tetanus shot before I open this? I tap on the email:

Hay, saw your profile and think we'd make a great match. I'm really into older women. They're hot. Email me.

Doesn't he know that older women could have bunions, fallen arches, and calluses as thick as tires? What does he mean a great match? I read his profile. Besides older women, he's into motor-cycles, hockey, and the New England Patriots. I want to write back:

Dude, did you actually READ my profile?

The next prospect is Mickey, age 73, whose photo must have been taken when he was 33, which apparently is where he stopped maturing. He writes:

You saw my age and thought, Forget it—too old. But I look and act at least 10 years younger. So I need someone young enough to keep up with me. I want someone who is warm and loving, very affection-ate and sensual, and willing and able to communicate on an intimate level. She should be age 40 to 55.

I'm tempted to respond to Mickey, pointing out that his math is off and there must be easier ways to get laid.

I get an email from a guy who immediately wants to know my long-term expectations because for legal reasons, he can't cohabi-tate, but he can do everything else—wink, wink. The winks are his.

I respond: *The only reason I can think of for not being able to cohabitate is that you're still married. Is that the case?*

I never hear back.

Eventually I do get a few dates.

The first is Giovanni, a 60-year-old Italian with a deep, sexy voice that lingers lovingly on his words, conjuring images of olive groves, wineries, and Tuscan villas. We agree to meet at a Starbucks on a Friday when I'm not working. Giovanni is 30 to 40 pounds heavier than in his photos but is dressed neatly in a navy blazer that once probably fit, a red and gray plaid shirt, and gray slacks. He has clearly made an effort to look good. That's in his favor.

Strands of gray hair stripe across his head, an attempt at comb-over, above a fleshy face. His lips are thick, but his eyes—deep, chocolate pools—are inviting.

I wonder what he thinks of me in my blue silk blouse and gray slacks, attempting to conceal a pound or two of my extra flesh.

We find a table in a relatively quiet corner of the café. Even at 10:30 on a Friday, it's crowded and noisy, so we have trouble hearing each other. Leaning forward and lip reading, I can make out what he's saying. Maybe he takes my body posture as a sign of encouragement, because I notice that he leans closer to me.

"I am widowed for 12 years," he confides, "cancer… my wife had cancer, died too young. He shakes his head. "I'm left with my two daughters, young, hard to raise without her."

"How old were your daughters?"

"The elder was 12, younger 10. Very hard."

"Did you ever think of remarrying?"

"No. I didn't want to bring a stranger into our family." He pauses, inching closer and reaching for my hand, which I slide over to my coffee cup.

"You don't like the physical contact?"

"Too soon," I say, feeling like a rabbit cornered by the fox.

"Now," he asserts, "I am ready for relationship. I am looking for a good Christian woman to love."

Thank god, I think, blurting out, "I'm Jewish! Too bad."

"I dated a Jewish woman before. We were going to live together until she changed her mind."

Was that after two dates, I wonder. This guy doesn't care who I am, so long as I have a warm body. "Giovanni, it's been nice meeting you, but I'm not the one you're looking for." I push my chair back to leave.

"So soon?" He says. "You won't stay to know me? Maybe cook me a nice meal?"

"That will be the next woman you meet," I promise as I back away.

I meet another man, Irv, who looks good on paper, although at 68, he falls outside my age specs. Hey, I'm open-minded. Our Starbucks conversation goes well, so I'm not surprised when he calls a few days later, inviting me to lunch.

Sitting across from each other at Lobster Bill's, we eat our seafood, chatting intermittently. More accurately, he drones, not allowing a two-way conversation, but giving me a chance to look him over. He's dressed casually in a hoodie, a Red Sox tee shirt and jeans. I wonder if this lunch is a pit stop before a game. His belly is bloated, perhaps by clam chowder and Crab Louie and the second glass of wine. In fact, his face is flushed Mateus rosé. His jaw, slackened into jowls, his sparse, gray hair pasted against a perfectly round head, his small ears flattened against his scalp.

He sits back, launching a complaint, "My computer crashed this morning. I left a technician working on it. I haven't got time for this nonsense."

Is he talking about his failing computer or this lunch date?

"My older daughter is asking me for another loan—just 'til her husband gets back on his feet. I'll never see that money again. They don't know how to manage their money, never have. I'm putting my foot down. I have a lifestyle to maintain."

I nibble at my salmon salad, which is losing its taste, the lettuce wilting on my fork, when he shifts nervously, beckoning to the waitress. "Can we have two cups of coffee and the check?"

After swigging his coffee and signing the check, he looks at me, hesitates, and says, "You're a very interesting woman, but I don't think there's any chemistry. If you'll excuse me, I've got to get back to my computer."

He scrapes back his chair and strides away, leaving me to stare at his back. I want to shout, "Chemistry? You mean the smell of rotten eggs we made in lab with hydrogen sulfide?"

At least now I can savor my salmon and ocean view without trying to extract humor or tenderness from this Cupid's Arrow match, revving his engine for flight.

• • •

Friday, August 11

Hi Ian,

Shh, I'm writing this letter from work.
How was your trip to Kyoto? Would love to hear about it.
I took your advice about having more fun and have embarked on an adventure I hope won't toss me into a pond full of toads! See, there I go, already doubting. I've got to kick this habit!

Are you ready? I signed up on a personals dating site. It's a three-month trial period, and I figure I'll know by then what's out there for me. True confession... I didn't sign up. My friend, Shelley, did it for me, because she knew I'd never follow through. She also helped me write the ad, which was an adventure, itself. I just signed up a couple of weeks ago and have already accumulated a few stories that someday will seem funny. I'm trying not to attach too much to this venture and plan to check for messages only once a day.

I don't know if you've ever tried online dating, but it seems pretty secure. You connect with prospects through the dating site and don't give out any personal contact information. You even use an alias like "Hot Lips, Cookie Baker, or Paige Turner," depending on what you want to say about yourself. Besides writing the ad, the hardest part was finding photos that looked like me and were flattering. That took hours.

My work has slowed to a crawl. The job search is creeping, and the scent of fading summer is already in the air. I have to do something to keep my fires burning. I'll let you know what happens.

Best,
Emily

• • •

Monday, Aug. 14

Emily,

Wow! Are you sure you want to go this route? Online dating? I haven't tried it, myself, but I've heard lots of stories. I'll bet you have, too. A lot of married guys and maybe women use those sites and scam artists, too. I don't mean to be a spoilsport, just want you to be careful.

If you decide to actually meet any of these guys, how do you plan to do that? Where will you meet and how will you take care of yourself? Jeez, I bet I sound like your father, don't I?

Speaking of your father, I know your mother is living in a retirement community in West Palm Beach and I'm wondering about your dad. I don't remember your mentioning him. My folks are both gone. They died in their early sixties, much too young. I miss them and wish they were still around.

Kyoto was great, and I'm really glad I took the extra time to see the city. I took some photos of incredibly beautiful temples and palaces, which I'm happy to share if you're interested. A funny thing happened outside of one of the temples. I was dressed in a suit and tie, carrying my camera, when I was stopped by a Japanese schoolteacher, leading her class of eight-year-olds. The boys were wearing navy jackets, long pants, white shirts, and bow ties, and the girls wore navy jumpers and white knee socks—quite impressive! The teacher asked if I'd speak a bit of English to the children. When I began with a bow and Japanese greeting, they all giggled and began snapping my picture, so I began snapping theirs.

Then I spoke to them in English. "Hello. How are you? I am happy to meet you. I am visiting Kyoto. I like it very much. The temples are beautiful. The people are so kind." Highlight of my afternoon!

Summer isn't fading here yet. August is one of our driest, warmest months, but in September it gets cloudier and cooler with some rain. That's when I'll stock wood for fires and begin to hunker down with good books. I've got a pile waiting for me on my night table. Have you read A Walk in the Woods by Bill Bryson or Guns, Germs and Steel: The Fate of Human Society by Jared Diamond? Sounds like a little light reading, doesn't it? That's just the top of the pile. Tell me if you're impressed.

Let me know how your manhunt goes and please be careful.

Best,
Ian

CHAPTER 11

—

LOVE FROM LEFT FIELD

Wishing I could meet a decent man who lives within whispering distance, I take charge of my search, sending email messages to likely prospects. Occasionally, I receive responses:

We'd make a good match?? I don't think so!!

Sorry, I found the love of my life 10 minutes ago.

Often, I get no response at all, as though my charming, literate messages hurtle into a black hole. Until one day, I open my email and see I have a new flirt.

• • •

Hello Wildflower,

You are so beautiful! I'm sure you have many men pursuing you, but I hope you'll give me a chance. Even though I don't exactly match your criteria, I think distance and age don't have to be barriers if two like minds find each other. I like what you say about yourself, the things you like to do, and the qualities you're looking for.

I have been a widower for almost 10 years, raising my son on my own. He's now at the University of London, studying for an advanced degree in economics. I'm so proud of him. It hasn't been easy for the two of us without a woman in our lives. I was married young to my high school sweetheart, the woman I thought I'd be with forever, but sometimes bad things happen. I'll tell you more when I know you better, so please send me a reply.

By the way, I have a law degree but have never practiced. I've had my own costume supply business for many years and have prospered, I'm happy to say. I travel worldwide for business and pleasure and would love to have a traveling companion.

I really hope I hear from you,

Nathaniel

• • •

I look at his profile. The guy is 45 and lives in Oklahoma! Forget it. Then I look at his photos. He's adorable—a little gray at the temples, lean face, strong jaw, lovely green? hazel? eyes and the most heart-fluttering smile. A bit of a rogue there, I can tell. I decide to read the rest of his profile. What harm can it do?

I'm intrigued that Nathaniel says he is a reader, loves theater, foreign films, and museums. It doesn't hurt that he was born in London and immigrated to America with his parents when he was 10 years old. How intriguing! My Anglophilic heart leaps!

I write back to him.

• • •

Hello, Nathaniel,

How nice to hear from you. While I do think our age difference and the geographic distance between us would make a relationship difficult, I appreciate your interest and am flattered, of course, by your email.

Ugh, much too formal. I sound like a stiff. I try again.

• • •

Hi Nathaniel,

Wow! Thanks so much for your email. I'm flattered, of course, and intrigued by our common interests and your fascinating background.

You must have wonderful stories to tell! Do you still have family in England? I love British mysteries, films and history, all fascinating. How did you end up in Oklahoma?

Please tell me more.

Thanks.
Emily

• • •

In the midst of this email exchange with Nathaniel, I receive an anxious note from Ian.

Thursday, Sept. 28

Hey, Emily,

Have you run off with one of those internet guys? Where are you? Last I heard, you were beginning your search for Mr. Right. That was more than a month ago. Not that I have any right to expect to hear from you, but I thought we had a nice communication line opened up, and I'm a bit concerned. Having two daughters has given me a hyperactive imagination and a hyper-vigilant attitude.

At least send me a postcard from Bali, Bora Bora, or wherever you are, letting me know you're okay. Or tell me to mind my own business.

Regards,
Ian, your fretful friend

Thursday, Oct. 5

Ian,

So sorry you've been worrying. I'm okay, just a little weary from the impossible quest, which I'll tell you about in a minute. I suspect you can't hold a candle to my father in the field of hyper-vigilism. By now, he would have notified the local and state police, FBI, and CIA! Once, when a friend and I drove to Florida, I made the mistake of calling my folks to tell them we'd crossed the Georgia/Florida state line and were wolfing down fried chicken in the famous Metro Diner in Jacksonville. Did I say we'd take our time and meander down the coast to get to them? I don't remember. My father assumed we'd take a direct route on I-95 and calculated the time we should arrive, By the time we drove in, hours late by his calculations, he had called the highway patrol! He was hyperventilating and ranting when he opened the door.

You thought perhaps I'd landed in Bali or Bora Bora with one of these characters? More likely it would have been Bellevue Psychiatric Hospital or San Quentin—not that any of my actual dates were criminals, but the psych part fits. Some of the men I heard from, like the foot fetishist or the polyamorous pansexual—could have had criminal intent, but I never gave them a chance. We never got past the initial email. I've also heard from octogenarians and adolescents, men in muscle shirts sitting on motorcycles, and did any of them read my profile???

I've been out with a few guys who seemed to fit my spectrum of relative normality but haven't found any keepers. For one coffee date, I wore my new plum colored blazer that brought out the blue in my eyes. When the guy began shuddering, I discovered he was a porphyrophobic who was afraid of the color purple—I'm not kidding! Another brutally honest lunch date said to me before he scurried away, "There's no chemistry." At least he paid the check.

I was about to give up but just responded to one last guy who contacted me hours ago. He's a bit younger and lives at a distance, but he has a way with words and is awfully cute. Shallow, aren't I?

I'll let you know how this 11th-hour fling goes and I'll keep in touch. Not to worry. I'm being careful.

Best,
Emily

• • •

Timing is interesting. I have just sent my letter off to Ian when gmail signals me that I have a new email from Nathaniel.

• • •

Dear Emily,

I am so taken with your profile. You sound like such an intelligent, caring woman. As I said in my profile, I lost my wife very young when my son was three and I raised him alone with a bit of help from my mother until she passed. I have not known many women since my wife's death, and think this is the time. Until recently, I was too busy building my business and raising my son. He and I have been through a great deal, but he's a fine young man and I miss him. We speak weekly on the phone, and I try to visit him as often as my work will allow. I also bring him home for holidays.

I am so pleased that you are interested in communicating. This could be a good beginning to something special, yes?

I must sign off now to prepare for a business meeting. Please write again and tell me a bit more about yourself. Are you living alone? What is it you do with your time? What is your gainful employment?

Many questions both ways, I am sure.

Until I hear from you again,
Nathaniel

• • •

I wait a couple of days before I answer, not wanting to appear too eager.

• • •

Hello, Nathaniel,

It sounds as though you have a close relationship with your son. What's his name?

About me, as I said in my profile, I'm divorced and have two sons in their 20s, out of school and trying to make their way in the world. My older son works in computers. My younger son is working on the pipeline in Alaska right now. Who knows what he'll be doing next. I miss them but enjoy my independence.

I'm about to finish graduate school, hoping to make a career change from marketing writer in a dead-end job to teacher in adult education, helping people improve their skills and make their way in this fast-changing world. Pretty idealistic, I know, but why not?

So, Nathaniel, I'm still curious to know about your life in England and how you came to live in Oklahoma. Do tell. Inquiring minds want to know.

Regards,
Emily

. . .

Emily Dear,

You ask about my life in England and how I came to Oklahoma. As a small child, I lived in London until my father, who was an international attorney, took a position with a large law firm, headquartered in Oklahoma City. I was 9 when we moved. That was a major upheaval, as you can imagine. I don't think my mother ever adjusted, so she returned to London a year after my father's passing. She remarried and lived in Woldingham.

By then, my home was here, and I was satisfied until recently. Now, I realize something is missing. That is a special person to be by my side and fill my heart.

Could you be that special someone?

Let us keep writing and learning more about each other. I think you must be a lovely woman, perhaps the one I'm looking for.

P.S. What is this "inquiring minds want to know?" I'm not familiar with that.

Yours,
Nathaniel

. . .

Hmm. This email gives me pause. "Yours?" That's a bit cozy, isn't it? Maybe it's my New England reserve. He isn't familiar with "Inquiring minds want to know?" Maybe that's an East Coast idiom?

Dear Nathaniel,

You are a flatterer, aren't you? I must tell you I'm a New England native with all that entails. You've heard of New England reserve? It just means I like to move slowly, get to know someone before I get too familiar. I hope you understand.

I've lived in the Boston area most of my life and love living near the coast, especially in the summer. Have you ever been to New England? I wonder what you'd think of Boston? I really like this city, but I'm not a winter lover and consider moving to warmer climes, although I'd hate to leave my friends.

Thanks to those friends, I have a busy social life and enjoy myself, especially away from work. After being on my own for many years, I think I'd enjoy a compatible, like-minded partner. That's why I placed a personals ad.

What kind of person and relationship are you looking for?

Take care,
Emily

I wonder if I'll hear from him again. What's his interest in me?

• • •

Dear Emily,

If you do not mind, I would like to give you my personal email address. I am being hounded by a woman who persists in contacting me and writing inappropriate messages despite my attempts to discourage her, so I would like to leave this personals site. Please, write to me at: abrit926@aol.com.

Yours in haste,
Nathaniel

• • •

Haste? Hounded? It sounds as though dogs are after him. Picky, picky, Emily. Give the guy a chance. I click onto his photo again. He is adorable. And we'll probably never meet anyway.

Dear Nathaniel,

It must be difficult to open up about such a trying part of your life. I'm sorry for your loss.

Your relationship with your son must bring comfort.

I have experienced loss, too, having struggled through a marriage that ended in disappointment and divorce—different, I know, from suddenly losing someone you love, but painful and wounding anyway. I know it takes great strength to get through these times. You're doing well now, it seems.

You're an interesting man, but I'm not anxious to get into an intense long-distance relationship. You may want to find someone closer to home. I hope this doesn't seem harsh. I'm just trying to be honest.

Take care,
Emily

• • •

I hesitate before clicking "Send" and reread the email. Satisfied I'm not being unkind, I press the key. I probably won't hear from him again, which is for the best. In fact, maybe it's time to take a break from this internet hunt for Mr. Just Right. Maybe I should dye my hair red instead.

Nathaniel is not so easily discouraged, sending me another email three days later.

• • •

Dear Emily,

I have exciting news! I must travel to Asia for business and have decided to first fly to England to visit my son. I haven't seen him since last summer, so this visit will give us a chance to catch up. My son promises me he'll take his nose out of his books and spend time with me. Perhaps we'll take the train to Paris for some R & R, which we both can use.

I must end this email so I can book my flights.
I will write again soon.

Your delighted Nathaniel

• • •

Dear Nathaniel,

That is good news! It's wonderful that you'll get to see your son.
When will you go to England? Where do you have business in Asia? I don't remember what kind of business you do.

Enjoy!
Emily

• • •

Emily, dear,

I have a wonderful idea if you'll indulge me. I know I'll fly many miles on an indirect route, but perhaps one into your heart… Since I am longing to meet you and can make my own schedule, I'd like to fly to Boston when my business is completed. I thought I'd told you I'm a manufacturer of costumes, work that requires travel abroad. Now, I'd like to "come home." I could stay in a nearby hotel and we could have a few days to become better acquainted. You could show me your city. I've never been to Boston and hear it's a historical gem and a beautiful place. We could explore it together.

Please say yes.

Your Nathaniel

• • •

Yikes! He wants to come here? He wants to explore the city? This isn't what I expected. What did I expect? Why am I even emailing this guy?

"Because you wanted to meet someone," Dr. Rothman chides, "but this isn't the one."

"Where did you come from? So he's a bit younger, so he lives in Oklahoma, so he comes on too strong, so what?"

"So, I think he's as phony as a facelift."

"But he's adorable and intriguing and interested in me. What's the harm? I don't have to marry him."

"Believe me, you won't. Listen, if finding a guy who's interested in you is your criterion, you can go down to Barney's Bar and Grill and line up five or six guys in no time."

"You know what? I'm tired of your cynicism. It's getting old and not getting me anywhere. Leave me alone!"

"That's what you should be saying to this Lothario from Oklahoma: 'Scram, Buster.'"

"Dr. Rothman, you scram please."

"Alright, since you asked so nicely, but don't say I didn't warn you."

"Arghh!"

• • •

Dear Nathaniel,

Whoa! That's quite an idea! It's tempting, but wouldn't that be a lot of travel and out of your way? Maybe you want to rethink that.

I'd like to meet you but can wait until a more convenient time. Besides, Boston in the winter is not at its most endearing.

Hesitantly,
Emily

• • •

Dearest,

If I'm willing to travel those miles to be with you, why don't you let me worry about the convenience? Besides, whoever said convenience should be part of the equation? I want to be with you and can make the time and travel arrangements.

Just say yes.

Your Nathaniel

• • •

Dear Nathaniel,

If I say yes, when would you be here? How long would you stay? Do you need names of hotels?

I think we should talk on the phone at least once before we meet. It would also be easier for us to make arrangements.

Please let me know when you can call or give me a number where I can reach you.

Ciao,
Emily

• • •

Dear one,

I am thrilled that you are consenting to my visit. It lightens my heart and will make the business portion of my trip, which I do not anticipate with pleasure, that much easier. I will tell you about my business sometime. It's a mixed bag.

Good idea for us to talk on the phone. I will call you Wednesday evening at 7 p.m. your time. I am leaving for London the next morning.

I cannot wait to be with you.

Yours,
Nathaniel

• • •

Dear Nathaniel,

I waited for your call Wednesday evening. What happened? Where are you now? Please send me an itinerary or some idea of your plans.

Thanks,
Emily

• • •

Dearest,
I could not call you on Wednesday. I had too much paperwork to do for my meetings. I will call you from abroad one evening.

Yours in haste,
Nathaniel

• • •

Emily, my dear,

My visit with Donald has been splendid. He's given me undivided attention and we've had a good time. I'm off to Asia tomorrow and will send you my itinerary, I promise.
Longing to see you and can't wait until I land at JFK.

Your devoted Nathaniel

• • •

Dear Nathaniel,

If you land at JFK, you will not see me. JFK is in New York and I live in Boston.

Puzzled,
Emily

• • •

My Dear,

My mistake. I have been working long hours here in Manila, trying to expedite shipment of materials out of port. It is not going well. It was weariness from long hours and little sleep that led to my writing JFK when I meant Logan Airport, of course.

With any luck, I will complete my business in the next two days and will fly to you on the next available flight. I will send you my itinerary as soon as I have booked my flights.

Please do not be impatient with me. I am anxious to be with you.

Yours,
Nathaniel

● ● ●

Dearest One,

I have booked my flights. Business is nearly complete and I am taking a leap of faith all will be clear for me to fly to you on Thursday, arriving at the airport at 4:00 p.m., ET. Will you meet me at the airport? I am so longing to be with you.

I have attached my itinerary.

With great joy,
Nathaniel

● ● ●

Dear Nathaniel,

Again, I'm confused. You wrote you were landing at 4:00 p.m., ET, but your itinerary says you land in Boston at 2100 hours. That's 9:00 p.m., isn't it? Please let me know which time is correct. And you still haven't told me which hotel you're staying at. Is it in Boston, near the airport?

Emily

● ● ●

"Hey, Snow White, what are you thinking?" Dr. Rothman's voice is loud, impatient. "Something is definitely fishy with this guy. He doesn't know which airport he's flying to? He can't tell 4 p.m. from 9 p.m. and he wants you to pick him up? Are you going to tell me a guy who flies around the world for business can't keep his airports and landing times straight? This world traveler can't get himself to a hotel? He needs you to hang around airports, waiting for him to figure out where he's at?"

"Not you again! He explained the airport mix-up. He was confused because he hasn't been sleeping. Business hasn't been going well. Something's gone wrong and he's been working night and day."

"I don't buy it. Something's wrong, but it's with Mr. Right. And why would you pick up a stranger in the middle of the night to drive him who knows where? Let him take a cab. Meet him at a crowded restaurant in broad daylight. You don't know him. Do you even know his last name? This lover boy could be the Son of Sam or the next Boston Strangler."

"That's ridiculous. It's not the middle of the night, and he's not exactly a stranger…"

"Oh, that's right. I forgot you've been exchanging intimate emails for what… three or four minutes? Something's not kosher about this guy."

"Okay, I won't meet him at the airport. I'll tell him to take a cab, but I think you're being paranoid."

"Leave the diagnoses to me, okay? You just use your head."

"Are you through?"

"Are you going to take care of yourself?"

"Yes, sigh."

"I'm through… for now. Lord, talk about working hard…"

• • •

Dear Sweet One,

Once again I slipped up. You're absolutely right, love, I've been so distracted, trying to get my goods shipped that I misstated the time of arrival. I land at 9 p.m. at Logan Airport and hope you'll be there to greet me. I can't wait to see your sweet face and can't believe that soon, very soon, we will be together. By the way, I told my son all about you.

Wish me luck tomorrow.

Ever yours,
Nathaniel

• • •

Dear Nathaniel,

What's happening tomorrow?

Thanks for clarifying time you'll arrive. Unfortunately, I won't be able to meet you at the airport because I take a class on Thursday evenings. Why don't you get a cab and call me when you get to your hotel. We can make plans to meet the next morning—and I'll take time off from work.

Have a safe flight. Or should I say "flights," since I see you'll have several. Looks exhausting. Not easy to get from there to here, is it?

I'm glad we'll finally get to meet.

Emily

• • •

Hello Sweets,

I have grown a love bond with you and it seems as though your name is recorded, inserted and on replay in my ears. I can't wait to get to Boston so that I hold you and tell you what I want for us, and also THAT MOMENT WHEN A MAN MUST BE ON HIS KNEE. I hope we get to that stage.

I am all smiley and happy thinking of you. Is it the same for you? However, I must speak of something other than love. I need your assistance to sort a little situation. And darling, I won't take NO for an answer.

I mentioned to you earlier that I had to get to the harbor to round up my shipment. Honey, that did not go well for me as there was an issue. I always purchase my materials in bulk and never pay tax because they're ordered in my name, not the company's. That way allows for an exemption. When I submitted my papers to the authorities, I was told new rules require that I pay tax on my goods before they are released for shipping.

Darling, I am so unsettled. I have contacted my bank and they cannot do anything as I am out of the country. A cheque of $40,000 deposited into my account from the UK must go through a clearing period of 10 to 14 working days.

They say the policy is for my own security because I am a frequent traveler. My worry is that I had signed a contract to deliver goods on Saturday. A breach would cost me well more than I was paid for the order and also cause a stain on my reputation. I tried to explain the situation to the representative of the companies, but they threatened to sue.

I have never been in such situation in my life, and I can't think of a way to sort this. You are the only one I think of, which leads me to ask you to grant me this favor.

Honey, I need you to assist me in form of a loan. The tax amount is $4000. Please help me with this amount, and I'll give it back to you upon my return, with interest if you want.

I know it is weird that I ask you, but you should understand that I have run out of options. I think it would help us bond more rather than just emotionally and would allow for our relationship to be based on trust, openness, and sacrifices. Thank you for understanding. I await your favourable response.

I am going for a meeting very early in the morning after which I will fly to the States. Emily, please send the funds via Western Union; they advised that it is the fastest way to get money here. I am leaving details to send the funds so that time is well managed.

Send to: Nathaniel D. Wilson

Address: Pedro Gil Corner MH Del Pilar, Manila, Philippines

You will be given a reference number and some information for me to collect the funds. I would like you to send the money as soon as you can. I would appreciate it more than any gesture in the world as I am in a desperate situation. I will be indebted to you, of course, for the rest of my life.

I can't even tell my son because he'll panic. I hope my decision to rely on you is the best I ever have made.

Love
Me

• • •

Oh my gawd! Holy hell! I whip my head around, expecting to hear Dr. Rothman, chanting, "I told you so." Nothing. Not a peep.

Okay, Emily, just breathe. "Deeply," I command aloud, hoping the sound of my voice will interrupt my hyperventilating. I realize I've been breathing irregularly since I read the sentence...what was it? Something about getting down on one knee?

"So, Cinderella, this is your Prince Charming."

I'm actually relieved to hear Dr. Rothman's voice.

"I don't believe this."

"What's not to believe? The guy's a scam artist."

"What should I do?"

"You're kidding, right? Call the cops."

"The cops? Why the cops?"

"On the off chance he might actually fly into Logan and show up on your doorstep."

"You don't think he'd do that?"

"I wouldn't think running a romance scam on middle-aged women was the most lucrative and satisfying way to earn a living either, but does it matter what I think? Call the cops."

CHAPTER 12

—

TRUE CONFESSIONS

I begin to wonder whether this guy could really show up on my doorstep some night when I'm alone, rob, and murder me in my bed.

I have to go to the police. What do I wear?

I dress conservatively in navy slacks, a long-sleeve white blouse and navy cardigan sweater. I wear my navy flats. I look like a visiting nurse.

The local precinct is four blocks from my apartment on Boylston Street, so I walk there, rehearsing my story, not that I won't be truthful, but maybe I can minimize the mortification.

You see, officer, it's not that I'm desperate or that lonely but I thought it would be nice to have a man in my life... hmm, maybe I doth protest too much.

I'm already at the station, climbing the dingy stone steps and heaving open the heavy door. I step into a small waiting area and approach the desk nearest the door. A head of red hair and blue police shoulders are hunched over paperwork.

"Ahem."

The head lifts and a young face with baby-blue eyes and a faint trace of freckles—I swear—peers at me. "Can I help you, Ma'am?"

At least he didn't say "Grandma."

"I hope so. I didn't really want to come here… no, that's not what I mean. I did want to come, but I was embarrassed. I'm afraid you'll think I'm a fool." I wait for him to protest, and he waits for me to say more.

I edge closer to his desk, not wanting to be overheard, looking over my shoulder before I begin speaking again. My heart is beating double-time as I spill the whole, ugly story, stopping occasionally to grab a breath. During one of these pauses, he offers me a chair and I sit, grateful because my knees have begun to tremble.

"So, what I'm afraid of is that he's going to show up at my door any minute," I finish plaintively.

Looking at me sympathetically, he says, "Ma'am, this kind of scam is happening all the time with the internet. You'd be surprised how many times we hear this story."

"Really?"

"Yeah, especially with…" he hesitates…"people of a certain age like yourself and especially on these personals sites. You're a prime target."

I'm not sure this is a comfort. "What should I do? What if he shows up?"

"He's not going to show up. This guy's running a scam and going through a list of women like yourself. Don't worry about him showing up. That's not what this is about. He's just looking for women to scam out of their money. In your case, he hasn't gotten any money out of you, so he hasn't committed a crime. There's not much we can do, but if you hear from him again, let us know."

"What do you mean he hasn't committed a crime?"

"You didn't send him the money, right? Then there's no crime."

"Well, that's something," I say, relieved and disappointed that the police can't hunt this Nathaniel down, rough him up, and toss him in the clink. As I get up and turn to leave, I hear the baby cop calling after me.

"Hey, you should feel good about yourself. You'd be amazed how many women have sent this guy money and guys like him. It's an epidemic."

Wearily trudging the four blocks back to my apartment, I review what baby cop has said. "It's an epidemic."

If it's an epidemic, why hasn't someone done anything to stop it? Where's the vaccine? Why aren't there signs on the sides of buses or warnings from the Surgeon General or anything to alert women of a certain age?

I speed up, hurrying to get onto my computer and do a little research, blessing the internet for being the source of all knowledge and forgiving it momentarily for being the source of dastardly scams by mean-spirited villains. By the time I reach my computer, my outrage is operating full throttle, so I dash off a hasty, irate last email.

• • •

Nathaniel, I know what you're up to. It's a scam and I've been to the cops. Your days are numbered, Buddy. Don't ever contact me again. You are an evil, mean-spirited bastard.

Emily

• • •

I needn't have bothered sending this email, because in the next two hours of online research, I learn there is no Nathaniel. He's the creation of a conglomerate—Frankenstein's monster, patched together from stolen internet photos, hard-luck stories, and a tub of romantic treacle by a bunch of guys at computers, working in the Philippines, Nigeria, and other exotic locales for companies making hundreds of thousands of dollars seducing suckers like me.

I watch a video interview of a guy in Nigeria, part of a group perpetrating this kind of scam. In the background, I see a row of computer operators tapping out their messages of seduction.

"We work on shifts and by script," this guy explains in an elegant British accent, "but then we have to vary our responses to accommodate the changes as the communications require. It necessitates careful attention to detail. Sometimes, it's difficult to keep up with what has transpired in the previous shifts. But with practice, we become quite proficient." He smiles modestly.

Oh, good lord, that's why "Nathaniel" confused details about airports and times. That's why the tone and language changes. A bunch of guys calling themselves Nathaniel were working their shifts, sending those emails.

It's hard for me to absorb this information and even harder to realize that lovelorn women may be anxiously waiting at airports all over the world for suitors who will never appear.

CHAPTER 13

—

RUMINATE AND REBOUND

I dread going into work today. I'm sure everyone can see the scarlet S for sucker emblazoned on my sweater. How can I survive the humiliation, ridicule, and scorn? I calm myself as I hang up my coat, realizing nobody knows about this debacle except Shelley, who doesn't know the latest and will keep her mouth shut, and Dr. Rothman, who doesn't count. I realize Ian has been waiting to hear from me, and I owe him an explanation—pathetic as the story is.

How could I have been such a fool? I sit at my desk, listening to voicemail, sharpening pencils, and fantasizing about stabbing him in the heart and other vital organs. But who is the "him" I want to eviscerate? There is no Nathaniel to loathe for being a slimy, treacherous bastard. Teams of trolls, sitting at computers, have seduced suckers like me, stealing our hearts and our life savings... wait a minute, I interrupt my rant... I didn't fall for it in the long run. I never gave them a cent.

Big, whooping deal! I did fall for his line. There I go again. There is no he. I begin to sniffle and grab for a tissue.

This is ridiculous, I snort. Nothing is hurt but my pride. Now I sound like my mother, the pragmatist, who doesn't believe in self-pity or wallowing. Think what she's missing! Pondering about anti-wallowers, I wonder why Dr. Rothman hasn't reared his chubby, round head. Never mind, I can do his part in my sleep.

"You can feel sorry for all the little old ladies who did part with their life savings, if it helps, but that's just a distraction. What about you? Why did you fall for this? Weren't there any red flags?"

"I suppose so," I nod and then stop jabbing my pencil into the small hole in my desk as I remember a story I heard in a recent career exploration workshop. The speaker was urging us aspiring job-changers to look for companies run with integrity, insisting that concept was not the oxymoron we might think. He told us to learn as much as we could about any organization we were considering by reading, doing research, and paying attention to all signals and clues during any interactions with staff and management; he urged us not to overlook any red flags in our eagerness to get a job, telling us this story.

"A woman came to me for career counseling, saying she was miserable in her job, hated the management, which was dishonest and exploitative, couldn't stand the back-biting culture and had to get out. She was unable to make a move because she was afraid she'd fall into another terrible situation.

"I asked her if she'd had any indication of what the company was like at her interviews. Had she seen any signs of trouble? She thought for a moment and said no; everyone seemed nice and helpful. We continued to talk and suddenly she said, 'I just remembered one thing. When I handed my application to the receptionist, she whispered, 'You don't want to work here.'"

I get up, grab my coat, and head for the door. I need fresh air. I remember Dr. Rothman's once saying to me, "You're so anxious to win the race, you don't think about whether or not you'd want to take the prize home with you."

I speed my pace to a trot as I circle the pond between buildings. It's damp and cold—good, maybe I'll catch a chill, develop pneumonia, and die. It would be hours before anyone found my frozen body. This path isn't used much. No one is around except one figure way off in the distance that doesn't seem to be moving.

Maybe it's a tree branch. Am I so desperate to find a man that I'm willing to overlook all warning signs? Am I that lonely? Hell, most of the time I'm not lonely at all. I'm busy and perfectly content… well, not with the job, but that's going to change. It's just a matter of time and work. Getting a new job is a lot of work. It's like a job.

It occurs to me that dating is very much like job hunting: the sighting, the chase, the desire to impress, the wait by the phone, the fear of rejection, the wish for acceptance—geez, all that sturm und drang without a thought about whether the prize is worth it. Still trying to win over Daddy? Argh.

Red flags, signals, paying attention… I'm so focused on these gnats buzzing around my brain that I don't notice the lone figure approaching on the path until we have almost collided. It's Will Slipway.

"Whoa, hey… Emily, is that you? What's your hurry?"

Of course it's me, I think. This guy is still playing games. "Sorry, I was so caught up in my thoughts that I didn't see you."

"I'm kind of glad. You couldn't turn in the other direction to avoid me."

"Avoid you? Why do you say that?"

"Probably because you've been avoiding me. I've been trying to reach you for a few weeks and have left messages. Haven't heard a word from you."

I could lie and say I haven't received them, but what would be the point? "Oh, sorry," I shrug, backing away slightly. "I've been distracted."

"Everything all right?" He actually looks concerned

"Yes, nothing new… it's just the job. Same old stuff."

"That's a bummer," he pauses and smiles, "but I've got good news. My wife has filed for divorce. We're separated. I'm living in the spare room at my sister's. Should be going to a final hearing soon."

"Congratulations. That's good news for you," I say without much enthusiasm.

"Hey, it is good news. I thought you'd be happy, too."

"Why?" I wrap my arms around my chest, shivering.

"For us. We can see each other now without sneaking around. I'm a free man."

"Look, Will, there is no us. I'm glad for your sake, but there never was an us, sneaking or otherwise. Sorry to be blunt, but I'm cold and not in the mood for this."

He reaches out to touch me, but I slip past him and head back up the path to my building.

"Hey, Emily," he shouts, "I'll catch you on another day when it's not so cold."

"Not if I see you first," I mutter.

CHAPTER 14

—

RESCUE ME

I sit in my cubicle, remembering past humiliations. One is particularly vivid. Eleven years old, midway through two weeks living in a tent at Camp Chippewa, I am homesick—missing TV, fresh fruit, my own bed, and reluctantly participating in the rigors of early morning swimming, archery, volleyball, and horseback riding. On this chilly afternoon, I sit astride a palomino named Trigger, waiting to set out on a trail ride for advanced beginners.

An apprehensive equestrienne, I fidget on the saddle, trying to get comfortable on the hard leather shell, clutching the reins and praying for heavy rains to wash out this ride. Trigger, sensing my discomfort, shifts his weight impatiently, pawing the ground, protesting that after all his years of service, this fidgety child is the best he can get. His uneasiness mirrors mine, but as the riders begin descending the trail toward a narrow, asphalt road bisecting the woods, we follow like dutiful soldiers.

A few minutes into the ride, a skinny, gray squirrel scurries across our path, spooking Trigger, who bolts with me bouncing on his back. He gallops down the road, ignoring my feeble attempts to rein him in. I scream in terror, which throws Trigger into a frenzy, pitching forward and toppling onto the rutty asphalt with me clinging to his neck. I roll off his back, scraping my face in grit. Voices shout, horses whinny, and I awaken in a narrow, lumpy cot in the camp infirmary. Concerned eyes are peering down at me.

"My throat is sore. I want my mother," I whisper, my voice thickened with gravel and defeat. I hold on to the sweet vision of my mother riding to my rescue in the battle-gray family Buick.

By early morning, I have managed to elevate my temperature to 100 degrees. Later that afternoon, the gray Buick rolls into camp and I am whisked away.

• • •

I punch my mother's number into the phone.

"Hi, Mum, how are you?" I whisper, relieved when I hear her voice, slightly short of breath. "And don't say 'How should I be?'"

"Why are you whispering?"

"I'm at work," I whisper slightly louder. "So how are you?"

"I'm fine, just a little winded. Raspberry and I were chasing each other around the dining room table."

"Who won?"

"So far, it's a draw. Why are you calling me in the middle of the day when the rates are so high? Are you okay?" Her voice leaks concern.

"Yes, I'm okay, but I was missing you, that's all. Haven't heard from you for a couple of weeks."

"The phone works both ways," she retorts.

"Okay, Smarty Pants, I know that. I've been…distracted." I feel tears pushing at the edges of my eyes.

"Oy, what's wrong? Are you sure you're okay? You're not sick, are you?"

Since my father's death, my mother has taken over his role as family physician. I still hear him asking, "How's your health? How are the kids? How's your job? How's the car? Here, I'll let you talk to your mother."

Still feeling blue, I send a letter to Ian, catching him up on my disasters, particularly the scam.

I think I've owed him a letter for ages, so I'm heartened to hear back from him.

• • •

Friday, November 28

Dear Emily,

I'm relieved to hear from you and am so sorry to hear what you've been through. Those miserable bastards! What happened to you is outrageous! It's hard to believe that anyone can prey on people that way. Who could believe that businesses have been created for just that purpose! Emily, I want you to know that I'm here for you. Please call anytime if you want to talk. We can use email for faster communication if you'd like. My address is flyingscotsman@aol.com. If you'd rather stick with letters, that's fine, too.

Also, I want you to know you have no reason to feel embarrassed or ashamed. This could happen to any of us, especially if we're not versed in the underhanded forms of cybercrime.

I know you've always thought of yourself as cynical, Emily, but you're not. A couple of things I appreciate about you are your kind heart and trusting nature. You try to disguise it with wit or humor, but you don't fool anyone who knows you well. I don't want you to change. I'd just like to see those bastards rotting in prison.

One more thing. You should give yourself credit for seeing through this scam. You didn't send the money. Think of how many people have been fooled and have sent thousands of dollars to these crooks. This has become big business. That should tell you something about how many people have fallen for it—how vulnerable we all are.

I hope you'll forgive yourself for being vulnerable, Emily, and please remember I'm always rooting for you.

Fondly,
Ian

• • •

Wednesday, December 3

Dear Ian,

How kind you are! Your words make me feel better and I have begun to forgive myself for being such a fool. I will recover. It would help my spirits immensely if those sleazebags are caught, tried, and sentenced to life, chained to computers in dark, dank prisons where they are forced to write essays on evil, sinfulness, purgatory, and hell until their fingers fall off. Then they should be forced to read the Bible, Old and New Testament, Dante's Divine Comedy and Milton's Paradise Lost to one another until they repent or go mad, whichever comes first.

As for me, I think it's time for me to finish my graduate program, as you so wisely have advised, and move on. Enough avoidance, distraction, and looking for love in all the wrong places!

To more pleasant topics—the holidays are fast approaching, and I'm wondering what you're doing for Christmas. Will you spend it with your daughters? I'm going to visit my mother next week. My older son and his girlfriend will be here later in the month, so we'll celebrate Hanukkah and Christmas together. That means we'll have a big roast and latkes and spin a dreidel under the Xmas tree.

Whatever you do, I wish you happy holidays and a wonderful New Year. I don't know about you, but I'm ready for this year to end and looking forward to a year without fetishists, frauds, and fortune hunters!

I'll let you know what happens with grad school. You can be sure I'll check out prospective internships to make sure the businesses aren't fronts for the Mafia or any other criminal group.

Thanks so much for your support and wise words. I appreciate your thoughtfulness and caring.

Fondly,
Emily

CHAPTER 15

—

MICHAELA, ROW THE BOAT AGROUND

I am checking job postings on Craigslist and Indeed when I sense a presence behind me. I close the screen and whip around in my chair, silently cursing cubicles and hoping my visitor hasn't seen what I'm doing.

It's Michaela, my manager, face puckered in her familiar scowl. Michaela has three facial expressions—scowling or opaque for staff; and unctuous for her boss, his boss, and up the ladder. She's a master at managing upward, which seems to be a winning attribute in this company.

"Emily, I hope I'm not interrupting anything important." She folds her arms against her ample chest. Michaela is short and stocky. The three-inch heels she wears tend to throw her off balance, so she looks as though she's going to lurch forward.

"No, I was just looking for an email. What can I do for you?" I back my chair against the computer desk in case Michaela comes tumbling at me.

"I'm checking to make sure everyone got the memo about the Friday at the end of quarter. I didn't get an acknowledgement from a few of you."

Stopping by in person? Talk about not having enough work! "No, I don't think I saw that memo. What about the Friday at the end of quarter?"

"It will be a mandatory workday this year. No exceptions."

"Wow! What's that about?"

She shrugs her broad shoulders. "Management decision."

Code for don't ask; we won't tell. "That seems pretty harsh."

Michaela shrugs again. "It is what it is." She's about to move on to the next cubicle.

"Michaela, speaking of quarter-end, I'd like to discuss another scheduling issue with you."

She sighs, her chest and shoulders heaving. Michaela is an advocate of body language. "How about 2 o'clock?"

"Good. Thanks." I turn to face my computer where tumble-weed rolls across the screen saver. I need a strategy.

At precisely 2 p.m., I knock on Michaela's door.

"Enter."

Michaela's desk is still stacked with papers, even more than before. Like Michaela, they seem to teeter precariously, threatening to topple over. Michaela is sitting at her computer table, adjacent to her desk. She turns to acknowledge me, opaque face in place.

"So, Emily. What other scheduling matter do we need to discuss?" Her tone is frosty.

"Thanks for seeing me. It looks as though you're really busy, so I won't take long. In fact, that's just what I want to talk about."

"My being busy?"

"Yes, in a way. You remember our conversation last month," I don't wait for a reply, plunging forward, "when I came to you, looking for work because I didn't have enough to do? Well, it may have seemed that I expected you to find work for me, putting an extra burden on you."

Her shoulders relax slightly. "I have been under a great deal of pressure. They keep asking for reports, asking for documentation, figures, and more reports. I'm up to my eyeballs and it just keeps coming…" She stops. "Sorry, I didn't mean to get carried away."

"That's okay. What I'm here to ask is how can I help you. Since I have time, can I take any work off your plate? I'd really like to do that."

Is Michaela's lip trembling? She turns her head away from me momentarily and then turns back. "Emily, that's really kind of you. I'd love to say yes and hand off a project to you, but I don't know if I can take the time to figure out which one and show you what to do."

Now, it's my turn to look away. I can't believe this. "But, Michaela, I'd like to help. I really would. I'm a quick study, so it wouldn't take that long to bring me up to speed." Now, I'm starting to whine. I stop talking.

"Emily, let me think about it, okay? In the meantime, if you want to make yourself useful, why don't you ask your colleagues if they need help? And you don't have to confine yourself to our team. Go ask other teams on this floor if they need help. Now, I really have to get back to this report. We'll talk when I'm less swamped. Close the door again after you, please."

That went well. I shudder and feel as though I just went six rounds with Rocky Balboa—so much for my strategy!

I walk toward Shelley's cubicle and peek in to see if she's got a shoulder to cry on.

"Shel, have you got a minute?"

She looks away from her computer, "For you, kiddo, always. What's up?"

I repeat the conversation between Michaela and me—verbatim, no editorializing.

Shelley says, "Maybe you should wear one of those sandwich board signs saying, 'Will work for… what's your favorite candy? Snickers? Will work for Snickers.'"

"Nice," I say. "Snickers says it all."

"What are you going to do?"

"I may ask if anyone on our team needs help, but I'm sure as hell not going to other groups begging for work. Is she nuts or am I?"

"A rhetorical question, I assume."

"I'm definitely going to step up my job search. I've got to get out of here."

"You may want to hang on for a while longer," Shelley says quietly.

"Why? Why would I want to do that?"

"There are rumors again… talk about layoffs. Sales are still down this quarter. I've heard the word 're-org' whispered in the wind…" She's whispering now.

"Are you serious? What else have you heard?"

"If layoffs come, some will probably be in this department."

CHAPTER 16

—

THE ESCAPE PLAN

If layoffs come again, maybe this time I'll get lucky and get the golden shoulder-tap. I have to think positively and start packing up again. Calm down, Emily. If layoffs come, you need a plan.

"What about finishing your graduate program?" Dr. Rothman's voice floats into my cubicle. "How many courses do you have left?"

"Two, but one of them is statistics. I was the only person who solved a trigonometry problem with my mineshaft going up into the air! Who knows what danger awaits me in statistics."

"You've got a point, but If you don't take it, you'll never pass," he chides.

"You're not the first person to tell me that."

"If it worries you so, why not get a tutor?"

"I've heard that before, too."

"Sounds like you've been getting good advice. What's the other course you're avoiding?"

"It's not really a course. It's an internship—10 hours a week somewhere. How can I do that when I'm stuck here?"

"Listen to you. Stuck here with no work to do. Told to lie low and stay out of the way. You probably spend 10 hours a week napping in your car, but I digress into thoughts of larceny. Take the statistics course. Get a tutor. Maybe, by the time you're ready for the internship, you'll have been laid off. Let me know when you have a plan."

I feel a rush of cool air. Dr. Rothman has left the building. I move papers around my desk, revisiting our conversation. He and Ian are right about finishing school. Then, instead of hiding from these middle management bottom feeders, I can teach real people how to read and write. What did he mean about larceny?

I get up from my chair, head for the soft-drink machine in the break room, drop my quarters into the slot, and listen with satisfaction to the thud of a Diet Coke dropping within reach. I sip on my soda, enjoying the tang and waiting for the familiar aftertaste, off the wagon after nearly a month. Can I do an internship while I'm supposed to be working here? Steal 10 hours a week from this place? I couldn't do that.

"Why not? You do that now." Dr. Rothman apparently hasn't quite left the building.

I return to my cubicle, grab my cellphone, and head for an empty conference room where I can make my call without an audience. I punch in the number for the graduate department of Adult Education. "Hello, this is Emily Rosenbloom. I'd like to make an appointment with Dr. Thayer to talk about internships for the next quarter."

I'm in the mood to celebrate. On the way home, I stop at Phun Duk to order pot stickers and spicy green beans, CVS drugstore to replenish my supply of Neutrogena bubble bath and Cherry Garcia ice cream, and finally at the library to borrow *Nine to Five*.

I'm about to dip my chopsticks into a juicy, hot pot sticker when the phone rings. I'm tempted not to answer, but it may be my mother.

"Hello, Emily, it's your mother." Raspberry yips in the background. "Shh, Mamala, I can't hear."

Now she calls the dog Mamala? Oy.

"Hi, Mum, how are you? Let me turn down the TV."

"Am I interrupting because I can call back after *Judge Judy*?"

"I'm not watching *Judge Judy*."

"No, I am."

"So why did you interrupt your program to call me?"

"I usually watch *The Wheel of Fortune*, but I can't stand how those dummies have to buy vowels before they've even tried."

"Mum, what's up?"

"I just wanted to check on you. The last time you called, you sounded blue, so I wanted to make sure you're okay."

"I'm more than okay. I'm going back to graduate school to finish my degree!"

"I thought you had finished."

"No, I had two courses left. It should take me another quarter or two."

"You know your father never wanted you to work too hard. He worried about you with the boys to raise, your job, and all."

"He worried about everything," I say dismissively. "Besides, the boys are raised, my job is practically nonexistent, and school will be fun."

"What do you mean your job is nonexistent? Were you fired?"

"Not yet, but I'm hoping… not to get fired, just laid off."

"What's the difference? You know jobs aren't easy to find right now. Did I tell you about Ethel Green's son? Been out of work for 10 months and not a nibble."

"That's why I want to finish graduate school so I can get work."

"You have work."

"Different work, something I like." I can hear my voice rising.

My mother sighs. "So long as you're happy. That's all I want. Just don't work too hard. I've got to finish *Judge Judy* and take Raspberry for a walk."

CHAPTER 17

—

SUFFERING IN STYLE

I can't believe how everything is falling into place. I've been able to arrange an internship in a workplace education program at Chemicon, Inc., a large, multinational conglomerate, once a corner oatmeal stand. And they're willing to let me fulfill my 10-hour weekly commitment in two afternoons a week, "as long as my employers are amenable to that schedule."

"My employers also find that schedule convenient," I lie, having no intention of letting my manager know anything about these AWOL excursions.

I'm going to sneak out of my cubicle Tuesday and Thursday afternoons for as long as I can get away with it. It's strange, but I feel no guilt, just relief and hints of exhilaration. I've already shadowed Val, the reading/writing teacher, who'll supervise me. I love her students. It's like the United Nations with such diversity and variety of learning issues. Sometimes, English is a student's third language; some students have learning disabilities; some are illiterate. The staff works with engineers whose writing is fit only for other engineers or admin assistants whose memos never get to the point. Val works with an Indian chemist who has a speech impediment and a Russian designer who wants to learn idiomatic

English. I can't wait to work with these people. I can feel my energy flowing again. I feel like Sleeping Beauty awakening from deep sleep—a self-help beauty—no princes need apply.

I'm enjoying a quiet Saturday at home, settling into my snug, little shell, when the phone rings and a voice from my past intrudes—this time, not Dr. Rothman.

"Emily, you're not easy to find at home. It's Will Slipway. How are you?"

I'm tempted to give him the classic answer of my ancestors, "So, how should I be?" Instead, I greet him with civility. "I'm just fine. How are you?"

"Bruised and battle-weary, but it's over! I have divorce papers in hand. I'm a free man and am looking to celebrate."

"Good for you." I want to tell him that I'm traveling down that road to freedom, too. Soon, one way or another, I'll be free of my crummy no-job and embarked on a new career, but I'm not sure I trust him not to blabber. "I'm glad for your sake and your wife's, too."

"Why are you glad for my wife?"

"No one wants to be trapped in a miserable marriage."

Silence. "I hadn't thought about that," he says. "I hadn't thought about her that way. All these years we've been unhappy but she's been against divorce. I guess I thought she'd settled for what we had and made her peace with it."

"Maybe so or maybe she's been waiting for you to take the big step. Eventually, I'll bet she sees she's better off," I reply. Am I projecting?

"Better off, for sure," he chuckles ruefully. "She got a good chunk of my change and future earnings."

"Well, you were married for how many years?"

"Twenty-seven long ones."

"So, what did you expect?" I ask, thinking of the father of my children who tried to weasel out of giving me any child support. He loved his boys but not enough to want to part with any of his change. "Look, this is a touchy subject for me, so let's drop it. I'm happy that you got what you wanted."

"Sorry if I hit a sore spot. I remember your ex-husband sounded like a schmo."

I laugh, "the original schmo."

"It's encouraging to me that you can laugh. Right now, I'm feeling like I had all my teeth extracted."

"It takes time but it gets better." I'm surprised at this urge to offer comfort, but he sounds real for once, not Mr. Man-on-the-Make.

"Thanks for the encouragement. I need to hear that kind of thing. Would you be willing to sit down and talk with me over a cup of coffee? No hidden agenda. It would cheer me up."

I hesitate, but I'm in an expansive mood, so I say, "Sure. Why not?"

• • •

I dress in sweatshirt, jeans, and my oldest running shoes to deliver a clear message. This is not a date. This is just one friend consoling another, sharing the enlightenment of experience.

Slipway wears a leather jacket, handsome brown and beige sweater, and charcoal brown slacks. His beard is trim and close to his chin. I'm surprised that he looks so good and wonder about his agenda.

But I dismiss my misgivings, determined to comfort, offer empathy and wisdom, and keep my distance.

"You look well," I say, shaking his hand and sitting in the chair he's pulled from the table.

"I am well, thanks. I feel like I've just come out of battle, a little bloody but unbowed."

"That's a good start, I suppose. Where are you living now—still at your sister's?"

"Until the end of the month. Then I've rented a two-bedroom place on Highland, not far from the Park Place Theater."

Two bedrooms in that neighborhood? He obviously didn't part with all his money. Why two bedrooms, I wonder. "That's a nice neighborhood."

"Yes, I was lucky to get the place. It's a rent control and I know the landlord. He's the brother-in-law of one of my tennis partners. It's a good deal."

Tennis, rent control, two bedrooms in an upscale area, new wardrobe—I should suffer in such comfort—so much for empathy for this guy. Meanwhile, his wife is probably buying groceries with food stamps, shopping for clothes at Goodwill, and taking in laundry. Now, I am projecting.

"Where's your wife living now? Are any of the kids with her?"

"Ex-wife," he corrects me. "She's still in the house, which is up for sale. With her half of the money, she'll probably buy a place in Stowe or Sugarbush. She loves to ski, and we've vacationed there for years."

Fine, I think, but what about the rest of the year? "Not an easy place to find a job, I'd guess."

He smiles. "She's never worked, at least not full-time. She'll find something in a dress boutique or gallery. She's good with the public."

Boutique or gallery? She clearly doesn't have to be good with the hoi polloi. How much money does this guy earn? I look at him again.

"So, I gather you're not suffering too much…at least not financially."

"No, there's some family money, a trust, that kind of thing."

"I see. What about your kids? Are they living with their mother?"

"No, they're away at school, just coming home for vacations and holidays. That's why I wanted a two bedroom to have a place for them."

School expenses, too. Good god, this guy must be rolling in dough.

"I'm relieved it's all over," he says, "but I have to admit I'm lonely. It's nice to be out, even in a coffee shop, and talk to a nice, sympathetic person like you."

Good thing he's not a mind reader. "My experience wasn't much like yours, but I know what you mean about the loneliness.

Even though my kids were still at home, I spent a lot of lonely hours, especially after they went to sleep. Sometimes, I even went to bed when they did."

"Then you know how it feels. But you seem fine, great even, so it gets better?"

"It gets better. Do you have any hobbies, things you like to do?"

"I used to sail, but I don't have a boat anymore."

"You can still sail. The guys with the boats are always looking for crews." Listen to me. I need Dramamine to stand on the dock.

"Really? Do you sail?" He looks hopeful.

"No, I have friends." I should say I have friends who know friends who know people who sail. "What else do you enjoy?"

"Dancing. I haven't been out dancing in years, except the night I met you. That was special. Do you like to dance?"

"No, I'm a klutz. I feel too self-conscious and clumsy to enjoy it."

Noticing his shoulders slump, I add, "but there are lots of dance classes. That's a great way to meet people."

"How do you know that?"

"Friends," I say and we both laugh.

"I might look into the dance classes," he says. "I don't suppose I could persuade you to join me? If you recall, I'm a bit of a klutz, myself."

"No, I wouldn't recognize myself if I learned to dance without tripping over my partner's toes. My nickname in high school was Oops, and I wouldn't want to relinquish my reputation. I think you'll have to do the dance bit on your own."

"What about your hobbies? What do you like to do?"

"I'm into more sedentary stuff like reading, movies, theater, music, although I've been known to work out and ride my trusty two-wheeler around the block, but I don't have time for much right now. I'm finishing grad school and have a couple of quarters to go."

"That's terrific. What are you getting, an MBA?"

"Me? Not bloody likely. Besides being a klutz, I'm numbers phobic. I get hives just thinking about the little devils. I'm in the adult education program. I want to teach other adults to fear and loath math as much as I do." Noticing his puzzled stare, I say, "Just kidding. I'm learning how to help people with reading and writing, two of my favorite sports."

"That's great. I really admire anyone who can write. It doesn't come easily to me."

"You're not alone. I know lots of people suffer when they have to write and I'd really like to make it easier."

"I'm also not much of a reader," he hesitates. "I had a hard time learning to read, so I never got turned on. When I read, it's mostly technical or science journals."

"Nothing wrong with that," I say, sensing more to the story.

"I have some dyslexia," he says quietly. "It wasn't diagnosed when I was a kid, so I struggled and nobody knew why."

"How did you figure it out?"

"When my son had trouble with reading. The testing and diagnosis made me wonder, so I got tested."

"That must have been a shock and a relief," I murmur.

"You're not kidding… but enough about me and my accomplishments. What kind of movies do you like, and can we find one we'd both enjoy?"

I hesitate, looking down at my empty cup. "I don't see why not. We can probably find something we'd both be willing to see. I'm not into horror or violence."

"Me neither," he grins. "What classes do you have left?"

I can't let him know about the internship on company time, so I prevaricate, "Right now, I'm working on experiential project design." That seems sufficiently obscure, I hope.

"Say what? I'm not sure I know what that means."

Neither do I, buddy, so I think fast. "Really? You haven't heard of that? I guess it's fairly new in the field. Maybe it's confined to adult education practice. That's probably it."

"I guess," he says, not sure if he should push for more information. "It sounds pretty mysterious."

Oy. "Basically, it's a research project. My teammates and I are working with adult volunteers." Crossing my fingers, I hope he's satisfied.

"Interesting, I guess. Maybe you'll tell me more sometime."

"Yes, sometime. Right now, I can't say too much about it."

"That's intriguing. What else are you taking?"

"It's actually what I'm not taking. Remember, I mentioned my math phobia? I've been successfully avoiding a basic statistics course required for the degree. Now, it's do or die," I say, miming a slash across my throat.

"That bad, huh?" He grins almost imperceptibly, but I catch it.

"I suppose it's like you with reading," I poke back.

"Maybe, maybe more a self-fulfilling prophecy, but I've got an idea. I've always been good at numbers, thank god. Maybe I could help you?"

"Tutor me, you mean?"

"Yes, why not? We could meet at a coffee shop or in one of the cafeterias at work if you feel more comfortable, or at the library."

"I could use the help. I know that without even buying the book. I was going to try to find someone at school…" I look at him as he leans forward, smiling encouragement. He really wants to help. "Why not," I say. "Thanks!"

• • •

Sunday, January 3

Dear Ian,

I hope your holidays were full of joy and love. I had a great time with my older son, Gabe, and his girlfriend. We invited friends to Xmas dinner, so my apartment was rocking with fun, laughter, and good spirits, not to mention a delicious prime rib, latkes, and—as I promised—Yorkshire pudding, vegetables, salad, an incredible chocolate soufflé, and home-baked pies for dessert, contributed by my friends. The day was exhausting and exhilarating.

Guess what?! I have great news! I'm back in my graduate program full force. I've signed up to take statistics and have an internship that begins later this month. I'll be spending two afternoons a week in a workplace education program at Chemicon, a large, research-based biopharmaceutical company. Have you heard of it?

It's like the UN with lots of diversity and learning issues. Sometimes, English is a student's third language; some students have learning disabilities. The staff helps chemists and engineers write so they can be understood. They also help admin assistants write memos that get to the point. I can't wait to work with these people!

Statistics begins in a week, and I've bought the book, which I haven't opened yet, since it will probably be Greek to me. At your suggestion, I've found a tutor. He's a colleague who likes math and is good at it. Apparently, he's helped his kids with algebra, calculus, and even statistics, so he's confident he can help me. I'm cautiously optimistic.

Again, I want to thank you for urging me to finish these grad school requirements and get on with my life. You've been really helpful.

Fondly,
Emily

CHAPTER 18
—
JUST ANOTHER STATISTIC

Encouraged by Will's offer to help me with statistics, I've enrolled in the class and ponder the probability of passing on the first go-round. We meet in the business library behind the cafeteria in his building. It's out-of-the-way, usually empty, and neutral territory. I'm satisfied that these meetings will be our secret.

My comfort is short-lived. The morning after our first tutorial, Shelley knocks on my cubicle wall and asks if I'd like to join her for a cup of coffee. We are barely out of earshot of curious colleagues when she says, "So, what were you doing with Slipway, the stalker, after hours yesterday? I thought you'd safely dodged that philanderer."

"How did you know I was with Slipway?" I sputter.

"My network, dearie, sees all and tells all. I have receptionists and staff assistants planted in every building. Nothing escapes our watchful eyes."

"If your network knows so much, why are you asking me what I was doing with him? You should have the answer, Smarty Pants!" I huff. "Besides, it's perfectly innocent."

"Really?" Shelley cocks her head and regards me suspiciously. "If it's so innocent, why are you getting so bent out of shape? Your face is as purple as an eggplant, and I can see steam coming out of your ears."

"First of all, Slipway is divorced, so he's not philandering. Second, we're just friends. Third, he's helping me with statistics. He's my tutor, that's all."

"Tutor? Since when do you use statistics and since when is he a tutor?" Shelley asks.

"Since I went back to graduate school. I'm surprised your network didn't know about that," I snap.

"Really, back to grad school? That's great!"

"Don't try to change the subject," I say. "You need to tell your network to back off."

"Okay, okay. But Slipway is your tutor?"

"Yes, and he's good—just the right blend of forbearance, fortitude, and perseverance to put up with me. And he hasn't made a single pass since we started the tutoring."

I can tell Shelley's not convinced, but she nods her head and says, "Okay, I'm glad for you. I'll tell my informers to chill."

Just to be safe, I call Will later that afternoon to suggest we find another meeting place. We settle on the Cambridge Public Library for our next rendezvous.

"In the meantime," I ask, "can I drop my homework off for you to look at? I have to hand it in before we're due to meet again, and I haven't the foggiest idea if I'm doing it right."

"Sure, just drop it off."

I climb the hill to the building where Will works and find him in the model-builders' lab, bent over a workbench, attaching two miniature wooden pieces to a complex-looking structure. He doesn't hear me approach, so I stop to watch him for a minute or two before I cough to announce my presence.

"Emily, hey, I didn't expect you so soon. It's good to see you."

"Not that I'm anxious about this assignment—hah! I thought I'd drop it off now, but if you don't have time to look at it, I'll leave it and pick it up tomorrow morning," I say, clutching the papers to me, feeling like a kid.

"I have time. Let me wash my hands to get the goop off."

As Will pulls his sleeves up and reaches for the soap, I notice his wrists and hands—strong and solid. I always notice a man's hands. I love strong hands but have never thought much about wrists. I stare.

"Emily, I'll take those papers now."

Will's voice interrupts my reverie and I release my grasp on the papers, handing them to him.

"Are you okay, Emily?" Will asks.

Feeling the heat rise in my cheeks, I back away slightly. "What? No, I'm fine. I just remembered I left my computer on. I've got to go back to my office."

I back up a few more steps, turn and flee, shouting over my shoulder, "Thanks again. I'll call you tomorrow."

Yikes! This is not happening.

CHAPTER 19

—

WRITTEN IN THE STARS

I call Will the minute I receive my statistics grade.

"Will, guess what? I just got my final grade in statistics—a B+! I can't believe it," I trill, giddy with delight.

"That's great! I knew you could do it." He's obviously pleased.

"I couldn't have done it without you! How can I thank you? How about a dinner to celebrate?"

"You don't have to do that. Just knowing how happy you are is thanks enough," he demurs.

"No way. Let's go to the Ritz. My treat. I'll make the reservations," I insist.

I wear my rose-colored sheath, the sleekest, chicest dress I own, and heels, low enough so I don't tower over him. He comes to the door, carrying a large bouquet of yellow and white tulips, and looks quite elegant in a navy suit.

"The tulips are gorgeous... and you don't look too bad either," I say, taking the bouquet into my arms.

When we arrive at the Ritz, I am delighted by the valet parking, doorman greeting us, tuxedoed maître d' leading us to a cozy corner table—treatment befitting a statistics star and her tutor. The dining room is large. Elegant crystal chandeliers hang from the high ceiling; gold damask drapes adorn the tall windows overlooking Boston Common. I can imagine horse carriages parked under gas-lit street lamps, waiting for diners to descend the stairs after their many-course meals and fine Bordeaux and Burgundy wines.

I'm tempted to order Champagne until I see the triple-digit pricing.

"Shall we order wine?" I ask, determined to be gracious and generous without my usual wary eye on my funds.

"I'll have to pass," Will replies, "but please have wine or whatever you'd like. I gave up alcohol for Lent."

"Lent? It's long past, isn't it? Besides, you're not Catholic," I protest.

"It's just a figure of speech," he says. "Actually, I started drinking too much when I was going through my divorce, so I decided to quit for a while."

"That makes sense," I say, wondering if he has a problem. He sounds so matter of fact and reasonable, but the alcohol must have been causing trouble. People don't usually quit otherwise.

"Find out more," Dr. Rothman barks at me. Who invited him?

"How did you know it was too much?" I ask tentatively.

"I was having trouble getting up the day after, and I'm too old for hangovers, so that was enough for me," he says dismissively.

"Maybe I'll have iced tea," I say, looking at the menu.

Rothman barks again, "Find out how much he was drinking. Get details."

Oh, great, this nudge expects me to get a drinking history. Will recognized he was drinking too much, so he quit. Seems logical to me. What's the big deal?

I cough violently, hoping to jar Rothman loose from my head. Will jumps up, ready to do the Heimlich. "Are you okay?"

"Yes, fine. It's just an annoying scratchiness, like something's caught in my throat. It comes and goes."

"Maybe an allergy?" he asks.

"Exactly," I say, "a reaction to an irritant in the air. I'm ready to order. Are you?"

Will nods to our dashing waiter, who has been waiting at a respectful distance. The staff doesn't hover at the Ritz.

I order "line-caught" North Atlantic salmon, better, I'm sure, than a spear-chucked salmon or one that has wandered mistakenly into a lobster trap. Will orders short rib bourguignon.

"So, now that you have triumphed over statistics, what's in the future for you?" Will asks between bites of his tender-looking beef.

"Immediate future, get my master's at the end of June and blow off this dead-end, mind-numbing job. Of course, it would be perfect if I could get laid off and end up with a little bankroll to sustain me while I find my dream job."

"I've heard layoffs are coming, so you may get your wish," Will says.

"When? When are the layoffs coming? What's the scuttlebutt?"

"Soon, I hear, so hang in there."

"I've been hanging so long that my neck is two inches longer," I say, exasperated.

"It's tough when you feel stuck," Will agrees.

"What about you? You like what you do, I know. Any danger of your being laid off?"

"My astrologer says not," he replies, "and the scuttlebutt is that layoffs will be in the soft areas like marketing, events, and maybe HR."

"Excuse me, your astrologer? You consult an astrologer?"

"Oh, Christ!" Dr. Rothman bleats.

Will grins sheepishly. "I know it's hard for some people to believe, not everyone's cup of tea, but I've been working with Astrid for years and she almost never steers me wrong."

"Okay, ask for the check, pay the bill, and get out of here now," Rothman demands.

"Wait a minute. What do you mean you work with her? How often do you consult this Astrid? What kinds of things do you consult her about?"

"I used to talk with her weekly. Now, it's on an as-needed basis. She's really terrific. She predicted the last stock market crash… unfortunately, that was the one time I didn't pay enough attention, but she's guided me with my investments and most major decisions."

"You consult with a woman who consults the stars for your major decisions?"

"Not exactly. She uses computers and other technology, not just readings of astral charts. She calls herself a techno-wizard."

"And I listen to the Cosmic Muffin on WBCN to find out when Mercury is in Retrograde and I should stay in bed. You're kidding, right?"

"Well, maybe a little," Will backpedals. "It's not as though I can't make my own decisions. I just like to run some things by her. Don't knock it 'til you've tried it."

CHAPTER 20

—

MAN THE LIFEBOATS

I'm at work at 8:00 a.m. today because this is one of the days I sneak out to do my internship at Chemicon. Shelley is the only person who knows what I'm up to, and no one else has even missed me.

As I head toward the ladies room to repair my wind-blown hair, I check to see if Shelley's in yet. Maybe she'd like a cup of coffee. I peek over the top of her cubicle and see her head bent over her computer. She's whispering into her phone. Tiptoeing away, I decide I'll stop by when I hear her hang up her phone, confident the sound will carry. I can even hear when Gertie is wheezing three cubicles away.

"Hi, Shel, do you want to go over to the caf for a cup of coffee?"

Shelley's face is pale and she's not smiling.

"What's the matter?" I ask, concerned. Maybe her husband is sick or one of the kids.

"Not here," she whispers, grabbing her bag. "Let's get that coffee."

She waits until we're in the elevator. "Is today one of your afternoons at Chemicon?"

"Yes, you've got a great memory," I reply.

"Don't go."

"What do you mean, don't go?" I ask, puzzled. "I go every Tuesday and Thursday."

"You can't go today," she insists.

"Shelley, what's going on? Why are you acting so weird?"

We're at the entrance to the cafeteria, but I don't go in, waiting for her response.

"Let's get our coffee and grab a table over there," she says, pointing to a far corner.

Once we have our coffee and are seated, I ask again, "What's going on? Why the melodrama?"

Shelley sips her coffee, grimacing, "burnt. Never mind." She leans toward me and hisses, "Layoffs. Today."

"You're kidding!" I look at her face, seeing pain in her eyes. "You're not kidding. When? How? How do you know?"

I feel a hot, prickling sensation as though I've been zapped with a cattle prod, and it isn't a hot flash.

Shelley, unaware of my excitement, says, "Michaela. She asked me to make sure everyone's available for a meeting later today. She was closeted in her office with her boss and HR all afternoon yesterday. When they came out, I was at the fax machine behind Gina's cubicle. They didn't know I was there and I heard the HR rep saying something like, "We'll schedule all of the appointments, so we can process them tomorrow. The packages are ready."

"It could be something else," I speculate.

"Like what? What kind of packages do you think they're talking about—homemade fudge? The rumors have been floating around for weeks now."

"Wow! I hope they tell us soon and get it over with. I wonder who's going."

"It sounded big to me."

I return to my cubicle, resuming my mantra, "*lay* me off, lay *me* off, lay me *off*," interrupting it only long enough to call Chemicon with a story about an emergency dental appointment. Then I sit, murmuring my mantra, my hands sweaty, my stomach doing flip-flops as time crawls like an indolent snail. What if Shelley's wrong? I don't know if I can take the disappointment again.

At 1:50, Michaela appears at the entrance to my cubicle. "Emily, can you please meet me in Caracas in two minutes?" The conference rooms are named after major cities in no particular order. Caracas is next to Toronto. Go figure.

Oh my god, this is it! I nod without speaking, take my glasses and bag and head for Caracas. What if I'm the only one? So what? This is what I want, no time for ego to rear its ugly head.

I walk into the room and am stunned to see six morose faces, the whole team sitting at the table. David Dander, Michaela's big boss, sits at the head of the table like the wicked stepfather, and Michaela, his incompetent helpmate, sits at the other end. I sit in the empty seat next to David, who nods at me.

"Okay, is this everybody?" he asks Michaela.

Did he say every body? I stifle a snicker. I'm going to have to play this cool. I put on a glum mask to match those around the table.

"You probably have a sense of why we're here, so I'm going to get right to the point. For some time, the company has been swimming against the tide, trying to keep our Wooden Toy Division afloat..."

Yeah, I think, we're going down with the wooden toy ship. Watch out for splinters!

"But we've come to recognize that the market is shrinking. Wooden trains, building blocks, log fortresses are being replaced by plastic..."

Here's to you, Mrs. Robinson... I hum silently.

"We can no longer buck the trend. While our stuffed animal and electronic toys divisions are profitable, they can no longer carry the wooden toys..."

Yeah, waterlogged wood must be pretty heavy. Get to the point, dunderhead.

"So, we've decided to close the Wooden Toy Division and concentrate our efforts on the areas of profit. This means," he sighs theatrically, "we will also be reorganizing, outsourcing some functions, and downsizing support areas, including, unfortunately, your marketing department." He looks around the table, wearing his rueful mask. "I regret telling you that we are initiating layoffs in several areas, including yours."

I glance at Michaela, who is studying her cuticles. The only way I can contain my joy is by looking at my colleagues and trying to feel their pain.

"The company appreciates your hard work and years of loyalty. We regret having to take this action and want you to know this does not reflect on your performance. You have done good work, and you will be missed."

Oh, sure.

Stuart raises his hand. "When will this take effect?"

"Today. We've scheduled exit appointments for each of you with an HR representative, who will explain your package and benefits. We'll give you that schedule before you leave the room. You'll also find packing boxes waiting in your cubicles, and workers from Security will be available to carry those boxes to your vehicles.

"I think you'll find the packages generous. In addition to pay for your years of employment, the state requires we give you compensation for terminating your employment without 60 days' notice. You'll also be eligible for health benefits through COBRA.

"I know you must have many questions, so I'll take as many as I can," he says, looking at his watch.

Thunderous silence floods the room while I contemplate cartwheeling out the door.

• • •

Friday, March 19

Dear Ian,

Great news! I've been laid off! The whole department was sacked except for Michaela and her manager, whose incompetence will be rewarded with jobs in other divisions, since the entire Wooden Toy Division is kaput. Apparently, wooden toys are obsolete, soon to become extinct like the great auk, Tasmanian tiger and dodo bird. Hmm, I wonder what Michaela will do with her piles of toy trucks? Maybe she'll build a bonfire with her collection of wooden soldiers!

Since I was the only one to feel joy, I had to hide my feelings during the exit process, which was organized in perfect detail from the announcement to the packing boxes waiting in our cubicles to the exit interviews. By nightfall, all traces of our department had been erased. It was one of the most skillfully executed operations I've witnessed in that organization in my eight years there. You've gotta hand it to them—they know how to do layoffs.

The severance package will keep me in bubble bath and Ben and Jerry's for months, so I should be okay while I look for another job. I'm so close to getting my degree that I'm optimistic about getting work in my field. Tomorrow morning, I'm going to talk to my internship supervisor about employment. I'm loving that work.

Once again, wish me luck. I'll keep you posted.

Hope your life is saner than mine.

Fondly,
Emily

P.S. Did I tell you I got a B+ in statistics, just three points short of an A-!

•••

Wednesday, March 24

Dear Emily,

I like your spirit. This layoff is your chance to go for it: first woman on the moon, secretary of education, chief of quality control for Hershey's Kisses! I can't wait to see what happens next.

I am going to be traveling. Next week, I leave for Hong Kong and then on to Australia. After a brief visit to Sydney, I'll be in Melbourne, one of my favorite cities. I have friends in all these places, so I'll be mixing business with pleasure. I should be gone about two weeks.

Who knows what you'll be up to by then.

Safe travels to us both!

Best,
Ian

CHAPTER 21

—

AFTERMATH

"Mum, guess what! I've got the best news. I've been laid off. I'm free!"

I hear a sigh, then silence.

"Mum, are you still there? Did you hear what I said?"

"Of course I heard you. I'm not deaf, you know."

She is, in fact, very hard of hearing. "Anyway, this is such good news for me. I couldn't be happier," I say, hoping she'll catch some of my joy.

"How is this good news?" she asks.

I can hear insistent yipping in the background.

"Shh, Raspberry, I can't hear your sister."

Now the dog is my sister? "How is this good news?" I repeat. "Because I've been miserable there for ages. I haven't had enough work, I've been bored out of my skull and dying a slow, ugly death in my cubicle."

"That's a little dramatic, isn't it?" she chides. "What about a salary, health insurance? How are you going to live?"

"Not to worry. I got a terrific package—one month's salary for every year I've worked there. That's eight months' pay. And I get two months more because they didn't give us 60 days' notice."

"Who says?" she challenges.

"The state, and I can get my health insurance continued through COBRA for 18 months. It's a way for job changers and people who've lost jobs to hold onto their health insurance, so they don't lose benefits."

"Too good to be true," she says.

"I know... but it's not cheap, so I'm hoping to find another job before too long."

"In this job market? I'm worried for you. I told you about my neighbor's grandson—out of work..."

I interrupt, "Yes, Mum, you told me. But I'm finishing graduate school next month and I have prospects."

"What prospects? Raspberry, cut that out! He's scratching at the door. I've got to take him out. Call me back in an hour. We'll talk. I worry about you, you know." She hangs up, not waiting for my response.

That went well.

Forty minutes later, I pick up the phone, hoping to find a more encouraging reaction and then put it down again. Maybe I'll feel better if I do the laundry. I'm sorting whites from darks when the phone rings. I look at my watch. It hasn't been an hour and my mother wouldn't call anyway. She doesn't want to spend the money.

"Hello?" I ask.

"Hey, Emily, it's Will. I just heard the news about the layoffs and wanted to see how you're doing."

"Good news travels fast and bad news even faster," I comment.

"But this is still good news for you, right? I hear you all got pretty good packages."

"It's great news for me. I'm thrilled but I had to stop myself from doing a Fred Astaire on the ceiling when we heard the news. Not so hard when I looked at my co-workers. Quite a blow for most of them."

"How many went?"

"The whole department except Michaela and her boss. I guess they'll be 'redistributed.' Isn't that the euphemism?"

"Yeah," he chuckles, "they'll be scrambling to find jobs in other departments, bumping people with less seniority. That's how it goes."

"Yikes, I think I got the best of the deal."

"You did. I was calling to see if I had to commiserate or celebrate. Sounds like the latter. How about dinner on me this time?"

"Sounds great."

I let Will pick me up at my door—a first. I take it as a sign of liberation from bondage. No more suspicion and hyper-vigilance. I'm a new woman. I'm not surprised to see he drives an old, fading blue Volvo station wagon—the vehicle of choice in his suburban neighborhood. He holds the door for me. Nice, screw Women's Lib.

We dither back and forth about neighborhood restaurants and settle on Luigi's Two, a father/son operation on Boylston Street known for hefty portions of hearty old-world Italian cuisine. The meatballs are to die for.

Sitting comfortably in a small booth, inhaling fumes of marinara sauce, sizzling sausage, and garlic, I salivate with anticipation.

"Oh, my gawd, does that smell good!" I can't help grinning.

"You look like a new Emily," Will says, grinning back, "so relaxed and happy. Is getting laid off from a job all it takes?"

We both laugh and clink our iced-tea glasses.

"To layoffs," I cheer. "Oops, not so loud. This may not be an appropriate reaction."

"Not a typical one. That's for sure," Will chuckles.

The spaghetti and meatballs arrive steaming and fragrant. We dive in, occasionally coming up for air. Over coffee, we begin to talk.

"So, what's next on your agenda? Are you taking time off before you tackle the job market?"

"You bet," I smile, thinking about sleeping in and reading the morning paper. "Besides, I get my degree next month and will be steering my career in a whole new direction." I marvel at how confident I sound.

"I really admire your courage and energy," Will says, raising his coffee cup to me. "Here you are starting over while I labor away at the same job in the same place, not really challenged much anymore, satisfied with just making a living and looking forward to retiring soon."

"I didn't have much choice. Layoff, remember?"

"Yes, but you've been anticipating this and finishing your degree, so you'll have choices."

"You're right. I don't give myself credit. You know what—I may already have something in the works," I lower my voice, leaning toward him. "I may be able to get some work at the company where I'm doing my internship."

"Wow, that's terrific… if that's the kind of work you want," he says, leaning toward me and tentatively taking my hand. I don't pull away.

"Are you kidding? I love the work. The students are great, most of them motivated and so interesting. They come from all over the world and have great stories. The only drawback," I hesitate, "is that it probably won't be a full-time job, at least not in the beginning. The department doesn't have the funding right now."

"You'll have a foot in the door and you have the severance pay to hold you for a while," he reminds me.

"I like the way you think," I reply.

• • •

Thursday, April 8

Dear Ian,

I've been hired as an almost full-time employee in the Workplace Education Department at Chemicon! I've already begun the new job, which is much like the old one, except that it's almost full-time and I'm being paid!! I also have good health coverage and other benefits. I'm thrilled! To celebrate, Shelley and I are going on an overnight to Nantucket. Can't wait to get on that ferry!

What about you? How was your trip?

Gotta sign off now.

Emily

• • •

Wednesday, April 13

Dear Emily,

I can barely keep up with you! You're full of surprises. You sound excited and happy. I'm really glad you were able to land the job at Chemicon, since you enjoy the work there so much. They should know they're lucky to have you!

Hey, guess what? I'm training to be a literacy tutor at our library. As I hoped, my fluency in Mandarin and conversational Japanese is going to be an asset. I'll let you know how this goes.

My trip to Hong Kong and Australia was terrific. Business was good and catching up with old friends even better. In Sydney, I visited the Royal Botanic Gardens, 74 acres of all kinds of grand, gorgeous gardens. I loved it except for the infamous gray-headed flying foxes, a large species of fruit bat! These bats have reddish-brown neck fur and a wingspan of about three feet! Hundreds of them, hanging in the trees! Not a pretty sight for the faint of heart, including yours truly. For years, the authorities have been talking about getting these critters out of the gardens, but nothing has happened yet.

In Melbourne, offered the choice of swimming with sharks or taking a hot air balloon tour, I opted for the latter. I don't swim with anything that can eat me! We sailed over the vineyards in Yarra Valley at daybreak—wonderful views and just a light breeze. When we landed, a Champagne breakfast was waiting for us. After a generous helping of fruit, scones, and bubbly, I tottered around for a while.

It looks as though it's going to be hectic around here for a few months. My younger daughter, Nancy, is engaged, and wants me to help her plan the wedding. What do I know about that? I'm counting on her friends and her aunt for expert advice, but I'll do what I can in between traveling to Asia—a lot more of that coming up.

I'll be in touch when I can.

Fondly,
Ian

CHAPTER 22

—

SLIPPERY SLOPE

After dinner dates, lunches, movies, museum tours, and long walks around ponds, through neighborhoods, meadows and woods, one case of food poisoning, several allergy attacks, and a case of poison oak, Slipway and I have our first kiss.

We're sitting on an old army blanket near the water's edge at Plover Beach, one of my favorites, its silky, beige sand stretching for miles along the Atlantic Coast. High dunes, covered in beach grass, thickets of wild plums, and beach roses, rise along its perimeter. Luckily we're here before the famous piping plover season when the beach, a wild life refuge, closes to protect these sweet, nesting birds.

It's a perfect day, blue skies dipping into gray green ocean, waves breaking and tumbling into foam, sea breezes keeping the temperature in the mid-70s. I'm completely relaxed, leaning against Will's shoulder when I feel his arm slide around my waist, hand resting on my hip. It feels good, so when he kisses me, I kiss back.

We kiss and sigh and hug and kiss some more. Will begins murmuring in my bad ear—the left one where sounds aren't always distinct. I think I hear him say, "I'll court you forever." I wonder if I heard him right, but I'm reluctant to ask, "What's that?" I suspect it would kill the romantic moment, which I'm enjoying. We sit, wrapped around each other until the tide begins to come in, spraying the edge of our blanket.

By the time we cross the sand and follow the path back to Will's station wagon, the fog is lapping at our heels.

On the ride home, we're quiet until Will breaks the silence, saying, "I knew you were the one the minute I held you in my arms at the dance. I knew it! Remember I said that to you at coffee?"

Unease cracks my euphoria. Does he have to spoil the moment with silliness?

"I remember thinking you were a bit nuts," I reply lightly.

"And do you remember what I said? 'I know what I feel.'"

I'm about to retort but stop myself. Maybe he is one of those intuitive creatures who knows how he feels instantly and follows his heart. I can't imagine. But it is flattering… and I like his kisses… so what's the harm?

When he pulls the station wagon up to the curb in front of my door, we begin kissing again, our passion mounting. I don't know how long it's been for him, but I've lost count of the months, maybe years, since I've last been with a man. I'm into this and want to take our canoodling into the bedroom. He does, too.

I unlock the door, fling my jacket onto a chair. As he is flinging his jacket onto mine, I ask, "Do you have protection?"

He freezes mid-fling and says, "No, don't you?"

"No," I moan, flopping onto the chair.

We stare at each other. I'm ready to abandon the adventure. Got to give the guy credit. He's not giving up so easily.

"I'll go to a drugstore," he says.

I look at my watch. "Where are you going to find a drug store open at 11:30?"

"Aren't there any all-night pharmacies? There must be," he insists.

"Yes, I think, for sex emergencies like this one. Not bloody likely in Boston."

"Let me see your phone book," he says.

I watch him thumbing through the yellow pages.

"Eureka!" he shouts, 'Martin's 24-hour Pharmacy: Open for All Your Needs.' It's in Allston."

"I hope it has a drive-through window. You don't want to get out of your car in that neighborhood."

"Come on, Emily, where's your spirit of adventure?" He's struggling back into the sleeves of his jacket and halfway out the door, not waiting for an answer. Clearly, his spirit is afire.

It seems like hours later when the doorbell rings, awakening me from slumber. I hadn't intended to fall asleep, but the sun and sea air must have overridden my libido. Slapping my cheeks to get the blood flowing and smoothing my tousled hair, I stumble to the door before the bell wakes the rest of the building. Will stands before me, grinning manically and waving a pack of condoms triumphantly above his head.

"Oh, my god, were you asleep?" he asks, incredulous.

"No, of course not," I lie, "just resting and awaiting your return."

CHAPTER 23

—

ROAD TRIP

"Would you like to drive down to the Cape for the weekend?" Will asks from his supine position under the sink where he's replacing a leaky pipe. Since my building is under rent control, the landlord is the last person to ask for a speedy repair.

"The Cape? This weekend? Do you think we can get reservations?"

"Wrench, please, nurse," he says, extending his hand to receive the hefty instrument I'm holding. "We don't need reservations. I always just meander down Rte 6 and find something when I feel like stopping."

"In September, on the Cape? It's the nicest time of year and probably the busiest. I'd be nervous without a reservation."

"There. That should do it," Will says, wriggling out from under the sink. "Turn the water back on and then try the faucet…We'll find a place. Don't worry. The planets are aligned in our favor." He winks.

Now, I'm worried. Will really believes in the influence of the moon, stars and planets; he even consults an astrologer. I used to read my horoscope occasionally and listen to the Cosmic Muffin on the radio—for fun—until I realized no matter what the planets are up to, Virgos are deemed geeks, dweebs and undersexed nerds, always being advised to stick to business, balance our checkbooks, and squelch our perfectionist urges, particularly in relationships. I can get better advice from my mother.

I open the valve and turn on the faucet. The water streams out. Will checks the new piping and smiles triumphantly.

"Good work!" I say. "So your soothsayer thinks we can go without reservations?"

"If you're referring to my astrologer, her name is Astrid, and yes, she says it's okay," he replies.

"Who am I to naysay Astric? Let's do it! But I have to ask, 'How often do you consult this woman? Do you ask her about everything?'"

Will is packing his tools and doesn't look up. "No, of course not... maybe once a week... I just happened to be talking to her about another matter and the trip idea came up."

Another matter? Should I ask what that is? No, it's none of my business. If he wanted me to know, he'd tell me. Still, why so mysterious? This guy is a bit loosey-goosey. Geez, Emily, it's just a weekend on the Cape, warm salt water, a soft, sandy beach, fried clams. What's the big deal?

• • •

We are stuck in a long line of traffic crossing the Sagamore Bridge, but we've opened the car windows and I'm loving the warm, salty breeze tickling my cheek. I inhale slowly, sinking back into the comfortable leather seat. Maybe I'll nap.

"Emily, do you ever think about getting married again?"

There goes my nap. "No, not really," I say cautiously. "Why do you ask?"

"Just wondering, I guess. I was unhappy for so long, I should just be relieved to be free, but sometimes I wonder if I'm missing anything."

"Will, how long have you been divorced? Not even a year. And what do you think you're missing?"

"I don't know. Contentment? Commitment?"

"Confinement? Consternation?" I add.

"Wow, you sound like a sour lemon that wandered into the strawberry patch," Will says.

I'm tempted to respond with some good S words of my own but realize Will is right. I do sound bitter. "I was just being flip. Sorry. I'm not sure how I really feel about remarrying, but your nostalgia for something you didn't have must have pushed a button."

"You're right about nostalgia for some idealized relationship. Still, with the right woman…" he grins as the traffic begins to move more quickly at the end of the bridge. It begins to thin out as cars stop at campgrounds and motels set back in the woods that line the now sandy road.

"Let's see what we can find in Barnstable," Will suggests.

"Will, I didn't mean to be so harsh. I think it's sweet that you have such romantic notions about relationship and the possibility of a loving commitment. That's nice, actually. I tell myself that's what I'd like, but then I deny the possibility. That's probably why I'm still single."

"How long have you been single?"

"About 15 years. When my marriage ended, I was shell-shocked, struggling to get on my feet so I could take care of my kids. Eventually I started dating and had boyfriends, but my kids came first. Then came my work and graduate school and the timing was never right."

Will turns slightly to look at me. "You know what? I don't think we need to resolve this question now. We probably just need some sea and sand and a chance to relax. Have you ever been sailing?"

"I have, but not for a while."

"Good, let's rent a boat. I know a great place."

"First, we have to find a motel," I remind him, feeling very much like a Virgo mother.

We pass at least a dozen 'no vacancies,' and I am biting my lip to keep from saying, "See, I told you so." I read somewhere that it's better to be happy than always right.

We have driven through Sandwich, Barnstable, Yarmouth, and Dennis when I spot a vacancy sign on an old-style motel with small cottages nestled among the pines. By now, we're in Brewster, halfway down the Cape, and the sun is beginning to set.

Will pulls off the road and stops at the office. Cheerful and undaunted, he registers and we unpack the back of the station wagon. I'm traveling lightly for me with just two small bags. Will carries a backpack and shirt and slacks on a hanger.

The room is charming in a rustic Cape Cod way. A double bed, draped in white chenille spread, dominates the space. Gauzy white curtains dance in the warm breeze that slips through the open window. A large, rainbow-colored hooked rug covers most of the floor.

Will slips his arm around my waist. "This is nice, almost worth the wait?"

Feeling a rush of ardor, I turn toward him, so we can kiss. "Definitely worth the wait."

"We'll rent a boat tomorrow," Will murmurs in my neck. "We have more important matters to attend to right now."

"I love it when you talk dirty," I say, pulling him even closer.

• • •

The next afternoon, we are becalmed on the bay. Not a whisper of breeze. The sun beats down on the little Sunfish we've rented. Will is trying to work magic with the sail and I'm trying not to wring my hands. I'm attempting to focus on our little romantic interlude on a small, deserted island earlier in the afternoon.

"Will, do you want more sunscreen?" I ask as I slather my arms and legs with thick, white glop. Luckily, I'm wearing a large hat that shades my face and neck, but Will is wearing a baseball cap that shades his face but not much else. His neck is reddening to an ouch tone.

"Thanks. That's a good idea." He moves toward me, so I can slather him, too.

"I'm really sorry about this, Emily. The wind was good earlier. Now, it's just died."

"No need to apologize. You're not sorry about our romp on the island, are you? I'm not."

"Neither am I," he says, turning to hug me.

I return the hug, feeling a rush of tenderness and love. "Will, you are a sweetie and I really like being with you, even becalmed in this water, but do you have any idea how we'll get back to shore?"

In response, Will pulls a small paddle from the floor and lifts it for me to see.

"That? You're going to do it with that?" I can't disguise my doubt.

"Sure," he says. "Nothing like a little paddle and a lot of elbow grease to get us out of this jam."

"Do you have another of those things?" I ask, pointing skeptically at the paddle.

"Just seems to be this one, but you can use your hand. Just watch what I do and follow me."

"Put my hand in this water? What about sharks?"

Two hours later we've reached the shore and returned the sailboat, which is none the worse for wear. I wish I could say the same about us. We're sunburned to a fiery red, despite the sunscreen. My arm aches, from shoulder to pruned fingertips, my lips are as dry as a field in drought, and my vision is permanently blurred.

"I'm dying of dehydration," I moan as we climb the slope back to the parking lot.

"Nothing a nice, cool shower and tall vodka and tonic won't fix," Will chuckles.

"I thought you don't drink," I remind him.

"No harm in a drink now and then," he replies, tugging me up the last few steps.

CHAPTER 24

—

THE INQUISITION

Will and I are walking in my neighborhood as the sun is setting and the wind has calmed to a light breeze. We're holding hands and I'm enjoying the evening stillness and the comfort of his warm hand.

"My kids want to meet you." He tries to sound casual.

"Oh?" I respond in kind, trying to hide the dismay signals gurgling from my stomach.

"You're not still hungry?" Will asks in disbelief since we just left Pasquale's Pizzeria where we shared a large olive, mushroom, and pepper pie.

"No, I'm just digesting."

"So, what do you think? What should I tell Hallie and Hunter?"

"Do you think it's time to do that? Why do they want to meet me? What have you told them?"

I'm thinking about how fresh his divorce is and wondering how eager his kids are to meet the potential mother replacement. I'm probably getting ahead of myself.

"How happy you make me and how much they'll like you, too. Why shouldn't they want to meet you?"

"What I meant was do you think they're ready for that?"

"What is that?" He's sounding impatient.

"I'm not saying this well. I mean do you really think they're ready to meet the woman who may have taken their mother's place in your heart?"

"What do you mean 'may have taken?' In the first place, they know their mother has had no place in my heart for years and vice-versa. In the second place, they want me to be happy. Emily, what's this 'may have taken?' Why the hedging? You have the number one place in my heart, kiddo." He squeezes my hand.

I wonder if I've ever heard him so emphatic or eloquent.

"Where do you think we should meet?" I ask.

"Let's have dinner with them," he says.

"Do I meet them at the same time or one at a time?" You'd think I was preparing for an exam.

"I'd say together. They're so close they hiccup in unison, so together would be a lot easier for them."

What about me? I keep this thought to myself. I've already said enough.

• • •

Hallie and Hunter are waiting for us in front of Sloppy Joe's Hamburger Joint. They're gesticulating and both talking at once. They don't see us coming. Hallie notices us, says something to Hunter and they turn and grin as we approach, smiles so wide and teeth so polished, they backlight the freckles spattered across the bridges of their noses and cheeks. Hunter looks like a poster boy for Abercrombie and Fitch in a blue cotton, button-down shirt and chinos. Hallie is wearing a vintage, lacy beige blouse under a multi-colored vest and a long, wine-colored velvet skirt. Will introduces us and we go into the diner, sliding into a booth in the back where it's not too noisy.

"Dad's told us a lot about you," Hallie begins.

"Really?" I look sideways at Will.

"Good stuff," Hunter adds quickly, his cheeks flushing under the freckles.

"You know my dad. He can't keep anything secret," Hallie giggles.

"That's not true," Will protests.

"Oh, Daddy, I'm just teasing."

Is Hallie flirting with her father?

"He's talked about you two and he's really proud of you," I say, anxious to make sure father/child boundaries are in place.

The waitress strides to our table, pen and pad poised for business. "Ready to order?"

No time for amenities at this two-star burger joint. I order a turkey burger, fries, and coffee. Will orders a beef burger, slaw, and decaf coffee. The waitress looks at Hallie and Hunter.

"You go first, Hunter. I haven't decided," Hallie says, her head still in the menu.

"Okay, I'll have a double cheeseburger with onions and mushrooms, tomatoes, pickles, and lettuce with mayo, a double order of french fries, cole slaw, and a large Coke… and lots of ketchup," he grins.

I experience a sudden urge to belch.

"I'll have a garden salad with oil and vinegar on the side, please, with tuna but no mayonnaise… and a decaf coffee, black," Hallie pronounces as she closes her menu.

The waitress brings the drinks first, slopping coffee over the rim of the cups and grabbing a fistful of napkins to wipe up the spill.

When we're momentarily safe from her ministrations, we sip our drinks. Hallie, stirring her coffee, asks offhandedly, "So, how did you and Dad meet?"

"At a company event," I say. "I used to work in the same place as your dad. Didn't he tell you that?" I grin.

"I guess not," Hallie says. "Maybe he doesn't tell all. When was that?" Her blue eyes fix on me.

"When exactly was that, Will?"

"Last winter, after your mother and I separated. Why the third degree, Hallie? Hey, Hunter, how's your ankle? Are you going to be ready for track next month?"

Grateful for the shift, Hunter describes his ankle injury, physical therapy, and preparation for the track season. I sit back and reassess. These two may look alike but they're wired differently. Hallie is definitely digging. I'll let her father worry about that.

When Hunter has wound down and is sipping his Coke, Hallie asks, "So, what kind of work do you do? Are you and my dad in the same department?" She pokes at her salad and pushes it around her plate with her fork. I can see the lettuce wilting.

"I was a marketing writer in the Advertising Division—not the same division as your dad." I return her stare, feeling Will's weight shift on the padded bench.

"That sounds interesting," she says. "So what kind of event were you both at?"

"It was a holiday party, wasn't it, Will?"

"I think you're right," he mumbles.

"What holiday?" Hallie asks.

Did Hunter just elbow her? What's going on? I'm in the middle of something here and I don't like it.

"Will, do you remember when it was? Was it Christmas or Valentine's Day?" I ask, dumping the hot potato into his lap with a tinge of malice.

"Geez, Hallie, what's the big deal? I think it was Christmas." He lifts his coffee cup with two hands so his shaking is almost imperceptible.

"No big deal, Dad. I was curious. I love stories about how people meet. Excuse me, I need the restroom."

Hunter slides out of the booth so Hallie can leave and then unfolds back onto the bench across from us, shrugging his shoulders.

The silence is uncomfortable. It's our turn to push food around our plates. When Hallie returns, her face is flushed. I decide to try another approach.

"Hallie, your dad tells me you're an art major. I'd love to hear about that. Art history or practical art?"

She eyes me, then smiles. "A combination of both. I sculpt, but I don't know if I'll be good enough to earn a living, but I love the history, too, especially Renaissance Art. Did my dad tell you I'm going to Florence for a semester?"

Hallie's face is genuinely animated now and she reminds me of Botticelli's Primavera Maiden, minus the freckles.

Hunter chimes in, "Yeah, and I'm going to visit her spring break. I'm hoping she'll have checked out some hot spots by then… and maybe can introduce me to some beautiful Italian chicks."

"And what makes you think you can compete with Italian men?" Hallie teases.

"New guy in town," Hunter grins.

We talk more about school. Hunter is a math major and brighter than he first appears. Maybe my innate suspicion of jocks misled me. I have to watch out for that. Although Will isn't saying much, I can see he's beginning to relax and enjoy the banter.

At the end of the evening, Hallie and Hunter walk with us to Will's car. We hug awkwardly as we say our good-byes. Hallie and Hunter walk quickly in the other direction, heading toward Hallie's car.

"I'll call you soon," Will shouts into their backs.

"Now, what was that about?" I ask as we settle into Will's car.

"What was what about?" he asks, struggling with his twisted seat belt.

"You're joking, right? Your daughter's third degree about when we met and the layer of tension at our table."

"Now I really don't know what you're talking about."

"Does your daughter think I'm a home wrecker?" I ask, surprised at my shrill tone.

"Emily, you've got to understand Hallie. She's a drama queen, and," he pauses, fiddling with his keys, "she and her mother are pretty close."

"I thought you told me her mother was abusive and you stayed in your marriage to protect your children." I'm looking for a paper bag now, feeling a massive case of hyperventilation coming on. "If there's one thing I can't stand, Will, it's a liar."

"Hold on! I'm no liar. My ex wasn't always abusive. She had her good moments. It's just when she lost her temper, she could take her anger out on the kids. I couldn't let that happen. You know how it is."

"What do you mean I know how it is? Are you suggesting I abused my children?"

Now I'm out of control, no paper bag in sight.

"Jeezuz, that's not what I meant. I'm sure you were... are a wonderful mother. I don't know what you're getting so hopped up about. I'm just trying to explain," Will sounds wounded.

"Okay, please tell me what you told Hallie and Hunter about us. Explain why she's so upset and suspicious," I say, trying to modulate my tone.

Will is silent for so long, I wonder if he's gone narcoleptic. Finally, he speaks.

"I honestly don't remember what I told them. I may have been a little vague... I was still living at home when we met."

"In the basement," I say. "You told me you were living in the basement. Surely, your children must have noticed when they came home on visits."

"And... so?"

"And so, there would be no reason to hide the truth, especially since we didn't actually start 'dating' until you called to tell me you were divorced."

Dr. Rothman rears his moon-shaped face, waving me forward.

"You were divorced then, weren't you?"

"Not exactly."

Now I don't need a bag for hyperventilation. I need a barf bag. "Not exactly?"

"I had moved in with my sister and had filed for divorce. That's just about the same as divorce in my mind."

"Apparently not in Hallie's mind... nor in mine, by the way, in case you care."

Dr. Rothman, who can no longer butt out, intones, "Tell him that one relationship born in the shadow of another is doomed to failure. See what he says to that."

I repeat Rothman's words. Will eyes me suspiciously. "And," I add, "if you're not actually divorced, it's because you still have unfinished business… unresolved issues." Paraphrasing another Rothman pronouncement, I picture Will's issues dangling from a clothesline like wet underwear.

"What are you talking about?" Will is sputtering now. "I am divorced. I wasn't then because the courts take so damn long. That's all it was—unresolved issues, hah!"

"But that's not what you told me. You said you were divorced when you weren't. No wonder Hallie is so suspicious. Who knows what's true with you. This is too much. Please take me home. I have a splitting headache."

At the door as I fumble with my key, Will says, "I'll call you tomorrow when you're feeling better."

"No, call me when you've got your story straight," I say, slamming the door.

"Good girl," Rothman cheers.

• • •

Wednesday, June 24

Dear Ian,

Happy Birthday! I remember we used to celebrate the end of the school year and your birthday at the same time. How lucky you were! Even though we don't have two-month summer vacations anymore, ENJOY!

Have your ears been burning? Last Saturday, I went to the wedding of one of my friends' daughters and bumped into Ruth and Mason Rogers. You must remember them—the chubby, cheerful, little high school couple who got married on the carousel at Paragon Park? They'd wanted to exchange vows on the double ferris wheel, but their parents said absolutely not! That was a great wedding! I don't think any one thought the marriage would last because they were so young.

Here they were 40 years later—chubby, cheerful, and still holding hands. It was such fun catching up with them. They live in Milton where they own and operate a successful funeral parlor. Can you believe that? Those cheerful elves?

Since they missed our 40th, I filled them in on who was there, what they're doing now, and who had facelifts, hair weaves, and other enhancements. We reminisced about our senior year, the gang we hung out with, and they asked about you. I was happy to tell them what you're up to and that we're back in touch.

Isn't it remarkable that Ruth and Mason are still happily married after all these years? Do you think it's luck, hard work, or making a good choice to begin with? How did they get it right?

Present company excluded, I usually get it wrong. I fell in love with my husband because he was super bright, handsome, charming, and apparently carefree. He was so unlike my father, whom I saw as a hyper-responsible, honest worrywart. It turns out responsibility and honesty are important qualities. I learned that the hard way.

Since then, I seem to be attracted to men who are unavailable. Either they're emotionally frozen, married with 12 kids, or they're visiting from Alaska.

How did I get into this? Contrary to the impression I'm giving, life is good. Really. I love my job and am busy with friends and occasional visits from my mother and her dog, Raspberry, the Wonder Poodle. What's to complain?

How about you? When is your daughter's wedding? Are you ready?

Hope all's well.

Fondly,
Emily

• • •

Thursday, July 2

Dear Emily,

Good to hear from you. I remember Ruth and Mason and am glad to know they're still together and happy—not easy, we know. I recently met a couple who were celebrating their 65th anniversary and still playing tennis together! Can you imagine?

Makes me wonder. How did it work for them? Connie and I stayed in our marriage long after it had soured—I suppose for the girls. We weren't a great match to begin with, but who knew? We were too young, and people change and sometimes grow apart. I suppose it's the lucky ones who still enjoy each other after years. I'm not saying anything you don't know. Who says we're meant to mate for life, especially since we're living so much longer? A lot can happen in 50 to 60 years!

I have to admit I've been gun-shy since Connie's death. I'm probably one of those emotionally unavailable guys you're talking about— but I have learned never to say "never."

Meanwhile, my daughter, Nancy, is marrying her beloved next weekend. I'll be there to walk her down the aisle and wish them long life and happiness.

Take care,
Ian

• • •

Monday, July 28

Dear Ian,

How was Nancy's wedding? Did you cry? I remember my father tearing up at my wedding, which really surprised me. I didn't see him as sentimental.

Speaking of weddings, my older son, Gabe, and his girlfriend, Jocelyn, are moving to San Francisco next month and have begun talking about marriage! They've been going together since sophomore year in college, so they know the good, bad, and ugly about each other by now. You do hear stories, however, about couples who live together for years, think they know each other, marry and divorce within months! My friend recently quoted a comedian who says "you don't really meet people; you meet their representatives." I'm thinking that may be true. How well do you know anyone? When do you see the true person, not their rep? Geez, I'm getting cynical.

Gabe and Jocelyn's move has got me thinking about making a move, myself. I love my job and my friends, but I'm beginning to feel an itch. I've been in New England forever—at least two lifetimes—and I'd love to try another part of the country or even another country before I have "*shuffled off this mortal coil.*" *Just trying to impress you. It's one of the few quotes that I remember from the soliloquies we had to memorize in that class. Actually, I remember most of that soliloquy, having seen Hamlet more times than I care to count. My Doggie Hamlet award goes to the American Repertory Theater in Cambridge. Hamlet wore pajamas and delivered that "To be or not to be" soliloquy with his back to the audience! After a couple of hours of similar abuse, I wanted to get up and shout, "Enough already!!"*

I digress. Once Gabe and Jocelyn settle in, I'm going to invite myself for a visit and check out the Bay Area. I've been there only once in the late '70s to visit a boyfriend who had fled New England winters for San Francisco fog. Of course, by the time I got there, he'd met the man of his dreams! They very kindly let me stay on an air mattress in their living room, just below their sleeping loft. The three of us went to the symphony, museums, and ballet together. I've always wanted to return to San Francisco. A former college roommate has moved there and invited me to visit. I may take her up on that.

Do you ever get wanderlust? I don't know what that's about— midlife crisis maybe? Although as my son, Steven, reminded me when I complained about having a midlife crisis in my 40s, "you're optimistic if you think this is midlife."

What are you up to? Still traveling for business?

Write when you can.

Fondly,
Emily

• • •

Wednesday, August 26

Dear Emily,

Sorry it's taken me so long to get back to you. I've had a hectic summer. With business travel and my daughter's wedding, I lost track of time.

Nancy's wedding was lovely, everything she'd hoped for: perfect weather, so the ceremony could be outdoors in a vineyard. The reception on the patio of the winery spilled over onto the lawn overlooking the vineyard. Picture-perfect setting! Nancy looked beautiful, of course, and I did tear up when she and Paul said their vows, especially when I heard my daughter's sweet voice.

As to wanderlust, I've done so much traveling for work that I don't have that yen. I like the idea of being settled, and Seattle seems ideal. I don't mind the rainy season(s), and if I ever feel waterlogged, I can easily travel to dry ground.

I do sometimes miss New England and wish I were closer to family and friends still out there. I try to get back at least once a year. If you travel to the West Coast to visit your son, think about making a side trip to Seattle. I'd love to see you and show you my town. If you can't make it up here, let me know when you're coming to San Francisco, and I'll try to get down there. It would be a shame to be so close and not get together.

Thanks for being so good about staying in touch. I always like hearing from you.

Fondly,
Ian

CHAPTER 25

—

TRUST

I'm glad I'm busy at work. It takes my mind off my dismal love life. I like my new job, but I have to say the excursions into New Age take some getting used to. It's a trip! This afternoon I'm participating in a staff-development session. An outside consultant, Sven Skinner, a pudgy man with a scruffy beard, Hawaiian shirt covering his paunch, jeans, and leather sandals is leading us in trust exercises after a lengthy, jargon-laden introduction. Already I'm suspicious.

"Okay, folks, this exercise is called *Eye Contact*. Choose a partner and stand facing each other. Okay, everyone has a partner? Good."

I stand facing the substance abuse counselor, an older man, who is slightly cross-eyed. He smiles nervously at me.

"Okay, now I want you to stare into each other's eyes for 60 seconds."

Sixty seconds feels like an hour as I try to focus on my partner's eyes, which are intersecting despite his best efforts to look at me.

"Good job, everyone. Okay, stay in your pairs. This next exercise is called *Eye Contact with Touch*. Stand facing each other again, but this time, take each other's hands. Good. Now, holding hands, stare into each other's eyes for 60 seconds."

My partner's hands are damp and sticky, his eyes tearing now from the effort of staring into mine. Really, this is too much.

The trust session ends with the most harrowing exercise: *Trust Fall*, which Sven, the pudgy consultant, offers to illustrate with a volunteer.

He explains, "In pairs of people who are similar size, one becomes the Faller and the other becomes the Catcher. This exercise teaches methods for spotting, falling, and catching. We'll start with small falls and if that goes well, we can build to bigger falls and then swap. After that, we can talk about how this made you feel. Who wants to illustrate this one with me?"

No one steps forward. Finally, someone says, "Arthur, you do it."

Arthur is the largest in the group and stands a fair chance of being able to catch and, more importantly, hold onto Sven. We hold our collective breath as Sven lets his bulk fall backward into Arthur's arms.

"Okay, now," instructs Sven, wheezing slightly, "pair up with someone close to your size and decide who will be Faller and Catcher."

The session ends fairly well, all things considered, with only one strained back and a couple of sprained arms. I am limping slightly, but that's more from muscles tightened with fear.

In this weakened state, I answer my ringing phone before checking caller ID. I've been ducking Will's calls for the past few days. This time, I pick up.

"Emily. Thank goodness. I've been trying to reach you for days," Will says, his voice anxious.

"I know," I reply. "I thought a few days' respite might give you time to get your story straight."

"Emily, please don't be angry. I'm not a liar. I only said I was divorced because I was so afraid of losing you. I love you madly and want to spend the rest of my life with you. I couldn't risk losing you. Please give me one more chance."

"No more lies. Promise?"

"Promise."

I think I hear Dr. Rothman hyperventilating in the distance.

CHAPTER 26
—
EVERGREEN FOLLIES

Okay, so it isn't a rustic B&B in the woods surrounded by flower gardens. No large, fluffy canopied featherbed bedecked with soft pillows and downy quilts invites me to snuggle in. No home-cooked casseroles and freshly baked, grandmotherly cookies, served by a large, cheery, farm-fresh husband and wife await our arrival. No mammoth, deep Jacuzzi sits in the middle of the bathroom, beckoning me. No bathroom.

When Will suggested a weekend away in the New Hampshire woods, my first clue about what he had in mind could have been his recommending that I pack layers of casual, comfortable—emphasis on comfortable—clothes and sturdy shoes.

We drive for hours along winding roads, bordered by tall trees that gradually morph from oaks and elms to white birch and blue spruce. And we're climbing. I can tell because my ears occasionally pop.

"Where are we going?" I ask. "Did I forget to mention that I need to be back at work Monday morning at 8:30 sharp?"

Will chuckles. "We're almost there."

"Did I mention that I'm susceptible to nose bleeds at elevations above sea level?"

He slows the car and pulls off the highway at a large green and white sign reading "Evergreen Campgrounds."

"Campgrounds? What are we doing here?" I begin to wheeze and wonder if I can find an antihistamine in this car, which seems to be packed to the gills, now that I think about it. What's he carrying in here?

Will smiles and pats my knee. We are bumping along a rutted, dirt road. The woods are thinning, and I can see tents sitting among the pines. A large body of water suddenly looms ahead, too large to be a mirage. Will turns the car onto a small, gravel patch about 500 feet from a wooden platform. Whew, no tent! We're probably just turning around because he realizes he's made a wrong turn.

"Look at this view!" Will exclaims as he stops the car. "It's even better than I'd hoped. Come on, Emily, let's take a look around before we unpack our gear."

Gear? That's not what I'd call the black, lace nightgown, the carefully chosen shirts and slacks, the bubble bath, body oils, and sunscreen I've packed.

"Come on," Will repeats, taking my hand, "let's walk down to the lake. Mmm, smell that clean air! Smell the pine, too. It reminds me of camp when I was a kid."

That's the problem. It does smell suspiciously like camp… Camp Chippewa: the early morning compulsory swim class when Bub, the muscled, tanned, hunky waterfront director, had to fish me, floundering and flailing, out of the chilly lake with a long pole, leaving me dripping and mortified on the dock; the long walk to the bathroom in the chill and the dark, flashlight at the ready, when an unidentified flying insect flew into my open mouth and I swallowed; the hurricane, bringing fierce winds and lightning that lit the whole sky, turning night into a ghostly day while we huddled in a couple of lean-tos, watching our tents blow away.

"Yes," I say, "that's what it reminds me of, too."

The lake is beautiful, its gray-blue water lapping at the narrow strip of sand that must be the beach. I wonder what lurks on its muddy bottom, remembering another outing when I waded boldly into marsh water and emerged covered with leeches.

I shudder, still seeing the slimy, black, wormlike creatures attaching themselves affectionately to my flesh, but I decide to keep my concerns to myself, recognizing them as neurotic memories that don't have to be shared. I'm determined to enjoy the outing Will has planned.

When we've climbed back up the slight incline and returned to the car, I ask bravely, "What's next?"

"Next, we unpack our gear..."

There's that word again.

"And set up the tent. We want to do that before it gets too dark. Isn't it great that they have platforms for the tents?"

Ah, that's what the platform is for. I was afraid of that. "Great," I say, "you know, I haven't camped that much...not since I was a kid." I don't say that any camping I was exposed to occurred with friends' families, not my own. My father harbored a healthy aversion to sleeping on lumpy ground in drafty tents and loathed canned pork and beans, even prepared over an open fire. I'm pretty sure I've inherited those wilderness-averse genes.

But I'm determined to be a good sport. Maybe I'll even like camping now that I'm an adult. So many people do. There must be some good to it.

We set up the tent quickly and easily, or, rather, Will does, as I hold and hand him appropriate ropes and pegs. He unrolls a hefty camping mattress, sleeping bags, pillows and extra blankets. The tent is beginning to look almost cozy.

"Emily, you can help me unload the cooking utensils," Will says, hefting a large carton from the back of his car.

When we have finally unloaded pots, pans, cooking and eating utensils, camper stove, dried foods, canned foods, and the requisite can opener—enough equipment to stock an entire camping section at L. L. Bean, I need a break.

"Will, where's the bathroom?"

"What bathroom? You have all of this wonderful woods..." Noting my look of horror, he quickly says, "just kidding. This campground has a bathroom, hot and cold running water, even showers."

"All the amenities," I say. "Just point me toward that luxurious facility."

The primitive cement building housing the toilets, sinks, and shower stalls is exactly what I remember at Camp Chippewa. It's even at an uncomfortable distance from our tent; any nighttime visit will require a flashlight. Could it be? Have I been transported back to that childhood nightmare? Nonsense, I'm an adult and this is an adventure.

In the middle of the night, the cry of a hoot owl awakens me, and I recognize the discomfort of an overextended bladder. I need to go to the john. As I lie in the warmth of the down sleeping bag, reluctant to stir and debating how badly I need to go, I hear another sound. Is Will taking a shower? Wait a minute, there's no shower. We're in a tent. It's rain—not a gentle sprinkle. It's heavy rain, hitting at our canvas tent. Usually I love the sound of rain falling on a window or roof, but now the sound of running water is going to put me over the edge. Should I wake Will? No, better to let him sleep. After all, this isn't an emergency.

How am I going to cover myself? If Will brought raingear, I have no idea where to find it and don't have time to rummage around. I grope for my flashlight, lying somewhere to my right beside my sleeping bag. I find it and shine it around the tent, searching for something I can use as a cover. I spot a tarp, folded neatly on a stack of "gear" in the corner. This will do. When I unfold it, I discover it's huge, big enough to cover my bedroom floor. I fold it over and try draping it over my head and shoulders. The weight almost brings me to my knees, but I straighten up, determined to make it work. With the loop on my flashlight hanging off my wrist and my other hand clutching the tarp, I manage to lift the tent flap and struggle out of the tent.

The rain is heavy and wetter than I remember, but I gamely grasp the tarp and maneuver the flashlight loop off my wrist and the light into my hand. It's good I have it because no other light, not even a star, appears to guide me. With the rain slapping my face, I can't see much anyway, but I plod along the dirt path, headed, I hope, to the toilet. As I walk farther down the rutty road, my confidence mounts. I can do this. I'm no Annie Oakley, but I'm no wimp either.

I begin to walk more quickly and have just spotted the cement building that houses the toilet, have just exhaled a triumphant "Eureka," when my right foot finds a deep rut—the size of a city street pothole—digs into it, twisting my ankle, and I fall, shouting in shock and pain. I would writhe on the ground, but my foot is still stuck in the hole and the ground is too wet and soggy for writhing. Rather, I sink into the beginnings of mud, still covered in tarp. At least that's working. Since I didn't hear a snap, I don't think my ankle's broken, but I suspect it's badly sprained, and I can't extricate it from the hole. Now all I need is a mole or wood mouse to pop up the hole to find out what kind of critter is attempting a home invasion. What if he starts nibbling on my toes? What if I've fallen into a foxhole? Ignoring the pain, I begin wriggling and twisting my foot until I'm able to pull it out of the hole. I really want to writhe now, but all I can do is flop around in the muck.

When I try to lift myself to my knees, my ankle hurts too much. Collapsing back onto the ground, I realize I may drown or suffocate before another camper comes along this path in search of the toilet. At this point, my bladder gives way.

Time passes. I have no idea if it's minutes or hours. Again I try to lift myself off the ground, and this time, I'm able to get to my knees. I begin to crawl, dragging the tarp, burned out flashlight, and wounded ankle behind me.

It's slow going. The heavy, waterlogged tarp on my back doesn't make it any easier. Stopping to rest after every five or six knee jerks forward, I keep going. The wind has picked up and I can't tell if the moaning I hear comes from the wind, creaking tree limbs, or me. I'm just about to sink into the mud in weariness and despair when a voice reaches me.

"Emily, is that you? What in God's name happened? Where have you been?" Will shouts above the wind, grabbing me under my arms and heaving me to a standing position where I shriek in pain.

"What's happened? Are you hurt?"

"My ankle," I manage to groan, "twisted, get me off it!"

Will lifts me off the ground and carries me, tarp hanging off my mud-caked body, back up the path and into the tent not more than 50 feet away.

He removes the soggy tarp, dropping it outside the tent, and then carefully maneuvers me through the open flap and onto his sleeping bag.

"But it will get all wet and muddy," I protest.

"Don't worry about that. Let's get you warm and dry."

For the next couple of hours, Will ministers to me, getting me out of the soaked, muddy clothes and wrapping me in warm blankets; applying ice to my ankle; brewing me hot, soothing tea; dosing me with Ibuprofen; and sighing and shaking his head in disbelief as I tell my tale.

"Emily, try to sleep now. It's almost morning and we'll see how you are then. Maybe we'll need to find a hospital, but we'll see."

"Hospital? Why? Do I have hypothermia? Have I been bitten by a rabid animal? With all that was happening, I might not have noticed."

"No, you may want to have that ankle X-rayed, make sure nothing's broken."

"Oh, that," I mumble before falling asleep.

Too soon, the sky lightens into day. I open my eyes and groan.

Will, who looks as though he hasn't slept at all after a three-day binge, rolls over to my side. "What's wrong?"

"It's morning already." Listening for a moment, I add, "and it's still raining."

"Go back to sleep for a while. It's still early."

When I awaken again, it's still raining and my ankle is throbbing.

"Will," I say, "my ankle is killing me. Can I have more Ibuprofen?"

"Not on an empty stomach," he says, wriggling out of his sleeping bag and stumbling to the food supply where he fishes out crackers and peanut butter, serving them with hot tea and pills.

"Will, I think I'd like to go home now. This has been memorable and I think I've had enough."

"I'm so sorry," he says, applying fresh ice to my ankle, which has swollen to the size of a prize-winning pumpkin. "I'd wanted to make this a special weekend, taking you to one of my favorite spots, sharing the outdoors, and sleeping under the stars."

I sigh.

"You know, Emily, when I woke up and you were gone, I was terrified that something had happened to you."

"Your fears were justified."

"I don't know what I'd do if something had happened to you, if you were hurt," he pauses dramatically... "or worse."

"I'd say this came close."

"Emily, I'm trying to say that I love you and want to take care of you always."

My ankle throbs in response.

• • •

Thursday, September 17

Dear Ian,

I can't believe it's been a month since I last wrote. Lots to tell. Do you remember my writing about the colleague who tutored me in statistics? He was so patient and supportive and all those good things? I knew he had more than friendship in mind—long story—but he was newly divorced, and I wasn't interested.

We're now dating, despite my ambivalence. He loves sailing, hiking, and camping, all of which I've assiduously avoided until now. I'm game despite a disastrous camping adventure in the wilds of New Hampshire. We're so different. He's impetuous and wears his heart on his sleeve—so unlike me. He says he knew I was "the one" when we met. I tell him that's infatuation. He says he knows how he feels. That's so foreign to me, so I'm skeptical and attracted at the same time. I have to admit it's flattering to have so much attention and a living room filled with tulips. Never mind that my histamines are rampaging!

Who knows where this will go. I'm trying to keep it at a stroll while he wants to gallop.

I hope you're well. What are you up to?

Fondly,
Emily

P.S. He consults an astrologer. Should I worry?

• • •

Friday, September 25

Dear Emily,

You certainly know how to get my attention! I'm not surprised that you're being pursued. I'm actually surprised it doesn't happen more often, but it sounds like this guy's a fast mover—not to take away from your pleasure. If you're happy, I'm glad for you.

Tell me more about him. What's his story? As to astrology, I think it belongs to the same flake index as palm reading, fortune telling, and séances, but I know many follow it religiously—pun intended. It always surprises me when anyone asks me my sign, which is Gemini, by the way. How serious is this guy about astrology? What's his name?

Nothing dramatic to report on this front. After a summer break, I've started tutoring ESL students at the literacy center again. They've finally hooked me up with a couple of Mandarin speakers—males in their 20s. So far, our conversations center on the Seattle Mariners and dating practices in America. I contribute what I can.

Let me know how your relationship goes. I hope it continues to give you pleasure. My advice—take it slowly.

Best,
Ian

CHAPTER 27

—

CLASH OF THE TITANS?

"I'm asking you again. Will you marry me?"

Will is leaning on my shoulder, speaking in a stage whisper that I'm sure everyone can hear. We're crammed into window and center seats on a Delta 707, returning from a visit to my mother—a first meeting, actually, because "the mumbler," as my mother used to call him, and she had never met. Since Will and I are practically in each other's pockets, I thought it was time. Now, I'm not so sure.

"Let's not talk about that now," I whisper back. "It's not the time or place."

"Whoa, that doesn't sound like a 'yes'."

"I'd rather talk about your meeting with my mother," I say. "How do you think that went?"

"Pretty well. I like your mother despite the third degree she gave me."

"Okay, she did lay it on a little heavy, but why did you tease her that way?"

"What do you mean? When did I tease her?"

"You know perfectly well."

• • •

It's a warm autumn day and my mother, Will, and I are sitting on the screened patio, the only kind to have in West Palm Beach with all the mosquitoes, June bugs, geckos, poisonous frogs, and alligators on the prowl. We're sipping on my mother's Bloody Marys, her specialty brew, made with Clamato juice, vodka, horseradish, Worcestershire, a drop of Tabasco, and fresh-squeezed lime—a day's ration of veggies, spices, and alcohol. She has served a platter of Brie, Gouda, crackers, and celery sticks. It's a Florida version of afternoon tea.

"It's nice to put a face with a voice," my mother says to Will. "I'm glad you two could come for a visit, although five days is not nearly long enough, especially when the weather's so gorgeous this time of year. It must be pretty cold up north. I keep telling Emily she should move to Florida."

"But then we wouldn't have met," Will protests, slicing cheese for the crackers.

"That's true," my mother says, sipping her Bloody Mary.

"Mum, you know we've talked about this. My friends, my work, my network are all in Boston."

"I'm sure you can get work like that here. Look at all the elderly people. They always need help. And what do you need a network for? I'm sure we can find you a network here, too."

I notice my mother doesn't include herself among all the elderly people who need help.

"I'm awfully fond of your daughter, Mrs. Rosenbloom. I wouldn't want her to move away."

"That's all very nice, but I think it's up to Emily, don't you?"

"Mum, Will's just saying he'd miss me, and I'd miss him, too," I intercede, taking his hand.

"Besides, Mrs. Rosenbloom, I've been proposing weekly to your lovely daughter, and one of these days, she's bound to accept."

"Will!" I protest.

"And just what are you proposing, young man," my mother demands, "a live-in arrangement? That seems to be the trend these days."

"No, I'm talking about marriage. Don't you think we'd be a handsome couple and make beautiful babies?" Will asks.

"What? Don't be silly. Just how old are you?"

"Why not? I think Emily would be a wonderful mother."

"She is a wonderful mother, and, at this point, she'll be a better grandmother," my mother huffs.

"Mum, Will is just kidding, aren't you, Will?" I sputter, squeezing his hand.

"Ouch—yes, just kidding, although it would be nice, wouldn't it?" he replies, only slightly chastened.

"Well, that's nothing to kid about," my mother replies.

"You wouldn't mind if I married your daughter, would you?" Will ignores my hand squeeze this time.

"That depends," she says. "I haven't heard Emily say that's what she wants." She looks at me.

"Finally, one of you is thinking about what I want. You two stop talking about me as though I'm not here and stop planning my future. I'm not interested in moving or marrying right now, so let's drop it."

Like two chastened children, Will and my mother sit nursing their drinks while I get up to start dinner.

• • •

"I don't know why you had to provoke my mother that way. You can't think you were putting your best foot forward." I turn away from Will to look out the window into the night sky. I can see light at the end of the wing, and beyond it, only the dark.

"Look, Emily, I'm sorry. I don't think your mother took it as badly as you. And she certainly felt better when she trounced me at Scrabble. She even hugged me and thanked me again for fixing everything on her "to-do" list when we said goodbye."

On the second day of our visit, my mother, having learned that Will was handy with a hammer, screwdriver, and wrench, had slipped a list of chores across the table with a large slice of her scrumptious chocolate seven-layer cake.

"Will, since you're so handy, I wonder if you could do a quick fix for me on a couple of pesky, little household problems?"

In the next few days, Will had replaced a screen, replaced a door handle, unplugged a drain, fixed a faulty wire on a living room lamp, and rearranged the living room furniture.

"I know she appreciated all the work you did, so do I. That was really sweet of you, but I wish you hadn't pushed the marriage bit and teased her about our having babies. That was over-the-top."

"What can I say? I'm madly in love with you and want to spend the rest of my life with you. You're a very wonderful, desirable woman and a fine mother, I'm sure," he grins boyishly.

"Flattery will get you a few points but not the game, so let's just agree to slow down a bit."

"I've heard that one before. I'm developing a stutter and knee-joint pain from slowing down. Pretty soon I won't remember how to walk." Will's voice rises.

"Shh, the whole cabin can hear you. I just don't want to rush into anything."

"I know. You've said that before, too. You said I should have other interests, hobbies, so I took up ballroom dancing, joined a sailing club, and am taking a photography course. I'm getting so well rounded I'm going to start rolling soon, so it won't matter if I remember how to walk. Emily, what more can I do?" he asks.

"Be patient," I respond half-heartedly. Besides, why are you so fired up about getting married again?"

"I told you. I love you and want to spend my life with you. I want to wake up beside you, sit across from you at the breakfast table…"

I interrupt his list, which is threatening to be infinite. "We already do all that… not every day, but…"

This time he interrupts, "I'm old-fashioned and want us to make a commitment to each other."

How do you argue with that? I turn back to the window.

CHAPTER 28

—

THE PERFECT STORM

A staff meeting has been called for 9:30. I shuffle into the conference room with my teammates; we have no idea why we're here. I hope it's not bad news. Things have been going so well. The clients are great, mostly non-natives, eager to learn English so they can get ahead in their jobs. I can't believe that I'm getting paid to work with these people. It doesn't feel like work.

I look around the room at my colleagues, who nod and smile hesitantly, question marks across their brows. I really like these people; they're supportive and good at their work. For once, I feel as though I'm working on a real team and that I belong here.

And Will—he's been so thoughtful since we came back from visiting my mother. He appears at my door with tulips, which I adore—so graceful and spirited, such a sign of promise. He hands them to me, grinning like a kid. Sweet. He's also been making dinners and fixing things around my apartment, a tactic he picked up at my mother's. Best of all, he's not pressuring me to marry him. In fact, he's stopped proposing, which is a relief. He's looking better to me.

I'm surprised to see Ziggy, our managing director, bustle through the door, his hairpiece slightly askew. What's he doing here?

"Good morning, all. I apologize for calling you together on such short notice, but I just left the executive committee meeting and wanted to share this information with you before rumors begin to fly."

Rumors? This can't be good. I wiggle around on my seat, trying to find a comfortable position. Stuart, my office mate, begins drumming his fingers on the table. Alice, his supervisor, nudges him, while others cough and clear their throats. The room sounds like a frog pond.

"As you know, Chemicon Industries has always been a pioneer, leading the corporate world, heads and shoulders above our competitors, in creating a workplace that works for its workers." He pauses, allowing time for us to absorb his weighty words, delivered with perfect diction. Someone snorts.

"We have developed the best workplace education program, bar none, in the country, perhaps the globe. We are the model for worker education, envied and imitated by many. And that's all no small thanks to you, our A#1 Staff. We couldn't have achieved this standing without you..." He pauses, glancing around the room, his brow furrowed with sincerity, dripping it, in fact. He wipes his forehead with a freshly ironed handkerchief from his breast pocket.

"This is why my task is so difficult."

I tune out, watching Lillian, the admin, shredding tissues and heaping them in a pile on the table as Ziggy drones on.

"Flagging economy... precipitous downswing... downward spiral... survival..."

My stomach is churning as I look at the stricken faces around the table.

"In this spirit, we are calling on you all to join us in making sacrifices now so we may be stronger in the future. As of close of business today, we are disbanding our workplace education program..."

Groans and cries of despair interrupt his oration. He looks surprised.

"Wait, people, please. Hear me out. We firmly believe that this is only a temporary measure. When the economy rebounds, we will rebuild. In the meantime, you will all be given generous severance packages, the amount based on your years of service."

Years of service? Try months! Five, to be exact. What will that be worth?

"Our fondest hope is that this is only a temporary stopgap and that we'll be calling you all back into service before year-end. We understand, of course, that you have no obligation to wait for that to happen and that some of you will need to seek other employment, but we hope the package we offer will make your waiting not out of the question."

Double negative… double talk.

"And we are still exploring other options, so please take heart and understand that we feel your pain."

"Now, I'm asking you to return to your desks until you're called into the HR office where you'll be given your termination papers and a full description of the resources and benefits available to you."

This layoff feels so different from the one at my previous job. That was a godsend, at least for me. Now, I know how my colleagues felt. I don't want to lose this job, and I didn't see this coming! I feel sick.

I wander back to my cubicle to find a stack of boxes waiting to be assembled, filled, and carried away. I slump into my chair and stare at my computer screen, finally tapping a key to see if the computer's still working. It's still connected to the internet. They're not as efficient as they think. I can send out messages about unfair practices, but who would care or be surprised? Layoffs are the swine flu right now. Anyone who hasn't been hit wants to duck and hide.

I call Will and leave a message, asking him to meet me at Dinty's, a neighborhood bar, after work. The office is eerily quiet and I just want to get out as fast as I can, so I begin throwing files, folders, photos, and books into boxes. I'll have time to sort them later. Then I sit, waiting until I'm called into HR.

The HR Rep, smartly dressed in a navy business suit and pumps, her auburn hair perfectly coiffed in a flawless pageboy, ushers me into her office. After a few scripted words of condolence, she describes my severance package, which isn't bad for the few months I've worked at this company. I get a couple of months' pay and access to COBRA health insurance, which eats up most of the severance pay—unless I get a new job with insurance tomorrow. Since I'm not willing to go without health insurance, I sign on. I also sign up for the free workshops on resume writing and interviewing. At least I know what I'll be doing for those few hours in the coming weeks.

At 5:30, Will strolls through the door of Dinty's where I've been sitting at the bar, nursing a glass of Chablis. I've promised not to share my sad story with the bartender, and in return, he hasn't hassled me about ordering another drink. He's had to replenish my pretzel bowl twice, but I'm planning to leave a generous tip.

"I'm so glad to see you." I hug Will, holding onto him.

"Me, too, but at Dinty's? I thought you hated the smell of smoke and stale beer."

"No, it's the sawdust on the floor I really hate. But I couldn't think of any other place. I was too upset."

"Ah," he says as if he understands. "Let's go sit at a table."

I order another glass of Chablis. Will orders seltzer water. We take our drinks to a booth near the end of the bar away from after-work drinkers lining up for a magic elixir that will make another day in purgatory disappear.

"So, what's up?" Will asks.

I tell him my sad story, omitting no details. He listens patiently. I've noticed before that he's a good listener. I like that.

"I'm so sorry. I know you liked that job."

"Yes, I did." I can feel the tears assembling for descent and fight them back. I sigh as he takes my hand.

"It's so discouraging. I thought I'd found the perfect job."

"I know. It sucks. But if you found that one, you'll find others. They're out there and you have so much to offer."

Now, the tears tumble down my cheeks.

Will offers me a handkerchief from his pocket. It's fresh and smells like the soap he uses, a woodsy scent, slightly pine. I sniffle and snort into the soft cloth.

"I'll wash it for you," I say, tucking the handkerchief into my bag.

"That's the least of my worries. What are we going to do about you? No, let me say that another way. What can I do for you?"

"Just be here and listen. That's a lot. Here I thought everything was going so well—my work, our relationship…"

"Whoa! Your work may have taken a nosedive, but what's wrong with our relationship? You've made me happy."

"You've made me happy, too. I didn't mean anything was wrong with us."

"That's a relief."

"I'm just worried about bills, health insurance, all the shit I thought I had handled."

I'm feeling the effect of two glasses of wine and no food except for pretzels. How many nutrients are in dough and salt?

"I think I should probably eat. I'm going to the restroom and then maybe we can order something."

I feel a little woozy and make my way carefully to the women's room, use the toilet, wash my hands, and douse my face with cold water. When I return to the table, Will is grinning above the Dinty's menu.

"Are you smiling because we both know there's nothing good on that menu but Irish stew?"

"The hamburgers aren't that bad, but no, that's not why I'm grinning. I think I've come up with the solution to your problem."

"Which is?"

"Marry me! Now, listen, before you say no and tell me to stop asking, this is different. I haven't asked in weeks, maybe months, so this is not just my broken record. You've hit a rough patch, and

I love you and want to take care of you. You know eventually I'll get you to say 'yes,' so why not now?"

"I want to take care of myself. I want a career. I don't want to depend on you."

"I want the same, but wouldn't it be nice if we could take care of each other, too?"

I close my eyes, imagining what it would be like to share a life with this man. He's sweet, devoted, a good lover, funny, a bit crazy maybe, but who isn't? What would it be like to have someone take care of me?

I wouldn't have to deplete my meager savings and start from scratch. And I'm not getting any younger. My birthday is approaching at warp speed, only two months away. Gray hairs are proliferating like weeds; wrinkles are eroding my cover girl complexion; and I'm beginning to yearn for afternoon naps. I'm tired of worrying about money, sharing a basement apartment with roaches and mice, and I dread having to continue my fruitless search for Mr. Right, which has succeeded only in unearthing a horde of Mr. Horrifics.

"Let me think about it," I say.

"That's not a no?"

"It's a strong maybe."

CHAPTER 29

—

STAR-STRUCK

Emily and Will
invite you to celebrate
their marriage
Saturday, September 20
2:00 p.m.
Saltwater Tide Inn
Barnstable, Cape Cod, Massachusetts
Reception is a clambake on the beach.
Bring swimsuit and sunscreen!
RSVP on card enclosed.

I hope this doesn't come as a shock. You could probably see it coming.

In the months after my layoff, while I searched for a new job in an ever-tightening market, Will managed to endear himself to me with his constancy, thoughtfulness, and delicious, home-cooked dinners. One evening, after serving me two generous portions of vegetable lasagna, dripping with mozzarella and ricotta cheese, fresh zucchini, yellow squash, carrots, spinach, garlic, and onions, and before I could fall into a food coma, Will fell to one knee.

"Marry me," he urged, bending over to retrieve the napkin that had fallen onto the floor at my feet. "I'll cook like this forever, a different dish every night."

Who could say no?

• • •

Now, Will and I are sitting at my kitchen table in our sweats, addressing our wedding invitations, painstakingly writing in our best script. It's taking hours while time seems to be hurtling ahead. I can't believe the wedding will be in six weeks!—the second wedding, that is, the one with our families and friends.

The first wedding, the secret ceremony, will be 10 days earlier on Wednesday, September 10 at 10:00 a.m.—the exact moment when stars, planets, and even asteroids are aligned most favorably for good fortune in our union, according to Will's astrologer, Astrid Farthingale.

It seems that Astrid and Will have been stargazing together for several years and Astrid has led Will through some hairy episodes when Mercury must have been in big-time retrograde, including the last stock market crash and his divorce. Will has total faith in Astrid's ability to steer his path by the light of the planets. I have resisted pointing out the flaws in that thinking. He apparently lost a good portion of his shirt—at least a sleeve and cuff—in that latest stock market dive—a loss that helped precipitate his divorce, but maybe that's why he considers it good fortune.

• • •

I'm wondering about this astrological penchant, which I had dismissed as a harmless hobby until now.

"Will, who gets married at 10 on a Wednesday morning?" I don't wait for an answer. "No one who wants anyone to come to his wedding, that's who!"

"Emily, calm down. I'm just telling you what Astrid advises. She says that's the most propitious time for our marriage… if we want good fortune and happiness."

"How many times has Astrid been married? Never mind, I don't care. I just don't see how we can expect our family and friends to come. If you recall, I wanted to elope with no fuss and no muss. You're the one who insisted we should share our joy with a multitude."

"Emily... Emily... I'm sure we can come up with a way to do this."

• • •

So we're marrying twice, once for Astrid and her planets and once for family and friends, who will never know about the first rites for a variety of reasons; for one, I'd never hear the end of it and that's enough for me.

I might not have agreed to these machinations if I weren't afraid that Will might believe our marriage doomed without the "I do's" on the stroke of 10 on that celestially ordained Wednesday. Besides, he's enjoying all this plotting and scheming so whole-heartedly I don't want to spoil his fun. What harm can it do?

• • •

Thursday, April 29

Dear Emily,

It's a gray, rainy day and I'm stuck at home, nursing a cold instead of hiking in Seward Park. It's probably just as well. My to-do list is yellowing with age and neglect.

Before I'm buried in de-cluttering my hall closet or replacing rotting drainpipes, I'm reaching out to see how you're doing. It's been a long time since I last heard from you and I'm wondering what's happening in your world.

Please write.

Best,
Ian

• • •

Tuesday, May 3

Dear Ian,

So sorry about the long silence! So much has happened I don't know where to begin.

Yes, I do. His name is Will Slipway and we're getting married!

He's won my heart, despite the fact that he walks like a duck and sometimes begins a story in its middle. He's dear, sweet, and loves me unconditionally! What more could a girl want? Seriously, I think we're a good match. He's unflappable while I tend to flop about in a stiff breeze. He's cheerful and optimistic, not a worrier like me. I think he adds balance to my life.

He has some quirks, but at our age, who hasn't? I've decided his attention to astrology is harmless. Who am I to naysay? I like his spirit and his good nature.

Will has a steady job and health insurance—not to be sneezed at! I was laid off again a few weeks ago. This time, I didn't see it coming or wish for it, so it was a blow. I've been able to pick myself off the dusty floor with Will's help and have begun the job hunt again, without much success so far. At least now I have Will's support and don't have to panic. He says he'd be happy if I didn't work or just worked part-time so we'd have more time together, but I didn't go to graduate school to be a stay-at-home wife. Besides, I loved my work with adult learners and am itching to do more.

More about Will. He's divorced and has twins in college—a boy and a girl. I've met them and after a rocky start with his daughter, I think we'll be okay. As I think I told you, Will and I met at my old workplace. He designs electronic toys, so his job is probably secure. More to the point, he seems to enjoy his work. He's a native Bostonian and has two sisters living in the area. Nice people.

We weathered another rocky start when I took Will to meet my mother. Without boring you with details, I'll just say he jammed both feet into his mouth more than once, and I was afraid the damage was irreversible. Fortunately, my mother's memory isn't that great. She still has reservations about him, I think, but she'll be happy if I am. She's hard of hearing and calls him "the mumbler."

I wanted to elope and Will wanted a gala with friends, family, and strays. He's getting his gala, toned down to a beach party, and I'm eliminating his strays. We'll need until next September to iron out some of the details.

The next step is to bring our families together—oy!

I hope your cold has subsided, and your closets win the Good Housekeeping Award..

Fondly,
Emily

CHAPTER 30

—

PRENUPTIAL PORTENTS

At 9 a. m. on a glorious September morn, Will and I meet my friend Jessie, a Boston attorney who can perform marriages in the eyes of God and the Commonwealth of Massachusetts, her husband, Cal, and their oldest daughter, Nicky, who will be our witnesses. We exchange vows under a weeping willow tree in Boston Public Garden, near the Swan Boats and famous family of Mallards, whom I can almost hear quacking and honking their delight.

Now, we are 10 days away from wedding #2, the biggy. My mother and kids, who have met Will only once before, will be arriving in four days. Since I'm still in my tiny basement apartment and Will is living at his sister's, my family will stay with my friends, who have generously offered them bed and board. Raspberry, my mother's poodle, will not accompany my mother but will board in a kennel where he belongs.

I feel besieged by last-minute details and am trying to hold myself together. I have to lose three to four pounds so my dress drapes gracefully instead of clinging like plaster to my mid-section. I have to cover the gray strands threatening territorial domination of my hair. I have to go over the menu with the Clamshuckers Catering Service, make sure I've reserved enough cabanas for guests to change in and out of swimsuits... the list runs on, haunting my nights and dogging my days.

At least Will is in charge of the DJ and music.

Why the hell are we doing this? The Wednesday wedding in the Public Garden was perfect. We are married. We're planning to move into a house big enough for Will's stuff, my stuff, and stuff yet to be. We're going on a honeymoon trip to Italy. Why complicate things with a large wedding where I'll be too excited and nervous to eat, talk to anyone for more than three seconds, or remember much of anything that happens?

What if it rains?

This is just jitters.

• • •

The families have gathered this evening for a prenuptial celebration and get-acquainted dinner in the back room of Carlo's, a neighborhood Italian restaurant that Will and I chose after spending hours planning our Italian honeymoon and drooling at photos of pasta, garlic bread, and gelato.

It's kind of exciting to see my kids, his kids, our siblings, and my mother all at the same table, but I'd be more excited if I were a fly on the wall instead of the focus of so much familial attention and last-minute advice.

• • •

My mother and Will have already locked horns once today over hot pastrami sandwiches while I nibble my salad, still trying to whittle off those four pounds.

"Mrs. Rosenbloom... what should I call you now that you're my mother-in-law?"

In alarm, I kick Will's leg under the table. He looks puzzled and then chagrined.

"Let's not jump the gun on that mother-in-law bit, but you can call me Adele."

"Not Mother?"

"Am I your mother? Certainly not."

I'd like to leave the table but am afraid I'll return to find them wrestling on top of it. Like the little Dutch boy, I have to keep my finger in the dike.

Will forges ahead. "I don't want you to worry, Adele. I intend to take good care of Emily and make sure she has everything she needs."

"Emily doesn't need to be taken care of. She's done a fine job, herself."

"If you want to talk about me, wait until I leave the room," I protest.

"Adele, I know she's a competent adult. I just want to make her life easier. I tell her not to worry about finding another full-time job. Part-time would be fine. I want us to have more time for each other, and I want to take care of her."

• • •

Now, while we wait for our dinner to be served, Alan, my older brother, dressed in emerald green and gold Hawaiian shirt and jeans, lifts his lanky body out of his chair, raising his glass of Chianti.

"Well, sistah, you're finally tying the knot again and in this century," he pauses to enjoy giggles from nieces and nephews followed by a humph from our mother. "Seriously, we're all happy for you and Will and have come from near and far to celebrate with you and make sure you show up at the ceremony."

Chuckles reward him, including mine, although he'll never get the irony. Not to be outdone, Will's brother-in-law, Brian, dressed in preppy, navy blazer, lifts his 6'3" bulk and his glass.

"Emily and Will, we toast you today, welcoming you, Emily, to our family and congratulating you, Will, on your good taste and good fortune. May your union be blessed." He glances at Alan.

My younger son, Steven, stands wearing an impish grin. "It's great to be here with you, Mom. I'm glad you and Will are committing to love, honor, and take care of one another." He hesitates, wipes his brow with an exaggerated sweep of his hand and utters a loud, "Whew!"

More laughter. I turn to Will and stage whisper, "I didn't think this was supposed to be a roast."

Mercifully, the waiters arrive with platters of food and we all dig in. The food, served family style, is good, hearty Italian peasant food: antipasto of cold cuts, vegetables, and cheeses, white bean and pasta soup, spaghetti tossed with olive oil, garlic, mushrooms, and olives, Italian peasant chicken casserole, ripe summer tomatoes and basil heaped on toasted country bread, garlic risotto and almond, apricot, and cream cheese crostata and gelato for dessert.

I'm sure I'm forgetting one or two courses, but you get the gist. When Congreve said, "Music hath charms to soothe the savage breast," he hadn't met my family and didn't realize the power of gastronomic persuasion. By the fourth or fifth course, my brother and Will's brother-in-law are exchanging business cards; Will's sister is exchanging spaghetti sauce recipes with my mother; and our heirs are checking out neighborhood clubs for après-dinner dancing and drinking.

I don't know about Will, but I'm exhausted and wondering if we can still call the whole thing off. We are married, after all. Maybe we can fess up about our ceremony in the Public Garden and be done with it. We can take everyone bowling instead.

But no, we've signed contracts, paid deposits, and issued invitations. It's going to be "a Real Nice Clambake," just like the one in Rogers' and Hammerstein's musical, *Carousel*.

• • •

Today, my mother and I are at the Left Bank Beauty Studio, choosing nail polish shades for our manicures and pedicures to be followed by facials and hair styling.

My mother points to a livid purplish-red nail polish. "What do you think of this Forever Fuchsia?"

"Not you. How about Cantaloupe Crush? That would be perfect with your hair and skin." My mother, at 88, still dyes her hair herself; the shades vary, depending on what's on sale. Today, her hair is a muted strawberry blonde, which is flattering.

"Really? It looks a bit bland to me... but if you say so. You're the blushing bride."

"The blush is off this rose. How does it feel to be the mother of a middle-aged bride?"

"Fine, if you're sure this is what you want."

"What do you mean? What are you saying?"

"It's nothing... I just wonder if this Will really knows who you are."

"You're worried about your conversation at lunch, aren't you? Don't. Will's just... enthusiastic. He's generous and sweet and wants the best for me."

"You have to decide what's best for you."

"I am doing that. Don't worry, Mum." I kiss her cheek. "Speaking of blushing roses, I'm going to use this Rose Red polish. Do you like it?"

"It's nice," my mother replies half-heartedly.

"Mum, what do you think Dad would have thought of Will?"

"He would have liked him well enough, I guess, because he's quiet and has good manners, but he would have said he's short, and he wouldn't have liked the beard."

"Short and bad beard? That's all he'd have to say?"

"Your father always thought men who grew beards had something to hide."

"Dad certainly did have some unusual prejudices, not the usual run-of-the-mill, racist, sexist kind of stuff. You've got to give him that."

"Don't knock your father. You'd do well to find someone like him. They broke the mold when they made him."

"Amen to that."

Having filed, moisturized, and painted our nails at just below warp speed, Brittany and Tiffany lead us to the nail dryers and place us next to each other, our hands and feet under the jets of warm air. "Just relax, ladies. Can we bring you tea?"

My mother says, "I'm not a tea drinker unless it's iced. Do you have decaf coffee?"

Brittany and Tiffany wander away, mumbling something about siphoning coffee from the boss's thermos.

"Mum, you're awfully quiet. Is everything okay?"

"I'm fine… I don't want to talk about it."

My mother is the mistress of mixed messages.

"What do you mean, you don't want to talk about *it*? What is *it*?"

"Nothing. Forget about it."

But I can't. I'm hooked. "Please don't do this. Just tell me what's wrong."

She sighs, looking at me sideways, a sure sign she's about to say something I don't want to hear. "I'm just not sure about this Will."

I groan. "Why? What's wrong with him?"

"I didn't say anything was wrong… it's just a feeling I get."

"Like what?" I don't want to hear her response, but I feel like a spectator at a train wreck, repelled by the mayhem and mangled bodies but unable to look away.

"Can you be more specific? A feeling you get doesn't tell me anything." My voice is rising.

"Calm down. Everyone can hear you."

I take a deep breath, then another, fighting the urge to hyperventilate.

"He doesn't look at me when we're talking. He mumbles. It's like he has something to hide."

"He's not mumbling. You're hard of hearing. Or maybe the beard Dad would have hated is muffling the sound." I'm being defensive but can't stop myself.

"This is exactly why I didn't want to say anything. You make me sound stupid."

"Sorry," I apologize. "I won't do that again. Anything else bothering you?"

"Emily, you know I want you to be happy, don't you?"

"Yes, of course."

"And your father would want you to be happy?"

"Mum, I know. Everyone wants me to be happy. Even your third cousins, twice removed, Ernest and Frances, want me to be happy…"

"You're being sarcastic again."

"Sorry, but I want to know what else is worrying you."

"How well do you know him?"

"Well enough. We've been together for more than a year. How well does anyone really know the person they marry? How well did you know Dad?"

"I just think this man has hidden layers."

"Does that mean you think he's deep?"

My mother looks at me and sighs again. "Oh, Emily. I just want the best for you. If you love the man, go marry him and be happy."

CHAPTER 31

—

NONPOTABLE PORTENT

The wind is racketing against the window and my mother is snoring in three-part harmony from her twin bed next to mine. Briefly, I wonder if I can shove her bed out into the hall or crawl into the bathtub and wrap towels around my head to muffle the noise. Of all nights for insomnia to plague me! Who ever heard of a blushing bride wearing deep, dark bags under her eyes and nodding off during the vows? I need my beauty sleep.

I turn onto my left side, away from my mother and am just drifting off when I hear voices arguing—two men or a man and a woman with a low, smoker's voice that's familiar—my mother? The man's voice sounds like someone I know, too, but his face is shadowed and his name is eluding me. If I listen for a while, maybe it will come to me...

"You were supposed to do something about this. Isn't that your job?"

"Madam, nowhere in the DSM-5 or *Journal of Psychiatry* does it state that preventing a marriage is part of my job."

"Don't get smart with me, my dear young man. Just what is your job if it isn't to prevent disasters?"

My god, it is my mother!

"I have an obligation to intervene when a patient threatens harm to herself or another. I am neither responsible for, nor can I prevent the choices or behavior of my patients. I can counsel, interpret, and help patients gain insight, nothing more… and I am not your dear young man," the man harrumphs.

My god, it's Dr. Rothman!

"I never wanted Emily to see you in the first place. I knew you'd stir up trouble. We were good parents. We did the best we could, gave her a warm, loving home, a good education and up-bringing, nice clothes, and now look at what you've done. A lot of help you are!"

"I am beginning to understand the problem," Rothman says, folding his hands against his ample belly and sitting back in his chair.

I notice for the first time that my mother's sitting on Rothman's brown leather couch and he's sitting in his armchair across from her, a box of tissue on the coffee table between them, but they're not in his office. They're floating on the ocean, waves cresting beneath them and foghorns belching behind them. Dr. Rothman slaps at a school of minnows swimming around his chair.

"Well, maybe that's where the trouble lies," my mother replies. "How could you help my daughter if you hadn't figured out the problem?" It's her turn to harrumph.

"An interesting point. Tell me, what do you see as the problem?"

"Now you want me to do your work? I thought you had just finally figured it out."

"Maybe, but I'd like to hear your thoughts," he purrs.

"My daughter is making a mistake, and it's not her first. You know she was married before?"

Dr. Rothman nods.

"He turned out badly—completely irresponsible, wouldn't work, left her and the kids penniless. My husband and I helped her get back on her feet. She's done a good job, too. Now, she wants to throw it all away on a strange character with a beard!"

Dr. Rothman rubs his whiskerless chin, "a beard, eh? That's the problem?"

"What do we know about him? Are you saying this marriage is a good thing?" My mother challenges, kicking away a cod that's nibbling at her toes.

"I'm not saying that, but this isn't about me. It's about your concerns."

"How did this get turned around?" My mother sputters, "We're not talking about me. This is about how you're not doing your job."

She and Dr. Rothman glare at each other.

My mother breaks the silence. "I think he works for the CIA or some other undercover branch of the government. Or maybe he's a spy," she whispers.

"A spy? Interesting. What makes you say that?"

"He's shifty. Her first husband was shiftless. This one's shifty."

I can hear myself laughing. My mother and Dr. Rothman hear me, too.

"Emily, what are you doing here? This is my session with your shrink. Go back to bed."

"You don't seem to be getting anywhere," I protest, splashing a jellyfish in her direction.

"What makes you think we're not getting anywhere, Emily?" Dr. Rothman asks.

"Oh, good lord! Do you see what he does, Mum?"

"Yes, I see only too well. What did you ever see in him is my question."

"Mine, too," Rothman chimes in.

I begin to back paddle away from them, the waves spilling over me. I'm swallowing water. I can hear Rothman and my mother shouting at me, "Come back. You'll drown. Emily! Emily!"

I open my eyes to see my mother standing over my bed. "Emily, the window isn't closed at the top and the rain is coming in. Can't you feel it?"

CHAPTER 32

—

SPOSA BAGNATA, SPOSA FORTUNATA:
WET BRIDE, HAPPY BRIDE

At 5 a.m., I give up my battle to sleep and tiptoe over to the window, hoping not to disturb my mother, who is snoring softly now, her head covered by blankets. Ominous dark clouds are gathering for a second assault. I watch them creep up over the horizon, thickening as they roll toward land. I wonder if Astrid Farthingale, Will's astrologer, has summoned them to plague this second ceremony—her way of saying the 10 a.m. Wednesday wedding should have been enough. Good god, next I'll be watching for her to streak the sky on a broomstick, trailing a stream of howling black cats!

I shudder and close the drapes. It's only 5:03. The wedding is not until 2. The clouds could blow over by then. I slide back under the covers.

At 7 a.m., an angry wind splatters rain against the window, which rattles in protest. I moan, tugging the covers up over my head.

"What's that?" my mother asks, sitting upright, looking like Medusa with her hair wound tightly around oversized curlers.

"It's a monsoon," I howl, "on my wedding day!"

"Maybe it will blow over."

"Or maybe it will blow the wedding tent over!"

Because it's a September wedding and this is Massachusetts, my fantasy beach wedding and clambake have already been down-scaled to a New England seafood dinner under a tent on a sturdy platform between the inn and the beach—just in case. At least the menu has pretty much endured.

Now, I'm afraid that's not enough and a strong gust will whip the tent, the food, and the guests into the ocean. Maybe we should pass out life jackets as people take their seats.

The guests begin arriving at 1:30, looking as though they've been run through a car wash: umbrellas sprung inside out, hair, makeup, and beach attire dripping puddles onto the floor. Inn staffers scurry to find towels to absorb the water; one rushes in with a large mop and bucket.

Guests continue to dribble in for the next two hours with tales of hydroplaning on the highway, navigating puddles the size of Lake Ontario, and slowing to a 5-mph-crawl along the two-lane road down to Barnstable.

The ceremony finally begins at 3:30. My mouth is trembling from maintaining a smile and a stiff upper lip. Will has been handing out beach towels and hot toddies for the last half hour. I think I notice a quiver in his lip, too. My left eye has begun to twitch, but the show must go on.

Jessie, the friend and attorney who performed our secret ceremony, stands before us again, smiling bravely. She opens with a few words of greeting and acknowledgment of the courage and fortitude of the family and friends gathered for the festivities in the midst of a gale. Will and I exchange vows, accompanied by the mournful soundings of a nearby foghorn, balefully moaning in the wind.

After the ceremony, Will and I enjoy endless hugging from damp well-wishers, toasts shouted to be heard above the storm, and good-natured family and friends, diving enthusiastically into steamed clams, baked potatoes, corn on the cob, lobster, salmon or steak, washed down with beer, wine, or lemonade, laughter, motion, and flashing cameras.

Will, who is in charge of the music, has hired a local DJ, who stands, grinning ruefully under a large blue and white umbrella supplied by the inn. A steady trickle of water dribbles through a slight tear at the top of the tent onto that umbrella. Every packet of wedding photos sent by friends includes shots of the DJ under the umbrella, his long hair scooped into a pony tail, wearing a black tee shirt, advertising his services in fluorescent pink lettering, KSTB's *Manny, the Manic Music Man.*

Manny introduces us for the first dance, "Ladies and Lads, may I present the bride and groom, Emily and Will Slipway."

"Who told him my name is Slipway?" I ask Will as he leads me to the space allotted for dance floor. "That's not my name. I'm still Emily Rosenbloom."

"Does it matter? Let's relax and enjoy our dance," Will murmurs drawing me closer as Manny presses the button to play our song, my choice, "At Last," sung by the inimitable Etta James. But it's not "At Last." Instead, I hear Frank Sinatra crooning, "I Did It My Way!"

What the hell? I hesitate, inadvertently tripping Will and we stumble across the dance floor, taking a few phrases to regain our balance. "That's not the song I wanted," I snivel. "What happened to Etta James?"

Frankie warbles, "I traveled each and ev'ry highway,

And more, much more than this, I did it my way."

"I couldn't find the CD, so this is what I came up with," Will replies, "What's the big deal?"

"I hate this song. It sounds like a dirge."

"Now, you're being dramatic," he says, spinning me into a dip.

I hear Frankie taunting me, "For what is a man, what has he got?"

The good news is that the storm has passed, leaving a whimpering wind and a few half-hearted rain showers. Guests who haven't joined in the dancing, wander outside as the tent flaps are lifted.

"Look," someone shouts, "there's a rainbow!"

I take Will's hand, relieved to exit the dance floor, and lead him out to the patio. A magnificent rainbow arcs the sky. He squeezes my hand.

"That's good luck, you know," he whispers. "A rainbow means fresh beginnings."

I resist asking him if he's quoting Astrid, his trusty astrologer. Instead, I say, "I hope so. I could use a little magic right about now."

"And there's more to come," he says, leering at me as he pulls me closer.

"Emily, it's time to cut the cake," my mother says, appearing at our side. "You two will have plenty of time for canoodling later."

CHAPTER 33
—
GONDOLAS AND CASA ISABELLA

A honeymoon in Venice seemed such a splendid idea when we planned the trip months ago. What could be more romantic than Venice? That was before the wedding deluge. Now, I'm not eager to see water of any kind, and living on a canal, even for a few days, seems foolhardy. I have nightmares of being washed away in a tsunami, my bridal veil wrapped around my neck like Isadora Duncan's scarf.

Since we're already on the plane to Paris where we'll have 40 minutes—if we're lucky—to charge through the airport and board the plane to Venice, I suppose it's too late to back out. Besides, Will is as excited as a kid on Christmas Eve and has none of my qualms.

We fly over the Adriatic into Marco Polo Airport, which sits on the edge of a lagoon. The day is so clear and the mountains and sea so brilliant green, navy, and turquoise, I vow to relish every moment in Venice, abandoning my budding aquaphobia. As we begin our descent, another phobia surfaces—my fear of landing from any distance higher than five feet. I clutch Will's hand. Mistaking my fear for excitement and affection, Will begins to nuzzle my neck. I squeeze his hand. He begins to nibble my ear.

"Not here, Will," I whisper, kissing him lightly on the cheek.

Anxious to get to the hotel, we splurge on a water taxi to carry us the eight miles into Venice and along the Grand Canal—the ancient waterway that snakes through the city.

Despite all the photos I've seen of Venice, my mouth is agape as we pass magnificent, old palazzi—buildings constructed by the wealthy, some dating back to the 13th century—their once brilliant colors faded, facades worn down by age and harsh weather. I turn to Will. He's frantically snapping photos as though he's afraid these ancient buildings will suddenly disappear. It is happening, but not that quickly. I sigh and turn back to absorb what I'm seeing: Byzantine architecture abutting Baroque next to Gothic, next to Renaissance—a wild reflection of centuries of Venetian history. We pass under footbridges that arch gracefully over the Canal. I want to hold this moment forever.

Soon after we glide under the Rialto Bridge, our taxi slows and draws up to a landing. The driver announces the Hotel Palazzo Abagonza, the accommodations we've chosen based on the eloquent description issued by the hotel.

Set in a former Doge's 16th-century residence, Hotel Palazzo Abagonza overlooks the Santa Sofia Canal in Cannaregio. It offers a peaceful garden and rooms with Venetian views and antique furnishings. Most rooms feature original 18th-century furniture, frescoed ceilings, and silk wallpaper. The Palazzo Abagonza's public areas feature Murano-glass lamps and Persian carpets.

Guests can sip a drink in the bar while admiring views of the canal, and free Wi-Fi is available.

Will pays the driver, helps me onto the dock, hoists our luggage: a medium-sized roll-on and backpack for me and a larger, somewhat unwieldy leather suitcase and backpack for him. Apparently, it's a case he used on his last trip to Europe 15 years earlier and he's formed an inexplicable attachment to it, despite the streamlining of newer luggage.

We walk the stone path to the hotel's entrance and step into the lobby, where we find ourselves standing on marble flooring, staring at the wooden coffered ceiling and leaded-glass windows, looking out on a canal, certain we have time-traveled to the 16th century.

"Will," I say, grabbing his arm, "isn't this fabulous!"

"Better than that."

Our room is sumptuous. A canopied king-size bed, smothered in large, plush pillows, commands center stage. Silver and gold silk damask covers the walls. The velvet ruby-red drapes have been drawn aside like theater curtains, opening onto a garden scene of lavender, ruby and blue impatiens, plumbago, and hydrangea, and beyond the garden, the Santa Sofia Canal.

It's late afternoon, the sun dipping slowly toward the water. We stand arm-in-arm, gazing at the garden and water, inhaling the fragrance of the flowers. Still, our excitement at arriving in Venice is overlaid with a tinge of weariness tinted with ardor.

"Let's nap," Will suggests, moving away from me to draw the drapes.

"Leave a window open. The air feels so good," I say, having noticed a hint of mildew in our splendid room.

We tumble into bed, tossing pillows aside, and are soon asleep.

A buzz saw is cutting the limb off a perfectly healthy apple tree in full blossom. What the hell is wrong with that guy, whacking off the arm of a tree in bloom, and why is he working in the dark? Must be up to no good—an act of retribution against a neighbor.

In the dark? What time is it? Where am I? I move my left arm, which has fallen asleep and open my eyes. I'm lying in a strange bed in a large, unfamiliar room. I hear the buzz saw again, this time closer and sounding more like a drone heading for my… ear! It's a mosquito! I slap at it, catching my cheek but missing the mosquito, which darts angrily away and then back at me. Or is that another one? I give it a mighty swat, hitting it broadside and imagining it tumbling to the carpet.

"Take that, you miserable insect!"

Another buzzing Messerschmitt dive-bombs at my head and I swing at it with my pillow, hitting Will on the down-swat. I begin to scratch my arm, my shoulder, my chin, realizing these bloodsuckers have been eating me!

"What's going on?" Will shouts, startled by the blow to his head.

"Mosquitoes," I yell. "Close the windows! If the Venetians are smart enough to invent blinds, why can't they make screens?"

Will slams the windows and walks toward me, scratching furiously at his mosquito-ravaged flesh. I lie back onto the bed, pulling the sheet up over my head.

"They could at least warn us," Will mutters, "or supply mosquito netting."

I nod in agreement. At the same time, I'm distracted by another sensation.

"Will, the sheets are damp!"

"Don't look at me. I stopped wetting the bed ages ago."

"What is that?"

"We're right on a canal, aren't we? It's probably damp air from the water. Another reason to keep the windows closed."

"A fine, romantic setting," I scoff, burrowing farther down under the moist covers.

We awaken in an overheated room flooded by the midday sun. We had closed the windows against the invading mosquitoes but had forgotten to close the heavy drapes, hanging like sheets on a clothesline, grateful for the drying rays of the sun.

It's almost noon. We're hungry and dress quickly, trying to ignore the slight dampness clinging to our clothes. I cannot ignore, however, the frightening image confronting me in the mirror. Gad, what is that? My recently straightened hair, gracefully sculpted around my face, has sprung loose, Medusa-like, filling the mirror. I push on it with my hands in an attempt to flatten it into place. It springs back to occupy all available space. I think I hear hissing!

"Emily, what are you doing in there? Let's get going."

"Don't come in here. A dangerous animal has been let loose!"

Will flings open the door, "What the hell are you talking about?"

He stops short when he sees me wrestling with my Medusa locks. "Oh, my." He backs away.

"What am I going to do?"

"Just comb it. You'll look fine."

"You think I can get a comb through this?"

"Well, brush it then. I'll wait for you in the garden."

I notice he's still inching away, afraid to turn his back on the beast that threatens to devour Venice.

Despite our dubious beginning and the occasional rain clouds that trundle across the sky, our days in Venice are a tourist-book delight: we tour palazzi, attend *La Traviata* at the Palazzo Barbarigo Minotto on the Grand Canal. We take a photo walking tour with Marco, a native of Venice and professional photographer who knows all the out-of-the-way spots in Venice, their history, and best photo opportunities. We watch glass-blowing at the Murano Glass Factory, admire elderly women embroidering lace on the Isle of Burano, cuddle discreetly on night-lit gondolas gliding through the canals, make love in the moonlight under damp sheets.

Reluctantly, we depart Venice and travel by train to Florence, where we make our way, dragging our luggage over the cobblestones to Casa Isabella, the inn just steps away from the Duomo, the historical center of Florence.

We ring the bell on the massive wooden door, wondering if we should use the oversized wrought-iron knocker instead. Moments later, the door opens and a statuesque brunette, all leg and bosom, crammed into a peasant blouse and tight black skirt à la Sophia Loren, stands before us.

"Ciao," she says in a whiskey voice.

Will has been rendered dumb, so I say in my huskiest voice, "Ciao, parli Inglesi?"

"Si, how can I help you?" She responds, eyeing us, particularly Will, who has straightened himself to his full 5'8".

Satisfied with my explanation of who we are, she leads us to a small cage, the inn's shaky elevator, and the three of us plus luggage squeeze into its narrow confines. Will is grinning like a cat that has swallowed multiple canaries. I frown at him. His grin subsides.

Our room is small but cozy with a double bed covered by a pink and white rose-print chenille spread, matching the pink and white rose-print drapes and armchair. A large, carved wooden armoire occupies most of the remaining space in the room. Our window overlooks a rose-filled garden. I try to remember where I packed my Claritin. On the plus side, we seem to be in the back of the building off the narrow, busy street. I'm also pleased that the air is dry and fresh-smelling, no hint of mildew.

"Did you hear Isabella say they serve tea at 4? We can just make it."

"Isabella, how did you know that's her name?"

"Isn't this the Casa Isabella? Besides, I noticed it on her nametag."

I'll bet you did, I think, but keep it to myself.

"I'd like to unpack and freshen up a bit, so if you are so anxious for tea, go ahead. I'll catch up."

I have barely finished my sentence when Will is out the door. By the time I descend to the parlor in Isabella's apartment on the main floor, she is cleaning away the remnants of tea.

"Ciao," I venture, "is it still possible to have a cup of tea?"

Will is sitting on a floral sofa, glancing through tour brochures.

"Si, certamente," she purrs, wiggling out of the room.

I look quickly at Will, whose head is studiously buried in a brochure. What could be that fascinating?

"Does Isabella come with a Mr. Isabella?"

Will looks up. "Oh, Emily, I didn't realize you were here."

"Engrossed in your reading, eh?"

Will ignores this snide query and asks, "What did you say about Isabella?"

"I asked if there's a Mr. attached to our voluptuous hostess."

"Your guess is as good as mine," he replies.

"I doubt that."

Isabella returns, bearing a fresh pot of tea and cup and saucer in a floral design of lily and iris. I notice the not-so-pleasant fragrance of lily past its prime wafting from our hostess. Her Italian perfume?

"Grazie." I'm using up all my Italian pretty quickly. "This is such a lovely place. Very cozy. I love all the fresh flowers and floral prints. Do you manage it all yourself?"

"No. Mio marito, Guido, he helps me."

"How nice for you. Will we be meeting Guido?"

"No, unfortunately. His mother is ill in Napoli and he visits her."

"Too bad," I say, glancing at Will, who pretends not to listen. "I understand you and Guido own this inn. Has it been in your family long?"

"I own Casa Isabella, only me. It has been in my family, the Donatella Manginares for generations, but not always it was an inn. Once it was the family home in Firenze until times and circumstances, they change," she sighs. "We keep the inn to help support our farm in Poppi. That has been ours for centuries."

"How very interesting," I remark, impressed by Isabella's fluency in English and her family history. I still don't think anyone with a body like hers can be trusted.

"Have you seen Poppi? La più bella!" She kisses her fingers.

"We've been thinking about seeing some of the countryside," Will pipes up. "We'd love to hear more about Poppi."

"But we mustn't keep you any longer," I intervene. "We did want to see the Duomo before sunset."

"We'll do that, Emily, when I'm through helping out here."

Isabella chimes in, "No, no, Guglielmo, you have been so helpful and I am filled with gratitude."

And a few other things, I think.

"You go now with your lovely bride. I can do the rest myself."

"Just let me carry this tray of cups and saucers into your kitchen," Will insists. Mr. Gallant. Mr. Goo Elmo.

He lifts the floral tray, which he has stacked precariously with Isabella's china tea set, turns around to follow her to the kitchen, is distracted by her ample ass, trips and falls to the floor, scattering cups and saucers that shatter when they hit the hardwood floor. A couple of lucky cups land on the rug and remain intact. Not so my courtly, helpful husband, who stutters his apology.

"Oh, my god, I'm so sorry. I tripped over something."

Probably your tongue, which is hanging out of your lecherous mouth.

"Please forgive me. Emily and I will be happy to reimburse you whatever it costs to replace these dishes. I can't tell you how sorry we are."

So now it's we, is it?

Isabella, who has said nothing, stares at shards of cups and saucers, scattered at her feet, her chin beginning to quiver. "This tea set has been in the Donatella Manginare family longer than I have been alive. It was my great-grandmother's. It cannot be replaced."

Will looks at me as if to say, 'What now?'

I shrug my shoulders, tempted to let him squirm, but I can't be that mean. "Will, let's help Isabella clean this up and then we can figure out what to do. Perhaps they still sell this beautiful pattern. I think I've seen it before."

Will nods gratefully and is lifting his chagrined body off the floor when Isabella turns on him.

"Ay mid dio," she howls, "is irreplaceable! You shatter my heart when you break the dish of my great-grandmother! Do not touch another thing. Just go away," she sobs, her bosom heaving, a sight not easily forgotten.

"No good deed goes unpunished," I say to Will as we push open the heavy front door. "Let's go atone at the Duomo. We can light a few candles and say a few "Our Fathers." Just don't knock over any precious relics or we may end up in prigione, doing laundry for the guards!"

• • •

Chastened and penitent, we tiptoe around the cathedral, light a few candles, and drop coins into a collection box. When we finally can take our leave, we head for the nearest café. It's still light so we sit outdoors at the edge of the piazza, sipping cappuccinos and watching the parade of tourists, students, and workers on foot and motor scooters. Earlier I would have found charm in the color, movement, and sounds in this famous square, would have delighted in its bustle and cobblestone beauty. Now, I'd just like to hop on the back of one of those scooters and ride off into the Tuscan hills.

"Thanks for having my back, Emily. I really appreciate your support," Will stammers, reaching for my hand.

"What was that all about?" I demand, pulling away.

"What was what about?"

Detecting a sheepish grin, I fire a withering stare.

"Okay, I was just trying to be helpful."

"Helpful? No wonder you fell on that floor. It was slick with your drool."

"Don't be absurd. Since Isabella was gracious enough to make an extra pot of tea for you, I was just trying to repay the favor," Will huffs.

"Puhleez! I saw you ogling her class-act bodice and throwing yourself at her. Maybe you didn't trip at all. You lunged and missed."

"Now, Emily, you have to admit she has a great body. What red-blooded male wouldn't ogle? You're blowing this all out of proportion."

I'm about to respond when I feel a slight breeze at my shoulder.

"Tell this libidinous lothario he's got no class," Dr. Rothman whispers in my ear. "Tell the old dog he's behaving like an adolescent in heat."

Oh, my god, he's here!

"You have no class," I sputter. "You're like an adolescent in heat." I sit back in my chair, folding my arms across my chest.

"Good work," Dr. Rothman coaches.

"Come on. Don't be ridiculous. It was just harmless flirting. Besides, she was coming onto me."

"He's got to be kidding," Rothman snorts. "Don't bother arguing with this boob. Just give him a timeout and send him to his room."

"Will, I don't want to argue. I just want you to know I'm unhappy about this, and I hope my feelings count for something with you."

"Not bad," Rothman comments.

"Sorry, Emily. I didn't think it was such a big deal. You know your feelings matter to me." Will reaches for my hand again.

I let him take it but am wary, listening for Dr. Rothman's reaction. Apparently he has drifted away in search of hazelnut-chocolate gelato.

CHAPTER 34

—

BLAST FROM THE PAST

A month back from our honeymoon, which we somehow survived, we've moved into a two-bedroom townhouse on Liberty Street in Brookline, just west of Boston. Since Will is back at work and I'm still unemployed, the brunt of the move has fallen on me. For the umpteenth time in my life, I'm overwhelmed by stacks of boxes, waiting to be unpacked. I wouldn't mind so much if I were 30 years younger when I could schlep boxes in the afternoon and still go out dancing with friends in the evening. Now, my lower back aches, sending out sparks of distress, and my sinuses quiver and snort, protesting a steady diet of dust.

I inhale deeply with a handkerchief over my nose and mouth, creaking at my weary knees, ready to heft another box when the phone rings. Not immediately spotting it, I follow the cord to its source.

"Hello, Slipway-Rosenbloom residence," I say, surprising myself, but liking the way it sounds.

"Emily Rosenbloom? I don't know if you remember me. It's Ziggy Windward, managing director of People as Assets Division of Chemicon Industries."

"Of course, I remember you! How are you?" As if I care. This is the guy who cut costs by laying us off, decimating the workplace education program.

"Fine, just fine. In fact, I'm calling with good news."

I wait, unwilling to bite.

"As you probably know, the economy's finally turning around. Things are looking good for our third quarter."

How nice for you, I think, with rancor in my heart.

"This means, we're able to rehire staff and I'm calling to offer you a role if you're available and interested."

A soupçon of excitement tickles my neck, but I ask, "A role? What does that mean?"

I can picture Dr. Rothman punching the air triumphantly. The girl is asking questions.

"Well, what it means…" Ziggy stammers, "is I can offer you a contract position doing exactly the work you were doing. In fact, you may even have some of the same clients. You know how long this kind of training can take."

"A contract position… not a full-time staff position?"

"No, we're not prepared to do that at this point. You weren't working full-time yet, were you?"

"Thirty-two hours with benefits. That was close enough," I retort.

"You can probably still have close to those hours," he replies, "but it would be on a contract basis. This is the deal we're offering everyone we're asking back. It's the best we can do."

Is he whining? I decide to rub the sore spot. "I thought you said the economy's reviving."

"It's still got a way to go. We're hesitantly optimistic," he backpedals.

"I see. Things are good, but not that good."

"Exactly," he replies, missing my irony.

"One other question, what is the contract rate?"

He gives me a figure, which seems okay, but I don't trust him. "Is that the same rate for everyone?"

"I think there may be some differential based on seniority and longevity, but that can all be worked out. Besides, I understand your status has changed. Am I right that you recently married? Congratulations—all the more reason for you to jump at this opportunity. You don't need to worry. Your hubby can pick up the slack and cover health insurance and other benefits. We'd love to have you back in the fold."

"Thanks for the offer. I am interested but want to think about it, and I may even run it past my 'hubby.' Can I get back to you in the next day or two?"

"Of course, the offer's on the table. You'd be smart to grab it. I'll expect to hear from you soon."

I hang up, tempted to rant about this incorrigibly arrogant, chauvinistic, prehistoric throwback, but the offer is tempting. I like the work and rarely have to deal with Ziggy or his staff. Besides, I can use the money. This will be my escape from nonstop household chores. It certainly beats unpacking boxes and deciding what to do with things that should have been discarded two moves earlier.

• • •

"So, Will, what do you think?"

We're sitting at the small patio table where we've had dinner, sipping our iced coffee and stalling before we return to unpacking. It's a warm fall evening, possibly one of the last before autumn chill sets in. I hate to let it go.

"It sounds like a good deal to me, despite the fact the company is taking advantage of you. Nice deal getting a bunch of trained professionals to work without benefits. That's corporate America," he sighs. "It's probably good for us, because it gives you flexibility in your schedule. If you're a contract employee, you probably can have more time off so we can travel. You just won't get paid when you're out."

"That doesn't sound like a great deal to me. I like getting paid."

Will pulls his chair closer to mine, reaching for my hand, "but, Emily, you don't have to worry about that. You have me. I make a decent income, enough to support us both. Besides, I don't want you working so hard. Eventually, we'll want to spend more time traveling." He pats my hand.

"I do want a career," I counter, "besides, what do you mean, you don't want me working so hard?"

He looks perplexed, "I just want us to have a good time together, that's all."

I sip my iced coffee, thinking this may not be such a bad deal, although the idea of travel triggers a slight twitch in my left eyelid. Will has been his sweet, attentive self since the unfortunate scene with the temptress of Florence, but I still wonder. Maybe he was just acting out some sort of newlywed jitters? I want to give him the benefit of the doubt, but I'm wary. "I'll probably take the offer. I'll call Ziggy tomorrow."

• • •

Saturday, August 1

Dear Ian,

To quote Yogi Berra, "Dèja vu all over again." I'm married, unpacking boxes in my new home, and about to return to the job at Chemicon—fewer hours and less pay than before—the corporation's way of caring for their workers, but it's a foot back in the half-open door. I'll take it.

I feel as though I've neglected you and don't want to lose our connection. I got so wrapped up in wedding planning and family stuff that I overlooked friends and other parts of my life. Sorry about that.

I'm adjusting to married life, and it's mostly good. I'm sure I'll feel better once we're settled into our new place and I'm back at work. Right now, I'm tired of unpacking and organizing. I'm still carrying 20-year-old cosmetics, 30-year-old cancelled checks, and moldy college essays with me and am tempted to toss some of the boxes into a giant dumpster without even opening them. Then I think what if I'm dumping my high school yearbook or other mementos? That's when I decided to take a break and write this long overdue letter.

How are you? I'm sending this letter to your Seattle address, as-suming you haven't made any major moves. I'm anxious to hear from you and hope all is well.

Please write when you can and give me an update.

Best,
Emily

• • •

Wednesday, August 19

Dear Emily,

I was off on a camping trip on North Vancouver Island when your letter arrived, so I'm just getting to it.

Good to hear from you and get all your news. Congratulations on your marriage! I heard about it from classmates, who told me you'd actually taken the plunge and were honeymooning in Italy. That must have been an adventure!

I hope you'll be happy in your new life. As you said, it's an adjust-ment—new marriage, new home, and sort of new job. I hope those guys have their act together now and the job is more secure.

I commend you for your bravery in taking on a new relationship in such a major way. I may be too gun-shy and comfortable with my own ways. I'm still in the same house in Seattle, enjoying friends, my daughters, and some travel. It's always nice to come home. I have a new family member—my rescue dog, Max, part golden, part shepherd and who knows what else. I met him at the local humane society and fell in love. At first, I hesitated about adopting him because I travel so much, but my daughters have promised to dog-sit when I'm away. He's four and still thinks he's a puppy—keeps me young.

That's probably the biggest change in my life. I'm enclosing a photo of him.

Be well and happy.

Best,
Ian

CHAPTER 35

—

LOVE THY NEIGHBORS

N ow that we're unpacked, we're like kids celebrating summer vacation. We've been trying local restaurants and coffee shops, roaming the aisles of a large bookstore a couple of blocks from us, and taking walks around our complex and the neighborhood, an old, established New England one with single-family Victorian houses, Dutch Colonials with their mansard roofs, and an occasional Cape Cod. The lawns are shaded by large oaks and elms—lots of raking coming up, I think, grateful for the small patio and patch of grass we own with the condo association taking care of leaf removal.

We've been meeting neighbors and have been invited to participate in a progressive dinner party in a couple of weeks. We're in charge of appetizers. I think Will's more excited about this evening than I am. He's the one who has been studying cookbooks and going through my recipe box.

When he isn't working, Will spends most of his time preparing for the dinner party, which is only a week away now. He has taken over dinner prep, too.

I've returned to work and am having to readapt to the schedule, so I'm grateful to find a warm meal waiting, complete with samples of appetizers he's considering for the fête. Every evening, two or three new delights appear on the table: asparagus wrapped in prosciutto, crab-stuffed mushroom caps—not my favorite—Shrimp Louie, scampi, shrimp with cocktail sauce, crudités with a variety of dips, my favorite, the candied ginger and onion dip, spinach with filo dough, spinach dip, spinach soufflé. It seems difficult for Will to know when enough is enough.

"Will, you are the unvanquished appetizer king!"

"No half measures with me! When I set out to do something, I go whole hog."

"Don't be surprised if that's the next thing to come out of the kitchen," Dr. Rothman grumbles.

Trying to ignore Rothman, I say, "At some point, however, don't you have to stop trying new recipes and narrow down the field? You can't possibly serve all these creations. It wouldn't be fair to the neighbors who have to follow us with entrees, salads, and desserts."

"It doesn't hurt to awe the neighbors."

When the evening finally arrives, our dining table has been transformed into a groaning board of culinary delights. Our roles are set and I don't mind mine. Since Will has done most of the preparation, he should enjoy the accolades. So while he greets and schmoozes, I shuttle back and forth from the dining room to the kitchen, replenishing platters, refilling the punch bowl, handing out extra napkins, and occasionally stopping to chat with a familiar face or meet a new one.

I'm pleased to hear guests extolling Will's appetizers and asking for recipes. I'm not so pleased in one of my passes to notice a brunette I've never seen before, tightly sheathed in a black, satiny jumpsuit, rubbing Will's arm as she whispers in his ear. I do not like the slow grin widening his mouth or the blush tingeing his cheeks. I rush into the kitchen, push the oven timer ahead, and run back into the dining room to announce, "Time to move on to Les and Betty's for the second course. Soup, is it?"

Hours later, I'm finally able to undo my belt, unstrap my sandals, and collapse onto our couch with a sigh.

"I should have worn a Hawaiian muumuu. Why did I eat so much?"

"It was great, wasn't it?" Will asks, admiring himself in the hall mirror as he strokes his upper lip.

I sit up straighter and peer at him. "Will, are you growing a mustache?" I walk closer to him to see what he's gazing at. I can see a few limp wisps of hair above his upper lip.

"Why not? I thought I'd give it a try."

"Don't you think the beard is enough? Why go to all that trouble?"

"What trouble? It's no big deal. The big deal was our debut this evening. Don't you think our course was the best? People were drooling all over the table."

"And over you, too."

"What's that supposed to mean?"

"The bimbo with dyed raven locks and the black jumpsuit."

"Who?" Will feigns innocence but his left eyelid twitches.

"The one all in black, who looked like a crow, fondling your arm and whispering in your ear."

"Velma? You mean Velma? She's harmless. She was just asking how I'd gotten the soufflé to rise so perfectly."

"How Freudian," I mutter.

"Listen, Emily, you've got an overactive imagination. That's your problem. I can't help it if people like me. I'm friendly, and maybe you should loosen up."

"Whoa, buddy, are you suggesting I'm unfriendly? I was just keeping things going behind the scenes so you could enjoy the party after all your work. I was busy. That doesn't mean I'm not friendly. I know how to be friendly. Maybe you'd like me to be more like Velma?"

"Let's just drop it," Will says.

Lying in bed hours later, unable to sleep, I concentrate on relaxing, running a meditation tape in my head, shifting my focus from my scalp to my forehead to my nose in an attempt to let go of worldly worries. It's not working. I realize I dropped the ball earlier, letting him distract me from questions about Velma with his accusation that I was unfriendly. He knew what he was doing. He's good at diversionary tactics, I think, as I finally drift into sleep.

CHAPTER 36
—
BIRD-WATCH

I'm sitting at the kitchen table with a second cup of coffee on a quiet Saturday morning. Will has gone sailing with friends for the weekend and I have nothing scheduled, so I can just relax. I look around the room, enjoying the sunlight and shadows. I really like our home, especially the light and the way it moves from room to room. I can't believe we've lived here for more than four years and neither of us can imagine living anywhere else. When we first moved in, we thought we'd be here for a year or two and then move out of the city, but we love being able to walk to movies, restaurants, shops, and cafés. I love our little urban nest.

In the early morning, when the alarm shrills into my bad ear, I tap the snooze button and lie awake, watching the sun filter through the leaves of the linden tree, creating patterns on the wall. It's a perfect meditation, something I anticipate with pleasure.

Will says his favorite room is our second bedroom, which doesn't get the morning sun but faces on the garden and courtyard that separate our house from the neighbors. He likes to watch the birds fly to the feeder our neighbors, Herb and Ellen, have hung from the tree in the courtyard. Occasionally, he spots a hummingbird on a second feeder by their dining room window. Will likes this room so much he's made it into a study with his grandfather's walnut wood desk near the window; he's set up some of his smaller work projects on it, careful to place padding on the desk to protect the wood. He has his ham radio on a table next to the desk.

He gets home from work before I do and often retreats to this room to work on his projects, read, or bird-watch before the sun sets. I'm happy he enjoys this private space and rarely bother him when he's up there. Occasionally, I venture in to dust or vacuum, careful not to disturb anything on his desk.

In fact, that's what I should do now. I rinse out my coffee cup and head up the stairs, lugging the vacuum behind me. I have just plugged the cord into the outlet when I look out the window, my attention drawn by sparrows perched on the feeder, pecking at the seeds. It's so sweet to watch them. I sit in Will's chair, positioning myself so my presence won't startle the birds.

Soon, I detect movement in a window across the courtyard. It's our neighbor, Ellen, at the window. She looks this way but can't see me, although she does seem to be looking for something. She pauses, begins to unbutton her blouse and then pulls it off her shoulders, letting it slide away to reveal bare breasts, which she lifts toward the window.

What the hell?! I hold my breath, closing my eyes as I lean back against my chair, willing myself to disappear. I don't dare move. I sit that way until my leg muscles begin to cramp. When I finally open my eyes, turning my head slowly back toward the window, Ellen has disappeared. Slowly, I slide off my chair onto the rug—just in case she's still there. I slither across the floor until I reach the hall where I stop, rest for a moment, and then crawl into my bedroom and lie on the floor in disbelief.

Did I just see what I think I saw? Was it a hallucination?

"Okay, that's enough," Dr. Rothman roars as he skids into the room and slides to a stop next to me. "What do you think you saw? Enough with the denial, Bambi."

"But why? What was she up to?"

"Not airing her breasts for their health, you can be sure. She was doing it for an audience and I doubt it was to titillate the birdies."

"You can't be suggesting that!" I protest feebly.

"Who is usually up in this room? I'll give you a clue. It's not Audubon."

When Will returns from his sailing weekend, I can barely look at him. I'm haunted by the vision of Ellen at the window and I don't know what to do. Dr. Rothman wants me to confront Will, but I'm afraid he'll duck and divert again. I can't bear hearing his excuses and lies, seeing that wounded expression of innocence on his sunburned, swollen, cherry-tomato face.

All I can say is, "Got a bit too much sun, didn't you? Does it smart?" I hope so, you bird-watching bastard.

I'm not ready to take him on, so I keep my ugly, angry thoughts to myself. Rescue comes in the form of a new work assignment for Will. His company has partnered with a Dallas firm that's working to develop a similar prototype for a 22nd century space station. Since Will has been the lead on this project, he'll be the primary partner with his counterpart in Dallas. The assignment means travel between Dallas and Boston with Will doing most of the travel since the other guy has young children and a pregnant wife. Suits me.

"You know I wouldn't accept this assignment if I thought I had a choice, Emily. But so close to retirement, it will be great for me to have this project under my belt. It will mean a promotion and raise, great for our retirement income."

"I can't argue with that, Will, but I'll really miss you," I lie, hoping that time and distance will heal the heel or diminish my anger and pain.

"I'll miss you, too, baby, but I won't be traveling every week. When I do, I'll come home on weekends."

"How long will this assignment last?"

"Too soon to tell—a few months, at least. Maybe you should have your mother come out for a visit. She hasn't seen our new place."

"Maybe I will ask her out, Raspberry, too. I'll give them your study so they can bird-watch."

I watch his left lid for the twitch but see nothing but an opaque lens.

• • •

Saturday, August 11

Dear Ian,

Don't be shocked. I know it's been at least a year since I've written. It seems I write only when I'm in crisis mode. For that, I apologize.

I've thought of you often, but something has kept me from getting in touch. Now, here I am when I desperately need a confidant.

Long story short, I think Will's cheating on me—not in the obvious way with an affair in a sleazy, by-the-hour motel. That would be too predictable. He and the neighbor across our courtyard appear to be engaged in a Rear Window strip poker match!

While Will was off on a sailing weekend, I went up to vacuum his "study." I opened the window for fresh air, pulled the curtains aside, and was just about to turn on the vacuum cleaner when what to my wonder should appear? Neighbor Ellen, bouncing her bountiful, bare boobs at her bedroom window! Oh my god! I was so shocked! I can't tell you how often I've left Will undisturbed in that room so he could bird-watch!

I jest, but I don't know what to do. I've seen Will flirt and ogle before, which has been painful, but this is so disturbing. I feel betrayed and nauseated. I want to throttle him.

Sorry to lay this on you, but I'm not ready to share this with anyone here. Maybe I don't want to see the look in their eyes when I tell them.

I don't know what to do. What do you think?

Thanks for any solace or advice you can offer.

Fondly,
Emily

• • •

Thursday, August 16

Dear Emily,

You don't deserve this! You're a wonderful, funny, caring woman who deserves love and appreciation. I don't understand hounds like this. I want to throttle this guy myself!

Never apologize for reaching out to me. I'm your friend. I understand why it may be hard for you to share this with friends who are nearby. You may want to be private until you figure it out and decide what to do.

I'm not sure what advice to give you. I can say that if this were happening to me, I'd confront my partner, describe what I saw, and ask what's going on.

Emily, I appreciate your trust and want you to know I've got your back. Write or call anytime.

Fondly,
Ian

CHAPTER 37

—

MAN YOUR BATTLE STATIONS

I have settled my mother and Raspberry in Will's study, as threatened. Who am I to interfere with the natural evolution of history? I'm ready for whatever happens; I just hope my mother is.

She'll sleep on Will's grandfather's brass bed, an antique, dating back to his boyhood, at least a century. The mattress, newly purchased at Mel's Slumber Land, dates back a month, so she should be comfortable. I have placed a small, carpeted dog bed on the floor for Raspberry, but I suspect he'll snuggle in next to her on the "slumber-perfect, easy sleeper."

Mum and Raspberry are both weary after a bumpy flight, and they're ready to tuck in right after dinner. My mother's hair is still a mélange of red and brown, cut in a short, somewhat haphazard style that requires little upkeep but more than she's giving it. She's lost weight, so her jacket and skirt droop on her slight frame. She's aged, I realize with a pang. Maybe I should move her to the small TV room on the first floor, so she doesn't have to climb the stairs.

"Don't be silly," she insists. "Raspberry and I need the exercise. I still try to walk with him every day, but he's not getting any younger. Sometimes, I have to carry him for the last block or two."

Reassured, I lead my visitors up the stairs and into their bedroom, help my mother unpack, turn on the nightlights in the hall and bathroom, and place a small bowl of water near the window for Raspberry.

"I'm so glad you're here, Mum. I've missed you."

"Me, too," she replies, pulling her flannel nightgown over her head, muffling her words.

"Sorry to miss your husband but happy to be here, aren't we, Raspberry?"

Raspberry cocks his head and replies, "woof."

We're busy the next few days, visiting relatives who still live in the area, shopping for new bathroom towels my mother insists on giving me, and gardening in my small patch. Today, we're headed for a dog park with a separate area for dogs under 15 pounds, where Raspberry can romp with other critters of like size and weight.

My mother unleashes Raspberry, who cocks his head quizzically. "Go ahead. Go run and play." She nudges him gently until he gets the message, turns and runs to join the troop of small dogs in the chase back and forth across the fenced area. We find an empty bench where we can sit and watch the action.

"So," my mother says, "how much does Will travel with this new job?"

"A fair amount," I concede.

"Is that okay with you?"

"Of course. It's an investment in our future," I explain, repeating Will's contention that it will give us more money for retirement. "I don't mind, really. It gives me time to catch up with friends after work, and he's home almost every weekend."

"Still, it can't be easy with him being away so much. It can't be good for your relationship."

I shift uneasily on the bench. "Don't they say absence makes the heart grow fonder?"

"Rubbish! Who believes that—traveling salesmen? If you want my advice…"

"Which I don't, but you'll give it to me anyway."

She looks at me. "Don't let this go on much longer."

"As if I can stop it. It's a work project. I don't have any say."

"That's a helluva way to run a business."

We sit silently. Finally, I sigh, "I agree."

Encouraged, my mother stirs another ember. "Another thing—you're talking about retirement. You're still young. Why would you want to retire? Didn't you go back to school so you could have a career?"

"That's true… but Will's been working steadily since college. He's ready for something new."

"It's not just about Will," she says. "I'm dying for a cigarette. You don't have any, do you?"

"I quit 20 years ago. You know that. Since when do you still smoke?" Didn't you quit after your last visit? I turn on the bench to look more closely at her. Has she started smoking again?

"I don't smoke either. I just get the urge now and then."

"Well, stifle it, Mum," I snap.

"Do you have any snacks?"

"Let's go home and fix an early dinner," I say, knowing why I'm so impatient with her.

I fix my mother a snack of pickled herring and crackers with a small Bloody Mary, her afternoon indulgence, give Raspberry a couple of dog treats, and pull out the ingredients for my mother's special chicken casserole, which she's promised to make. She moves more hesitantly in the kitchen now but pulls the dish together quickly and puts it into the preheated oven.

"Okay, that will take about 50 minutes. Will you make a salad? I think I'll go upstairs to put up my feet."

"No problem," I say gratefully.

I'm slicing cucumber when I hear a shriek, hysterical barking, and shouting above my head. I drop the knife, half-sliced cucumber, turn and dash to the stairs, climbing them two at a time.

"My god, what's happened? Are you all right?"

My mother stands at the window, pointing at the moving curtains across the courtyard. "What the hell was that?" she bellows, as Raspberry stands at the window on his back legs, yipping and jumping.

Could it be?

I run to my mother, putting my arms around her shoulders and easing her toward the bed.

"What happened?" I ask again.

"I bet I can guess," Dr. Rothman chimes in, peering out the window.

"What kind of neighborhood is this?" my mother demands.

"Mum, calm down and tell me what happened."

I was just going to open the window to get some fresh air. It's so stuffy in here... when I saw her, standing there, naked as a jay bird!"

"Interesting analogy," Dr. Rothman chuckles.

"Naked, bare-breasted, standing there so close I could almost touch her."

"Eww," I say loudly.

"I couldn't believe my eyes, so I started screaming, "Put on your clothes, you nuthatch! This is a family neighborhood. You should be ashamed."

Dr. Rothman is laughing now. I bite my lip.

"Is she still there?" my mother asks. "If she is, let's call the cops!"

"It's okay, Mum. She's gone, and I don't think she'll be back." I hug my mother affectionately.

Peering over my mother's shoulder, Dr. Rothman chuckles, "I don't think you've heard the end of this."

• • •

Monday, November 15

Dear Ian,

Doesn't time fly, even when you're not having fun!

To catch you up on my saga... I never confronted Will because fate intervened. He was sent to Dallas to collaborate on a big project with a company out there. It seems he'll be working there for several months. I have to admit this is a relief. He's coming home on weekends, so we still have time together. At some point, I'll confront him.

I suppose I'm resisting the confrontation because I'm afraid of what I'll hear. A heck of a way to live, eh?

Enough of my soap opera. How are you? I hope you're living a joyful, tranquil life. What are you doing for Thanksgiving? Will's kids and mine will be here for dinner. Should be a lovely holiday gathering—everyone pretending to be the Brady Bunch.

Take care,
Emily

• • •

Friday, November 19

Dear Emily,

You sound really down. I understand nobody wants to confront tough issues. It does seem, though, that you're prolonging the pain by not talking about the bedroom debacle with Will. Can the truth be worse than what you're imagining?

My life is good. While not necessarily joyful, it has its moments. I don't think I told you I'm going to be a grandfather. Can't wait! The baby is due in April. We're all excited, and Thanksgiving is going to be our first chance to celebrate the news together.

Be well, Emily, and take courage.

Fondly,
Ian

CHAPTER 38

—

WILL DOES DALLAS

It's early December. Mum and Raspberry are safely back in Florida, although Mum has been calling almost daily since they left. She's worried about leaving me alone in this "dubious neighborhood." Since spotting Ellen, the flasher/neighbor, she's been uneasy and suspicious. Nothing I've said has satisfied her—how could it unless I come clean with my own misgivings? I'm not ready to do that yet. I have to figure out what's going on.

I'm on a plane, flying to Dallas for a weekend with Will. My stomach is lurching despite the smooth flight, but I want to know what his life away from home is like. I've managed to subdue the chattering, uneasy voices that whisper to me at night by filling my days so completely that I fall into bed at day's end, too weary to hear anything but the sound of ocean waves slapping the shore of my white noise machine.

Besides working, taking art classes, and swim lessons, I've been redecorating our second bedroom. You wouldn't recognize it. I've moved Will's grandfather's desk down to the first-floor den in front of a window facing the street. In the bedroom, I've hung heavy navy drapes to complement the new navy-and-white-striped wallpaper and have placed a tall, antique bureau against the wall in place of Will's desk. The room is more of a guest room now. Will and I can share the downstairs den as our study. We'll work better with fewer distractions in that setting.

I've labored valiantly on the home front, but still, misgivings assail me like gnats at my ears. Will has been affectionate and attentive when he calls, but still…

I sigh and grip the edge of my seat as the plane bumps onto the runway at Dallas-Fort Worth Airport. Will is waiting at the gate, holding up a sign that reads, "Emily, my love."

I rush to his side and we hug enthusiastically.

I'm so glad to see you," he murmurs, holding me close.

"Me, too," I sigh.

"We've got a busy, fun weekend ahead," Will announces as we head for the airport garage. "These guys want to show us all the sights and make sure you want to come back."

Come back? I wonder. I just got here. What's the rush?

We drop my bag at the hotel and are off to meet Will's colleague Gary and his coworkers Billy Bob, Tommy Lou, and Harry Lee at Ricky Bob's Famous Barbeque and Hoedown for dinner. Their wives join us, but we don't have a chance to bond above the din of country music and clattering platters of ribs, corn, and coleslaw. Beer is flowing by the carload as we all put on big Ricky Bob bibs and begin to chow down.

The men all wear checked shirts, string ties, jeans, and leather boots. Some sport 10-gallon hats. The women wear checked blouses, matching skirts, and cowgirl boots. One wife, Frieda Mae, also wears a string tie. I'm about to comment on her attire to Will when he surprises me with my own string tie to match the one he's wearing.

He surprises me again when he tugs me out of my seat and onto the dance floor after dinner to dance a Texas Two-Step. I am all feet in the wrong places while he seems fairly nimble.

"I've been taking lessons," he explains, "when in Rome…"

The next evening, we attend a wannabe Grand Ole Opry Show in a vast auditorium in Fort Worth and then a local restaurant and watering hole, much like Ricky Bob's except for the nice touch of thick sawdust on the floor that wreaks havoc with my allergies. We're with another of Will's colleagues, Tammi, and her husband, Ike. To my surprise, Tammi, whom I've heard about from Will, is not 270 pounds of East Texas lard as Will described her, but a petite redhead with a soft Texas drawl and Loretta Lynn look. Her husband, Ike, is a drinker, his face reddening as the evening stretches into night, his voice growing louder and more insistent.

We leave them after too many hours, returning to our hotel.

"Nice couple," I say, "but Ike drinks too much."

"Tammi knows that, poor kid, but she doesn't know what to do."

"I liked her," I reply, "but was stunned to see such a petite, attractive woman. You'd told me she weighed close to 300 pounds!"

Will chuckles, "I said that?"

"Yes, why? That's the question."

"Guess I didn't want you to worry about me having an attractive coworker, since you've got such an overactive imagination."

Resisting the temptation to wallop him, I head for the shower, turn it on full blast, nearly scalding myself with hot steam. Only one more day before I can fly home.

One more day and one more outing with the Dallas crowd. This time, Gary and his wife, Clara Sue, have invited us to their home for some good ole home cookin'. It's an indoor barbecue of roast pork, corn on the cob, potato salad, baked beans, and more beer. Tammi arrives in a hot pink, hooded jacket. Under it, she wears a white peasant blouse, tight jeans, and snakeskin boots. She weighs maybe 110 pounds, soaking wet. Ike is not with her.

"Hi, Tammi. It's good to see you again," I trill. "Where's Ike?"

"He's a little under the weather," she replies, "so I told him he should stay to home."

The drawl seems heavier today and her makeup more obvious, a little too much green eye shadow.

"Too bad. You tell him I hope he's feeling better. Sorry not to see him again before I head for home."

"You leavin' already?" she asks sweetly. "That's too bad."

"But we'll get her back here," Gary chimes in, bringing another plate of roasted meat of some sort to the table. "We keep tellin' Will to get out of that liberal-ass, piss-chillin' northeast and come join us here in paradise. We're workin' on him and wearin' him down, you bet."

Paradise? I'm not sure how Adam and Eve would have felt if they had been expelled from this garden of gun-slinging Texas Two-Steppers, but I won't miss it. I know I'm an East Coast snob, but that attitude goes deep and I'm stuck with it.

I nudge Will. "What's this about moving to paradise?" I mutter under my breath. I've developed a pretty good mutter without moving my lips noticeably. When I was about 11, I wanted to be a ventriloquist and practiced for hours in front of my bedroom mirror.

"Later," he mumbles back. I can see his lips moving.

On our ride back to the airport, Will confesses that he's been approached by Dallas Futuristic to join their staff when the current project has been "put to bed."

"Live in Dallas?"

"Now, don't get excited. Nothing's been decided. That offer's on the table. That's all."

"When were you going to tell me?"

"I'm telling you now. But we don't have to decide right away. This project has a way to go before delivery. We'll have plenty of time to talk."

"Live in Dallas?" I repeat, remembering the live crèche scene in the parking lot of our hotel. All the players, Mary, Joseph, and the Three Wise Men, were walking, talking real people; even the animals were real. Only the Infant Jesus was a plastic baby doll, swaddled in a slightly worn, blue blanket. He reminded me of my Betsy Wetsy doll, who wet her diaper when you fed her water from a small, plastic bottle.

CHAPTER 39

—

TEXAS TWO-STEP

The work in Dallas is intensifying and Will is in Texas from Monday to Friday, flying home weekends. His frequent flyer miles could take us around the world. I like being on my own, but not this much. Ellen, the boob lady, has gone underground or maybe her husband has locked her in the basement. Since my mother's outburst, Ellen's curtains are drawn as tightly as mine.

Will and I haven't discussed the potential job waiting in the wings in Dallas when this project ends. We haven't talked about much at all. Our weekends feel so rushed and uncomfortable. It feels as though we're strangers having to get reacquainted. It feels like *Groundhog Day*.

"Will, how much longer is this Dallas project going to take?" I ask as we're weeding our small garden patch.

"As long as it takes," Will replies, not looking up from the thorny weed he's trying to wrest from the ground.

"What does that mean?"

"Sorry, Emily, I was distracted by this stubborn sucker. The work's slowed down. We've hit some snags. We probably won't be done for another few months."

"A few months?" I sigh. "Listen, I'm trying to be a supportive wife, but I don't like this deal anymore. It's going on too long. Aren't you sick of Dallas?"

I've been lighting candles that reek of sagebrush and deadly nightshade, exhorting the gods to make Will detest Dallas. I'm hexing the tumbleweed, cactus, and two-legged, gun-toting critters. Actually, I've tried to imagine living there. I've visited the Old West Emporium, trying on cowgirl skirts and shirts, even a pair of vermillion-red, Annie Oakley cowgirl boots, but I'm no Annie Oakley. In the westerns my friends and I watched on Saturday afternoons, I identified with the Boston school marm, who didn't know the front end of a horse from the rear.

Will interrupts my reverie, "I know you don't like this setup. What am I supposed to do about it? Quit now, two-thirds of the way through? Leave everyone in the lurch? This is my big chance to prove myself. Maybe it will lead to a promotion or something better. Be practical. We just have to make the best of it. It won't last forever."

"What do you mean by 'something better'? A job in Dallas? Is that what you call better?"

"Now, Emily, don't be so negative. We're supposed to be enjoying our weekend."

"That's just the problem. All we have now are weekends when we're both being so nice, walking on eggshells, not being real. This is not the way I want to live. It can't be good for our relationship."

Will puts down his spade, removes his gardening gloves, turns, and hugs me.

"Em, I know this is hard. Don't you think it's hard for me, too? It's important for my career and our future. We both have to make sacrifices, just for a while." He hesitates. "Maybe we need to stay in closer touch. I could call you every night just before you go to bed, around 10:30. Would you like that?"

"Yes. I can call you, too. You don't always have to be the one reaching out."

"No," Will says hastily. "I'll call you—the time difference. Sometimes, I might not be in."

"Where would you be?"

"At work... where I wouldn't hear the phone. Now, come on, let's go clean up, and I'll take you to Randy's Fish House for dinner. Maybe we catch a movie, too. Let's enjoy the evening."

True to his word, Will calls me every evening at 10:30. Sometimes, I can hear music or raucous laughter, and Will explains he's in a local bar with some of the guys, drinking an after-work beer or two. He's drinking tonic water and lime because he'd stopped drinking when we were dating, but I'm still not happy about the bar scene.

"Will, do you think it's a good idea for you to spend so much time in bars?"

"What are you talking about? I don't drink. You know that. Besides, I'm not in the bar that often. Remember the dance lessons? Next time we go dancing, I'll teach you the new steps I've learned. I've really perfected the Texas Two-Step."

Oh, my gawd, the Texas Two-Step again? I'd rather cross a floor of burning coals in my bare feet. I am not a Texas Two-Step kinda woman!

"Who do you dance with, some of the guys?"

"Yeh, sure—no, some of the guys bring their wives. And if I don't have a partner, there are plenty of single women who'll do a turn around the floor."

"Just make sure that's all you do," I reply, not happy with what I'm hearing.

"Geez, Emily, don't you have any faith in me? You don't want me in bars. You don't want me dancing with other women—what next? House arrest?"

"I'm just being cautious, that's all."

Will's tone softens, "Not to worry, Babe. I'm taking good care."

CHAPTER 40

—

SOMETHING STINKS IN
THE STATE OF TEXAS

I can't talk to anyone at work, and I don't want to talk with my mother. It would just be confirming her worst suspicions. Dr. Rothman seems to be on sabbatical, because he hasn't popped up for days. How much of this can I lay on poor Ian?

I call Shelley, my pal from my previous job, whom I used to see once a month for lunch and gossip. It's been longer than that and I'm a little embarrassed. She still works at Evil Corp., having weathered the last two purges, affectionately known as "re-orgs" in corporate lingo. Remembering her gang of spies, I'm pretty sure she'll know about the Dallas operation. We make a date for lunch at Chez Gourmet, miles from our workplaces so we won't be interrupted or overheard.

Shelley looks the same—wonderful smile, healthy glow, mischievous eyes and gorgeous auburn hair that curls rebelliously, despite her efforts to tame it. She's wearing a burgundy pants suit that highlights her long, lean frame.

"Emily, you look great! Lost a little weight?"

"A little maybe, not deliberately. But you look fabulous, a poster child for clean living."

"God, I hope not!" Shelley hugs me. "It's so good to see you. Glad you called, girl."

"Me, too," I sigh hugging her. I can feel tears hovering.

We sit at a corner table, away from the mainstream.

"How's Will? How's married life treating you?" Shelley asks as she unfolds her napkin.

I hesitate, "You know Will's working on that project in Dallas?"

Shelley nods. "Yes, sure. Not great for relationships, but it's almost over, isn't it?"

A tall, spindly waiter, wearing a black beret, gray ascot, and red Guccis, approaches and introduces himself.

"Hallo, Mesdames, I am Claude. I am happy to be your waiter today. Would either of you ladies care for a drink?"

Do I detect a wannabe French accent?

"Thanks, Claude," Shelley replies, smiling up at him. "I'll have iced tea."

"I'd like the same, and we'll need a minute or two to look at the menu."

"*Mais oui.* Take your time, Ladies."

The emphasis falls heavily on the last syllable, "Lay Deez." I wonder if Claude expects a tip in euros. I'm anxious for him to disappear so I can ask Shelley what she knows about Dallas.

I introduce the subject again. "Will says they're only two-thirds of the way through the work. What are you hearing?"

She looks at me, eyebrows slightly raised, "Two-thirds? That's not what I'm hearing."

Claude, who has been hovering at a distance, returns with our iced tea.

"Are the Mesdames ready to order?"

"Any specials today, Claude?" Shelley asks, suppressing a grin.

Claude's face flushes rosé. "*Mon Dieu*, did I not mention them?"

We let Claude stumble through the specials. Shelley orders a cup of French onion soup and a house salad. I order an artichoke quiche.

When Claude has safely scurried away, I say, "I'm hoping the chef has to start the onion soup or quiche from scratch, so we have time to talk before Claude's next onslaught."

Shelley giggles, "Eager, isn't he?"

"So, what are you hearing about this Dallas project, Shel?"

"Don't take my word for it, but I've heard the project has gone really well and is coming in before deadline, maybe by the end of the month."

The iced tea I'm drinking takes a wrong turn, and I begin to cough and sputter.

Shelley jumps up. "Emily, are you okay?"

Still sputtering, I nod my head affirmatively. "Wrong pipe. That's all." I motion for Shelley to sit before Claude notices her and rushes to my side.

When I have begun to breathe normally, Shelley asks, "Listen, kiddo, what's going on? You didn't just call to have a girl's lunch out. What's wrong?"

I begin to tear, dabbing my eyes hastily as Claude approaches again.

"Your lunch will soon be here. In the meantime, more *thé*?"

"More what?" Shelley asks as I continue to dab and sniffle.

"More *thé glacé*?... more iced tea?" Claude's accent slides away.

"*Bien sur*," Shelley replies.

I giggle despite my pain, setting off another coughing fit. When I have recovered, I sip slowly on the *thé glacé* while Claude serves our lunch and leaves us to stalk other tables.

"So, can we talk?" Shelley asks, touching my hand.

"I don't know, Shelley. Something's wrong. Will is different."

"We all knew that," she grins.

"No, that's not what I mean. He's changed since he started this assignment... maybe even before that," I realize as I speak.

"In what way?"

"He's not as affectionate. He flirts with other women. He wasn't like that before we married."

I reluctantly lift a piece of quiche onto my fork, no longer hungry.

Shelley puts down her fork. "Gee, kiddo, I don't know. Most men are flirts, don't you think? My Gene sometimes has a roving eye—a mental wolf, I call him."

"Will's become secretive and… sometimes he lies."

"What kind of lies?"

"He calls me every night but doesn't want me to call him. Half the time it sounds like he's calling from a bar. He tells me he isn't drinking, but I don't believe him."

Shelley looks puzzled, her eyebrows rising again.

"He was drinking too much during his divorce, so he had to stop," I explain.

"Ah," she nods. "Gene is in AA, has been for about 20 years."

"Will says he doesn't need it, just me." I smile weakly.

"Good line," Shelley chuckles. "Isn't he the clever, little devil?"

"That's not all. He has a coworker—an attractive woman. He's talked about her and said she weighed close to 300 pounds. When I went to Dallas, I met her and her husband. She probably weighs in at 110 soaking wet. She's a pretty little redhead. Now, why would he tell me a story like that?"

Shelley sips her iced tea. "Why would he tell you about her at all?"

"Especially since he must have figured I'd meet her."

"Emily, we can speculate from now 'til the cows come home, but that's not going to help. Do you want my advice?"

"Yes, of course."

"Talk to him the next time he's home. Tell him what's bothering you."

"Won't that just confirm what he already thinks… that I'm a paranoid loony bird?"

"Maybe, but if you can talk honestly about how you feel, you can hope he'll be honest, too. Maybe it's just a bad habit he developed in his first marriage—a protective cover that he doesn't need anymore. What can you lose? You sure aren't happy the way it is now."

She doesn't know the half of it.

• • •

Wednesday, January 6

Dear Ian,

Thanks for your support and concern. I'm sorry it's taken me this long to get back to you. I finally confronted Will about the flasher, and he denied any wrongdoing on his part. He claimed that Ellen was an oversexed exhibitionist and that he was as shocked as my mother and I had been. He also claimed he hadn't said anything because he didn't want to cause trouble. He insisted that he kept the curtains drawn once he knew what she was up to. Hah!

Since Will has been spending more and more time in Dallas, I decided to join him there for a weekend to get the lay of the land. I flew out just before Christmas. Oy! He's morphing into a Willie Nelson look-alike with the cowboy regalia, friends named Jim Boy and Jim Bob, and he's learning the Texas Two-Step with Tammi and Ike. Half the motel parking lot was inhabited by a live crèche!

All that wouldn't be so bad if it were temporary, but he's talking about a job offer there, which he's considering, I know—I can tell by his evasiveness when I raise the subject. I lie awake, tortured by visions of cattle being prodded into pens by the slaughterhouse, their woeful bellowing, and the odor of cow poop!

Why do I have the suspicion that my feelings won't have much impact on his decision? I can't imagine living in Dallas, and, at this point, I can't think of many reasons I'd want to.

Thanks again for your caring. Oh, I almost forgot! Congratulations on soon becoming a grandpa! I bet you'll love it!

With fondness and appreciation,
Emily

CHAPTER 41

—

THE OTHER SHOE DROPS

Apparently, I didn't know the other half of the story either, but a couple of days after our lunch, Shelley called, insisting we meet as soon as possible.

"Shall we do lunch again?" I ask.

"No time. I need to talk to you before the weekend."

Before Will comes home again, I realize, my stomach lurching.

"This isn't good, is it?" I whisper, having difficulty breathing.

"No, kiddo. It isn't. Can you do coffee later today?"

Again, we meet a distance from work and Shelley comes right to the point.

"I don't think I told you that the company's heading for another round of layoffs…?"

I interrupt, "That's what you had to tell me? Is your job at risk? Otherwise, I couldn't care less what that place does."

"No, Ms. Impatience, that's not it. They're also offering golden handshakes…"

"So?"

"Word is Will Slipway has accepted the offer."

I think my heart has stopped. I wait to see if I'll collapse in a heap on the dirty floor of this coffee shop. But I'm still breathing and shaking now.

"What?" I can't believe I've heard Shelley right.

She leans forward, taking my hand. "Your husband has taken the offer."

"When was this?" I ask, still incredulous.

"Two weeks ago," Shelley sighs. "I can't believe he hasn't told you."

"You can't believe it? I feel as though I've been hit by a tsunami!"

Shelley and I sit together for a while longer. She can't comfort me and we both know that, but I'm able to hold myself together long enough to ask if she knows any details...like when is this happening? I'd like to know in case he's planning to sell the house without telling me.

"It's happening soon," she says, "by the middle of March. I'm so sorry, kiddo. Are you going to be all right?"

"Once my heart stops fibrillating."

"Geez, I hate to leave you like this. I have to get home for dinner. Gene's cooking tonight."

"That's okay. I have to begin planning an execution."

"Do you want to come home with me? Gene will understand."

"No, thanks. I just need to sit with my tea for a while."

I'm not alone for more than five minutes when I feel a chill wind and rustling at my shoulder. It's Dr. Rothman.

"So, now what?" he asks.

"I can't believe this," I moan.

"Really? Just the other day you were telling your friend Shelley you don't trust the guy."

"Did I say that?"

"You said he lies. He calls from beer halls and has probably been drinking. You said he's changed—that I can dispute, but never mind. Do I need to quote your conversation verbatim?"

"Why were you listening to our conversation?"

"I was waiting for my order of crepes suzette to go. What do you care why I was there?"

"I think I'm going to die."

"I doubt that, Sarah Bernhardt. You're in pain, but you'll live.

This guy isn't worth dying over. He's going to end up drooling and in diapers. I know the type."

"You are no help," I grumble. "That's not what I need to hear."

"*Au contraire*, as my pal, Claude the waiter would say. It's just what you need. Now, what are you going to do about this guy?"

"Talk to him?"

"Talk to him? How about confronting his sneaky ass?"

"Can I just poison him and watch him writhe in agony on the kitchen floor?"

In the days before Will comes home, I alternate between denial and despair. How could he take the retirement package without telling me? Shelley has to be wrong. Why would he do that? I know, I know. Dr. Rothman would say the signs were all there. I just chose to ignore them. I can't sleep. I can't eat. I pace in the hallway between clients, at home in my bedroom, and in Hemingway Park near our house.

On Friday evening when Will comes through the front door, cheerful and tanned, I want to gag. He's taken up golf, he tells me. Some of the guys are teaching him.

"Anything else new?" I ask. "Anything you want to tell me?"

"What?" he asks, all innocence, rummaging in the refrigerator.

"What are you looking for? Dinner is almost ready—your favorite, meatloaf and mashed potatoes," I say, syrup dripping from my tongue.

"Wow, what's the occasion? It's not our anniversary or anyone's birthday, is it?"

"Does it have to be an anniversary or birthday?" I ask. "What about other occasions… like a new job, a promotion or, I don't know, a retirement?" I lean against the kitchen sink, my arms folded against my chest.

Will blanches, turning as pale as the mashed potatoes.

"What's wrong, Will? You look pale."

"What have you heard, Emily?"

"Nothing much, just that your company is offering golden handshakes and juicy packages to a bunch of employees and that your name is on that list."

Will lifts his hands in protest. "I've been offered a package, but I haven't made my final decision."

"I heard that you've accepted the offer."

"That's just not true. I wanted to talk with you first, of course. I just haven't had a chance."

I hear the air rushing out of the kitchen and smell the stench of sulphur wafting in.

"Is that so? Well, let me dish out this scrumptious dinner and we can talk at the table."

I watch Will wolfing down two large helpings of meatloaf and potatoes, marveling at the fortitude of his gut. I push my food around my plate, waiting for him to put down his fork in surrender.

"So," I say finally, "what's going on? When were you going to tell me?"

His cellphone vibrates, and, instead of ignoring it or turning it off, he says, "I have to take this. Problem at work." Picking up the phone, he walks out onto the patio.

I clear the plates from the table, scrape off the remains on my plate, flinging the plates into the dishwasher and letting one fall to the floor, hoping it will shatter. The china, boring white, embossed with gold, was his mother's, or so he says.

When he comes back into the house, I'm sitting in the living room, tucked into a corner of the couch. I've lit a fire. He sits on the chair, facing the couch, not next to me.

"So," I say, "where were we? If you wanted to take a job in Dallas and wanted us to move there, why haven't you told me? The last I knew, they'd made an offer that we really hadn't discussed, and you had months left on this project. What happened to change all that?"

"Things change," he mumbles.

"That's it? Things change? When were you going to tell me we're moving to Dallas?"

Silence.

"We're not moving," Will finally says.

"Really? That's a relief. I thought Shelley was mistaken..."

Will interrupts, "Emily. Stop. I want a divorce. I'm not in love with you anymore. It's been great, but it's time for me to move on."

For the second time in the past week, I feel as though I've been slammed by a 2 by 4.

"Is there someone else?" It feels so cliché to ask.

"No, there's no one else. It's time for me to move on, that's all."

"You said that already." I watch the flames sputter against the logs and feel the autumn chill.

"I don't have a good track record," he says. "I get restless and want to see what's around the corner."

"But you've worked for this same company for 25 years and you were married to your first wife for almost that long," I protest.

"I had affairs every four or five years during my marriage."

"Now you tell me. What about all the times you swore you'd love me forever? You'd found your soul mate? You never believed you could be so happy?"

"I say what women want to hear."

The fire hisses. Smoke and sulphur spin around the room.

CHAPTER 42

—

BATTLE READY

Will left for good with an Oscar-worthy parting scene. We're in the kitchen and he's pouring himself a drink—a full glass of Jim Beam. He's wearing jeans, a red plaid cowboy shirt, string tie and snakeskin gray boots. The only thing missing is the 10-gallon hat.

I stare at him in disbelief. "Since when are you drinking?"

"Since I remembered you're not my mother," he snarls.

I back toward the refrigerator.

"Listen, Em, I don't want this to get ugly," he says, softening his tone, "so I'll just say my piece and get outta here. I'm leaving tomorrow morning. I'll be back sometime to get my stuff." He takes a hefty slug of Jim Beam. "For a long time, I've felt like I'm suffocating. I've lost my life force. I need to unlock it to be me."

"What are you talking about? Where is this coming from?" I step toward him.

"You wouldn't understand and it's not worth trying to explain. The bottom line is I want to soar and live on the edge, and I can't do that here."

Reaching for the bottle of Jim Beam, Will utters his last words before he slithers back to Dallas, "You'd better get a lawyer because I'm suing for divorce, and I don't intend to give you anything."

• • •

Friday, January 24

Dear Ian,

My life is a disaster! Here's the quick and dirty version.

Slipway wants a divorce. He's taking a golden handshake next month, moving to Dallas, and going to live happily ever after in the Golden West! He told me he's been suffocating in his life with me and needs to be free. He denies having another woman, but I'm not sure. I don't believe anything he says. He made all the arrangements to take early retirement and leave me without a word. I found out from a friend at his work. He finally confessed when I confronted him about making retirement plans without me.

On top of this, he's drinking heavily. He's sleeping downstairs in the den, and it stinks of alcohol. I don't want to be alone in the house with him, so I put a deadbolt lock on my bedroom door. Thank god he says he's leaving by the end of the weekend. Oh, yes, he tells me to find a good lawyer.

Sorry to drop this on you! I haven't been able to tell anyone, not even my mother, and I'm afraid I'll explode if I can't at least write to you.

I'm going to crawl under the covers now.

Thank you, dear friend, for being out there.

Emily

• • •

Tuesday, January 27

Dear Emily,

I just got your letter. What a bastard! I want to fly out there and wring the idiot's neck! This guy never deserved you. Besides being an imbecile, he's a coward! I can't believe how he's treated you.

I'll stop ranting now.

What can I do for you? Do you want me to fly out? Please just ask.

Meanwhile, the prick's right—get a lawyer.

Forgive me if it's too soon to say this, but someday you'll be glad he's gone. You don't want that womanizing fraud in your life. Good riddance!

Emily, you're a wonderful, strong woman. You'll get through this and build the life you deserve. I believe in you.

Yours,
Ian

• • •

I've hunkered down in a state of paralysis since Sunday morning when he threw his travel bag over his shoulder—the one I'd given him for his birthday—shut the door behind him, and scuttled down the front walk to a waiting taxi.

I've called in sick to work and haven't gotten out of my favorite flannel pajamas, the pink ones with bunnies, for three days. I can't eat, sleep, or think straight, but I know I have to wake up and get moving. I've seen Will in action. When he wants something, he goes after it full throttle, so I can't afford to stay in mourning.

I begin to reach out to friends, whose reactions range from outrage and disbelief to speculation about what I might have done differently and what I can do to repair the damage and stop the flow of blood. The speculators make me sick, literally, sending me flying to the bathroom. I haven't told my family yet because I'm afraid I'll hear the same reactions and advice—not what I'm looking for.

On the fourth day after Will's declaration of independence, I get up, shower, dress in a clean tee shirt and jeans, and ready myself to deal with the debris. I call my friend Annie, not to ask for advice but for action. I tell her what's happened, listen to her expressions of empathy, and hear the question I'm now ready to answer.

"What can I do for you?"

"Help me find a divorce lawyer. I just got an email from Will. He's already hired someone—the attorney who represented his first wife and extracted a pound of flesh from his hide. She takes no prisoners."

"Not to worry. I know just who to call—a feminist attorney from my book group. She doesn't do divorces, but she'll know who does. I'll tell her we want the smartest, toughest attorney in Boston."

• • •

I haven't been eating well and have lost weight, so I fit nicely into my navy suit, appropriate for meeting with an attorney whom I hope can slay dragons. Her name is Gretchen Battle and she's a partner at Steele, Baumgartner, Battle and Malloy, a prestigious law firm in the financial district. I wonder how I can afford her but decide to meet her and worry about details later.

The offices of Steele, Baumgartner, et al. are on the 20th floor of a glass skyscraper that reaches into the murky city sky. I can feel my ears pop as the elevator ascends. A receptionist greets me from behind a large desk that reminds me of a fortress. She ushers me across thick, Oriental carpeting to a waiting area where I sink into a large, wine-colored leather chair.

I don't have to wait long when I hear a rich, melodious voice, "Mrs. Slipway?"

I stare up at a six-foot-tall woman, her long brown hair pulled into a ponytail that somehow doesn't fit with the black pantsuit and black horn-rimmed glasses. Her smile is friendly and her handshake firm but not aggressive.

Gretchen and I spend more than an hour together and I leave reassured that I have found the champion who can lead me into the fray and win a clean, clear victory without splattering the field with any more blood than necessary. Actually, a little might not be so bad.

I ask my questions:

"My husband is represented by Jean Hastings. I hear she's really tough and I need to know if you're tough," I say, trying not to sound as nervous as I feel.

"Jean? Oh, I know her. She's a junior partner in Spike and Parry. I usually go up against the senior partners there. Yes, I can handle Jean. You don't have to worry about that."

"What about your fees? How can I pay you? I don't have much money."

"I plan to collect your fees from Mr. Slipway, not to worry."

As we continue to exchange information, I have to resist the temptation to hug her and cover her with kisses. She is smart, self-assured, and kind. She tells me that she focuses on family law, particularly protecting women and children, ensuring they receive justice.

She is my guardian angel, my Athena, my Joan of Arc! I float out of her office, armed with her business card, another appointment, and instructions about papers I need to gather and tasks I need to attend to. I sing tunelessly, the best I can do, as I pay the parking attendant and head for home. I am not alone in this fight for justice.

At home, I begin to call my family to tell them what's happening.

My mother worries. "Are you sure you want to do this, take him to court and all? Wouldn't it be better just to have it done with? I worry about you and your health."

My parents have always worried about my health and I don't know why. Unless I have a mortal physical flaw I'm unaware of, I'm relatively healthy and sound.

"I need to do this for my mental health," I explain. "His behavior is outrageous and unforgivable. I'm not going to lie down and let him run over me. He's not going to get away with this."

Brave words I hope I can live up to.

Just as I'm beginning to soften in my stance and even think it's possible for Will and me to reconcile, that maybe his behavior is just a manifestation of a late-arriving midlife crisis, the gods signal me, "au contraire."

I return home on a Friday after a long, tiring week at work. Will is due home this weekend to pick up some of his clothes, tools, and who knows what else. I'm nervous about seeing him. When I open the door into our front hall and walk into the living room, I realize I've worried for nothing. Will has already come and gone. The large TV has disappeared from its customary place on the corner chest. A brass sailboat, a large serving platter, given him by his children, and some family photos are missing—not all things a burglar would covet.

I am angry and my stomach churns as I move from room to room to see what else is missing: some clothes, toiletries, and a few books. Not so terrible. But the idea that he's been here like a sneak thief enrages me.

I'm sitting in the armchair in our bedroom when I notice the bed looks rumpled. I didn't leave it that way. What the hell? I'm wondering what to do next when the phone rings.

"Emily? It's Shelley. I'm sorry to bother you, but I'm afraid I have more news."

"It can't be good. What is it, Shel?"

"Do you remember Maria DeSouza, who works in HR benefits?"

"Sure, she's the one who gave me my walking papers when I was laid off—bless her. Nice woman. What about her?"

"Well... Maria called me... about Will. Apparently, he was in the benefits office today to sign his retirement papers."

"Oh, geez!"

"There's more... he wasn't alone. He brought a woman with him, a real pushy type with a southern accent."

"You're kidding! What was her name? What was she doing there?"

"Apparently, she was trying to butt in and tell him what to do. Maria finally had to threaten to throw her out if she didn't butt out."

"Good Lord!" I'm breathing quickly now and have to put down the phone to catch my breath. "Hold on for a minute, will you?" Once again, I breathe in and out, trying to slow my breath.

"Okay, thanks. I'm back. Did Maria tell you her name?"

"She did, but all I remember is Tammi. Tammi something."

I yelp. Now I know why the bed was rumpled. "That bitch! That son of a bitch!"

"You don't sound that surprised," Shelley says, puzzled.

"That's right. You're absolutely right. Nothing can surprise me about that… Slipway anymore."

Shelley tells me that Will plans to take his retirement at the end of the month and will return from Dallas to attend the fare-well party for retirees.

I thank Shelley for her call and reassure her that telling me was the right thing to do and that I'm eternally grateful. We agree to get together after her son's wedding.

Hours later, I receive another email from Will:

Em, was home to pick up some of my stuff. Plan to return on the 25th for things I've left behind. Will.

I wait until Monday to call my attorney, who instructs me to change the locks immediately. I'll do that, but first, I have something else in mind.

CHAPTER 43

—

RETRIBUTION

I send a return email to Will, or rather, Slipway. I think of him that way now as a sign of scorn.

Will,
The 25th is fine. I'll be out of town, returning in the evening, so please take your things out by then. See you in court.
Emily

Although I dress for work on the 25th, I've taken the day off as a personal day, one of three we're allotted each year—rare, therefore, precious and not to be squandered.

I park my car down the street from our house where Slipway won't notice me, but I'll be able to spot him. I have to wait a couple of hours and have listened over and over to a CD of the *Eighteen Greatest Revenge Songs*, including "Mistreated" by Deep Purple, "Your Time Is Gonna Come" by Led Zeppelin, and "You Oughta Know" by Alanis Morissette. Just for good measure, I've listened to Fats Domino and Louis Armstrong rendering, "I'll Be Glad When You're Dead, You Rascal You!" I've mastered most of the lyrics and am fighting nausea when an unfamiliar black van pulls into our driveway. I slide down lower in my seat, lifting my binoculars to watch Slipway emerge from the driver's side. I watch the passenger side for movement and am rewarded when pert, pretty little Tammi bounces out and joins Slipway as he unlocks the garage door.

I force myself to wait, hoping I'm giving them enough time to slither their way to the bedroom and begin happily fornicating on our bed. I dial my neighbor, Lydia, who has agreed to be my co-conspirator after hearing my story. Apparently, her husband ran off with his secretary last year, and she has embarked on a vendetta against philanderers.

"Lydia, it's Emily. They've just gone into the house. You can see the van in the driveway. Call the cops and tell them there's a home invasion."

Moments later, lights flashing, two cop cars careen around the corner, screeching to a halt at the bottom of the driveway. Cops dash toward the front door and the open garage, disappearing out of view. I wait, my heart racing. Minutes pass and I begin to worry. Should I just drive away rather than risk being found here? What's taking them so long?

Just as I'm about to start my engine, the cops come out of the garage with slightly disheveled Slipway and his moll, Tammi, in tow, protesting loudly. A couple of neighbors have come out of their houses and are watching from across the street. Lydia is not among them.

Good girl, I think, no reason to get more involved than necessary.

Slipway is protesting, sputtering, and exclaiming, but Tammi outdoes him, screaming, swearing, and kicking at the cops, who have had enough. They usher the two miscreants into the back of the patrol car, wait for a truck to tow away the black van, check to ensure the property is secured, and satisfied with a good day's work, drive away.

Within minutes, I receive a voice message on my mobile phone, informing me that my house has been broken into and burglars were routed in the act of cleaning it out. The caller asks me to contact the precinct upon receiving this voice message.

First, I call a locksmith and arrange to meet him at the house. By the time I return the call to the police, the locksmith has completed his work, and Sergeant Flynn of Precinct 191 is chagrined to report that the capture and detainment of burglars at my home was a mistake, based on misinformation. In fact, one of the detainees turned out to be one Will Slipway, my husband. The sergeant offers his profuse apologies.

"These things can happen, I'm sure. I'm just grateful to know the Brookline Police are on the job... where is Mr. Slipway now, do you know?"

"Ma'am, he said something about returning to his hotel. His companion was a little distraught."

I'll bet she was.

"Thank you, Officer."

• • •

Friday, February 18

Dear Ian,

The tide is turning! Although victory is still at a distance, I can smell its sweet honey. After hiding under the covers for a weekend, I rallied, remembering your words, "Hire a smart lawyer." With the help of a smart friend, I hired a brilliant lawyer. Aptly, her name is Battle, Gretchen Battle, and she specializes in representing women and children. She should be wearing a Wonder Woman outfit or, better, the toga of a Goddess.

On my return from my first appointment with Gretchen, I discovered that Slipway and his moll had sneaked into the house, messed up my sheets, and absconded with a TV, his model sailboat, and other essentials. I immediately called Gretchen, who said she'd contact Slipway's attorney while I changed the locks.

First, however, I pulled off the caper of the century! Knowing when Slipway was due back to pick up more of his belongings, I conspired with a neighbor to have him and his moll carried away by the cops for breaking and entering. We didn't catch them in flagrante, but close enough to mortify him. I don't think his accomplice has enough brain cells to feel mortified, but she did give the cops a good fight.

I actually met the moll when I visited Dallas last December. She is Tammi, of the infamous Tammi and Ike duo, late of Dallas, Texas. I say late, because apparently Ike has been given his walking papers, and Tammi has hitched onto Slipway's star. According to reliable sources, she even tried to manage his exit interview with the Benefits Department!

   Stay tuned for the denouement.
I haven't felt this good in months!

Fondly,
Emily

   P. S. I don't want you to think I ignored your lovely offer to come out here to help, but I need to take care of this nasty matter myself. It's what I need to retrieve my self-esteem. Please know how much I appreciate your friendship. I'd really like to see you when we can celebrate victory.

• • •

Wednesday, February 23

Dear Emily,

BRAVA!!!!! You are a wonder! You and Gretchen Battle will knock this guy out of the ring! I'd love to be a fly on the wall when you have your day in court, but I'll have to settle for the details you want to share. Maybe you should write about this someday.

   I'll be delighted to celebrate with you when this is all over, so just say the word.
   You're almost there, friend, so go for it!

Your grinning fan,
Ian

CHAPTER 44

—

DAY IN COURT

S lipway and I are subpoenaed for depositions on consecutive days. Like the Japanese tale, "Rashomon," our stories differ radically.

In preparation for Slipway's deposition, Gretchen reviews the questions she'll include and then asks me, "Are there any other questions you'd like answered?"

"Yes, when he was leaving, he said he wanted to 'soar and live on the edge.' That's not his language. Ask him if he got that from his astrologer."

My deposition takes place in a small room at the courthouse—neutral territory, I suppose. Slipway's attorney, Jean Hastings, is a plain-looking, tailored woman in her 40s. She wears her shoulder-length, beige hair parted in the middle and tucked behind her ears, which bear the weight of heavy, gold-stud earrings. Her suit is beige, matching her low-heeled pumps. I imagine her fading into the beige walls of our narrow deposition cell. Gretchen's charcoal gray suit doesn't enliven the environment either. The court stenographer sits tucked into a corner in her navy blazer and gray slacks. I feel like a flashing neon sign in my new, royal blue suit, which looked adequately subdued on the rack at Filene's.

Slipway's attorney introduces herself and asks me relatively straightforward questions. Gretchen sits beside me, ready to support me and ask for clarification if necessary.

The only sticky queries concern my not working full-time. Apparently, Slipway has claimed that he wanted me to work full-time to "do my share," and I refused, despite his pleas. I do my best to refute his claim, describing our financial relationship, my layoffs, and search for full-time employment in a depressed economy. I also report Slipway's wish that I work only part-time so we could travel when he retired. I'm not sure I've convinced Jean, but Gretchen smiles encouragingly at me.

"Now, Mrs. Slipway, we have just one issue more to go over. I have Mr. Slipway's list of items he claims as his property and wants to remove from the home upon settlement of your divorce. Have you brought your list?"

I present my list to Jean with a copy for Gretchen. The list includes furniture, clothing, kitchenware, paintings and other decorative pieces, books, and miscellaneous items—all my possessions before the unfortunate merger. I also list the few pieces of jewelry he's given me, not sure who owns them now.

The two attorneys review my list while the stenographer and I wait. She smiles sympathetically, but I don't want to expect anything in this dreary place.

Jean hands me two sheets of paper, explaining, "This is Mr. Slipway's list. I'd like you to look at it to see if you dispute any of his property claims. I also would like to ask you one or two questions regarding his list, if I may."

"Sure," I reply, looking at the long, detailed list in my hands.

She asks why we both list the dining room table and chairs. I explain that while Slipway's small, mahogany table and chairs occupy the dining room, my older oak table and chairs are stored in the basement. We review a couple of similar items.

"One more question, Mrs. Slipway. If you look at the bottom of page 2, you see listed: 'One Power Strip.' Can you please tell me, what is a power strip?"

"Really? That's on the list?" I struggle for an explanation and finally say, "It's like a large extension cord with a series of outlets in it… so you can plug in several appliances at once."

Both attorneys roll their eyes.

They thank me for my time and put their papers back into their briefcases. The stenographer packs up her equipment and, as I walk around the large conference table toward the door, she hands me her card. "If you ever want to work in the court system, please call me. I may be able to help."

A week later, I receive a large manila envelope in the mail—the transcript of Slipway's deposition. Flipping through the pages, I spot his righteous indignation that I didn't carry my financial load, that I didn't support his career choices (?), that I demanded complete obedience (??), and other items of outrage. I want to stop reading when I see a reference to my indifferent housekeeping. I continue reading, looking for a specific question and answer segment.

"Mr. Slipway," my attorney asks, "is it true that when you were leaving Mrs. Slipway, you told her you 'wanted to soar and live on the edge?'"

"I might have said that."

"Was this something suggested to you by your astrologer?"

"Well… not exactly."

"Where exactly did you get this idea?"

"Uh, er, from my horoscope in the *American Airlines Magazine.*"

Now, I'm cringing in chagrin. I can feel the tsunami of hot flashes surging and enflaming my body. My attorney and his attorney, two smart, savvy women, have been witness to his idiocy and my excruciatingly bad judgment.

As if this mortification isn't enough to send me underground forever, my phone rings, and before I can get to it, I hear my mother's voice on the answering machine.

"Hello, Emily, this is your mother. Remember me? I haven't heard from you in days and I'm worried. Please call me the minute you get this message. I'm losing sleep. By the way, you need to change your message. You still have that jerk's voice on the phone. Get rid of it! Call me! Love, your mother."

My mother hasn't yet mastered the art of voice messaging. She's improving, however; at first, she'd hang up if she got the machine. I'd hear a pause and deep sigh before the click.

I'd like to ignore her message for a while, but she'll call the FBI. I return her call after 6:00 when I know she and Raspberry have finished dinner and their evening stroll.

"Hello, Mum."

"Who is this?" she replies. "I don't recognize the voice."

"Come on, Mum. It hasn't been that long."

"At least a week."

"Three days, and I've been busy."

"Too busy to call your mother who's been sitting by the phone, worrying? Emily, what's going on?"

"Slipway and I gave our depositions last week. I just got copies and have been reading the outrageous accusations he's made about me."

"You sound surprised. Why would you expect anything else from that slug?"

She sounds like Dr. Rothman.

"I don't know. I just didn't think he'd be so vindictive."

"You remind me of that saying, 'Fool me once, shame on you. Fool me twice, shame on me.'"

I sigh and feel my throat tightening and hot tears trickling down my cheeks. "I know."

"He says I demanded complete obedience."

I hear heavy breathing and a slight asthmatic whistle.

"Mum, are you okay?"

"Complete obedience? If anything, you haven't demanded enough. Your father and I always worried you were too much of a softy. What is he saying, you're Dora, the Dominatrix?"

"Dora?" I begin to giggle.

"Whatever. You know what I mean," she huffs. "That man is a no-good wimp. That's why he's such a sneak." She pauses, "What the hell is he talking about?"

"The only thing I can think of is that I didn't want him to drink because he said he'd had problems in the past. I thought he agreed his drinking wasn't a good idea, but it turns out he resented that."

"Now he can go drink himself loopy and good riddance to the *shikker*," my mother says. "*Abi gezunt dos leben ken men zikh ale mol nemen.*"

"What does that mean?"

"You know *shikker*. Means a lush."

"What about the rest of it?"

My mother chuckles, "stay healthy, because you can kill yourself later."

We both laugh.

"Since when do you use so much Yiddish?"

"Sometimes when I get angry, I talk like your grandmother. So what else did he say?"

"That I didn't keep up my financial end and didn't work full-time."

"That's what he wanted."

"He's saying otherwise and that may hurt me."

"You see he really is a *gonif*, a thief. Not enough to steal your heart. Now he's going for everything else."

"He also said I was a bad housekeeper. He mentioned dust bunnies on the stairs."

"You gotta give him that one."

"Mum!"

We laugh again.

"I've heard enough, Emily. The man is an idiot and you're well rid of him. He'd be nothing but more trouble down the road—a boozer, womanizer, and grifter. I wasn't impressed when I met him but you were happy and nothing I said would have made a difference. Right?"

"Right," I agree.

"Let him ride off into the sunset with his Texas-Two-Stepping Tootsie. Good luck to them."

"You know, for some strange reason, I feel a lot better, Mum. Thanks."

"Me, too," she says. "One more thing, Emily. Get rid of that ridiculous name."

I laugh. "I love you."

"Love you, too." My mother is laughing as she hangs up. "Keep me posted, please. Call once in a while."

CHAPTER 45

—

TWO MEETINGS
AND A FUNERAL

Two weeks before our meeting with Will and his attorney and appearance before the judge, Gretchen and I meet in her office for a final consultation.

"One sticking point," Gretchen says, smiling at me kindly from across her large mahogany desk. "Mr. Slipway still claims that you didn't carry your share of the financial load and refused to find full-time employment. I know you addressed this in your deposition, but it's still our Achilles heel."

I can feel despair and then indignation rising in my chest. I take a deep breath. "That's not true. He discouraged my working full-time."

"At this point," Gretchen replies, "it's your word against his. Do you have any witnesses? Anyone who heard him say he didn't want you to work full-time?"

She pauses thoughtfully, tapping her pen against her lower lip.

I close my eyes, trying to dig up a nugget I know must be buried in my memory.

"Wait… yes, I do have a friend, Callie Stephanotis. She's a perfect witness!" I hastily explain, "I remember she called me after I had taken Will to meet her. She wanted to apologize for her behavior."

• • •

"I'm so sorry, Em, I think I really blew it with Will. While you were basting the roast with my Fred, I grilled Will about his intentions. None of my business, I know. I just didn't want to see you hurt again. When he told me he wanted to take care of you and didn't want you to have to work, I think I lost it."

"Why? What did you say?"

"Something like, 'Emily doesn't need anyone to take care of her. She's perfectly capable of doing that herself. What she needs is someone who recognizes that and appreciates her for who she is.'"

• • •

I look at Gretchen, who is smiling. "Will this help?"

"You bet. Do you think she'll remember this conversation?"

"You bet," I reply. "Callie will remember verbatim. She's one of the sharpest women I know. Should have been a lawyer."

Gretchen grins. "Will she testify if we need her?"

"You betcha."

• • •

Gretchen and I meet outside the courthouse minutes before our encounter with Slipway and his attorney—a preliminary to the divorce hearing before the judge. I'm discouraged because we're no closer to agreement on the specifics of the settlement. Gretchen has been unable to move Jean or Slipway from their insistence that I deserve nothing from him. What can she do at this point? What if we have to go to trial? My stomach churns.

In her striped, gray pantsuit, Gretchen stands at the top of the granite steps, a monument of fortitude and strength. Her stature awes me. I, on the other hand, am trembling, anxious about today's outcome, and afraid I'll sweat right through my newly pressed, navy suit. I follow Gretchen into the courthouse, focusing on her mighty stride that promises to part the roiling waters.

Slipway and his attorney, Jean, are waiting in a court anteroom—a small, dingy, windowless cell. Slipway stands as we enter—the consummate gentleman, his manners a slick, outer skin, poised to shed when he strikes. He's wearing a navy blazer, wine-colored tie, and gray slacks. Is that the blazer I picked out at Bloomingdale's?

After polite preliminaries, Jean addresses Gretchen. "Judge Kaplan will want us to come in with a proposed settlement and figure. She has no patience for haggling, as you well know."

The judge is a woman! That could be good. Maybe not. Look at the crazy female bosses I've had—-Bethany, who talked about herself in the third person, Mallory, who spied on us, Liz, who slapped an employee…Wait, some have been great. Stop this. I'm making myself dizzy with speculation.

Gretchen, focused on her task, nods. "We're ready if you are."

Three sentences into her attorney jargon and jive, Jean comes to the point. "Since the marriage lasted barely five years, my client, although willing to pay Mrs. Slipway's court costs, does not believe she is entitled to more than that."

"My client sees it differently," Gretchen counters. "We've been over these grounds several times. Despite the recession and two layoffs, Mrs. Slipway has sought full-time work, determined to contribute financially to the marriage. It was Mr. Slipway who encouraged her part-time employment so they might enjoy more time together. She is due compensation and support to help her get reestablished."

"You know my client tells a different story," Jean rebuts. "He states that Mrs. Slipway was unwilling to pursue full-time employment despite his urging her to do so. Frankly, it's just her word against his."

I look at Slipway, searching for a twitch or any sign that he acknowledges this lie. Nothing but a smirk.

"On the contrary," Gretchen says, removing papers from her leather case. "Mrs. Slipway has a witness—someone who participated in a discussion with your client about Mrs. Slipway's future and career. The witness is willing to testify if necessary."

Handing the papers to Jean, Gretchen turns toward Will, the snake. "Mr. Slipway, do you remember talking with a Callie Stephanotis, a friend of Mrs. Slipway's?"

I look at Will, who frowns as if puzzled. "I'm not sure," he finally stammers.

"She remembers meeting you. In fact, she vividly remembers her conversation with you. Perhaps you should also look at the statement she gave me." Gretchen slides a set of papers across the table to him.

As Slipway reads the document, his face pales to ash, and his hands tremble. He whispers in his attorney's ear.

"I need a few moments to confer with my client," Jean says, pushing her chair back and signaling Slipway to follow her out of the room.

Once the door closes, I give Gretchen a high five. We both grin.

When the plaintiff's attorney and her client return from their caucus, they might as well be waving a white flag.

Waiting until Jean and Slipway are seated again, Gretchen says, "Let's talk about numbers."

• • •

We stand in the courtroom, waiting for Judge Kaplan's entrance. My knees are shaking. Judge Kaplan strides through a door to the left of the bench, her black robe flowing. I see an angel floating in on shimmering wings, a fairy godmother. Her silver hair is cut short around her ears. Her tortoise shell glasses rest halfway down her nose; her wrinkles and crow's feet signal hope. The woman is older than I am! I squeal under my breath. Gretchen peers at me.

"A slight wheeze," I murmur.

Slipway and I stand beside our attorneys as they hand documents to the judge. I struggle to focus on the words that are exchanged, distracted by my trembling limbs, the rivulet of perspiration trickling down my back, and my need to pee. Before total panic sets in, I begin to practice my kegel exercises, praying it's not too little, too late.

Judge Kaplan peers down at us. "I believe I've seen these financial statements already. Is there anything new I should consider?"

"Yes, Your Honor," Jean speaks, radiating respect, while Slipway shifts from one foot to the other.

"Mr. Slipway," the Judge asks, "are you all right?"

"Yes, Your Honor." Slipway stands still, frozen in place. Jean glares at him.

"Your Honor," Jean resumes, "recently Mr. Slipway has undergone a sudden and dramatic change in circumstances, having been retired by his company. These documents indicate the terms of his retirement. You will see his circumstances have been dramatically altered."

"Mr. Slipway was let go?"

"No, he was retired."

"So, this is not the same as a layoff?" Judge Kaplan reads the documents Jean has handed her. "Is this what you call a golden handshake, Counselor?"

"I'm not sure that term applies, Your Honor. You can see Mr. Slipway's income will be reduced with the change in employment status."

"It doesn't seem that he will suffer. The retirement benefits seem adequate to me. Do you have any more documents to offer, Counselor?"

"No, Your Honor." Jean steps back from the bench.

"Attorney Battle, do you have anything more?"

"Yes, Your Honor. When Mrs. Slipway married Mr. Slipway, she had just completed graduate school and was about to embark on a new career. However, Mr. Slipway did not want her to work full-time so that they could spend more time together and eventually travel. After experiencing two layoffs, my client reluctantly acquiesced. She has worked only part-time and has not established herself in her new career. Mrs. Slipway needs sufficient time and adequate monetary support to allow her to get back on her feet, establish her career, and maintain a reasonable lifestyle. We are asking for a lump-sum payment to enable her to achieve these goals."

I want to applaud but, instead, concentrate on my kegels.

Jean briefly protests, "The marriage lasted less than five years, Your Honor, and it was not meant to guarantee a lifetime annuity."

I think I hear Slipway silently snickering.

"No, it is not meant to do that, Counselor. However, when Mrs. Slipway entered this marriage, she was about to launch a new career, having just completed graduate school. Now, she has lost five valuable years and is at an age when it will be difficult to compensate for that loss of time and income. I believe that Mr. Slipway has an obligation to help Mrs. Slipway re-establish her career and become a self-sustaining member of society. Having reviewed all financial documents, I grant the defendant the amount of alimony requested—to be paid in total by the end of the calendar month. I hereby grant divorce according to the laws of the Commonwealth of Massachusetts."

"Thank you, Your Honor, one more matter if I may," Gretchen says.

"Yes, what is it?"

"Mrs. Slipway asks that she resume her maiden name."

"Request granted. Please handle that with the court clerk. Hearing dismissed."

CHAPTER 46

—

OVER THE MOON

I wait until we're outside the courthouse to plant an exuberant kiss on Gretchen's cheek.

"You are Wonder Woman, my superhero! How can I ever repay you?"

Gretchen chuckles, hugging me. "Just live well and enjoy."

I'm so excited I have to sit quietly in my car and calm myself before I dare to drive home. I list the people I have to call with my good news—my mother, my kids, Callie, Shelley, my book group—and I have to tell Dr. Rothman and Ian.

On cue, I feel a breeze and hear a harrumph. "You don't need to tell me anything. I saw it all. Congratulations, Ms. Rosenbloom. You and Ms. Battle whopped his ass," Dr. Rothman says.

"Is that clinical terminology for 'justice has been served?'"

"You could say that," he chuckles.

I put the car in gear, shouting, "Yahoo!" as I peel out of the parking lot—"Gunner Rosenbloom rides again!"

Once home, I leave the car in the driveway, too impatient to park in the garage. Besides, I've heaped trash bags full of Slipway's clothes, shoes, and electronics against the walls. It's not a pretty sight. He was supposed to pick them up a week ago but never showed. I'm hoping for a monsoon with flash flooding on our sloping driveway. I'd love to see those bags bobbing on oil-slicked waves.

I reach my mother on the first ring.

"I've been waiting on pins and needles. Have you been in court all this time?"

"Almost, it took a while to finalize the paperwork…"

"So, what's the bottom line?"

"We won!" I tell my mother all the details, my voice rising in excitement.

"I knew you could do it," my mother says. "I knew you wouldn't let that guy get away with anything."

"All he's getting away with is the junk I stuffed into garbage bags in the garage."

We hoot in unison.

"Send your attorney a big bunch of flowers," my mother says. "It's always good to say a special thank you."

"Good idea," I agree.

An hour later, I reach Callie and we arrange to meet at Joe's Hamburger Joint for a celebratory burger.

Callie lurches toward me on navy platform shoes, grinning triumphantly and carrying a large bouquet of red, yellow, and purple tulips.

"I should be giving you flowers," I protest, "not the other way around."

"That would look like a payoff, my dear." Callie places the bouquet carefully on the table. "You can give me a big hug, however."

"Thanks to you, Callie, and your big, brilliant mouth and memory, I have scored a major victory! We have skinned the snake."

Callie laughs. "Maybe we should make snake soup."

"Ew, I can't imagine."

"I'll have you know that snake soup has been considered a delicacy in China for over two thousand years. It's regarded as a high status dish, a symbol of wealth and bravery."

"This snake would poison the broth, but I appreciate the thought. Your brain is filled with amazing esoterica."

"My Fred has another word for it. He says I'm a hoarder with a headful of clutter."

"Thank goodness for that. If you hadn't remembered that conversation with Slipway, you wouldn't be sitting across from a wealthy woman now. I have enough dough to treat you to this hamburger, shake, and even dessert."

"I'll drink to that." Callie lifts her strawberry milkshake and takes a healthy swig.

I lift my coffee milkshake, a real splurge, and click my glass against hers.

"Let's drink to the defeat and downfall of all slimy creatures in the universe! God save the Commonwealth of Massachusetts and Judge Kaplan, the wisest, most ancient, and most honorable jurist in the land."

"And to the toughest, smartest attorney, too. What was her name?"

"Battle, Gretchen Battle."

"Perfect," Callie says, taking another swig.

We dive into our burgers, savoring every bite of medium-rare beef until Callie pauses to digest and ask, "So, what's next, pal?"

"Next, I throw a party for all my dear supporters. Then the townhouse goes up for sale. I move, probably into a month-to-month rental while I figure out what comes after that."

"Would you consider buying him out and staying where you are?"

"Nope. I have no love for the place, although some neighbors do put on a good show."

"Ah, the flasher," Callie giggles.

"I may be ready for a big move."

"What do you mean big? Florida, to be near your mother?"

"Neither of us is ready for that. Did I tell you an eight-foot-alligator showed up a week ago in her neighbor's pool?"

"What was it doing there?"

"The breaststroke. Who knows? Can you imagine me living with my mother, alligators, and 98% humidity? I'd be better off taking my chances with another two-legged snake."

"Bite your tongue," Callie snaps.

"I was kidding. I've learned my lesson. No more Slipways."

"What's a big move then?"

"I don't know yet, but I want adventure! I've lived most of my life within a 40-mile radius of Boston. It's time to move out of my comfort zone. Time's a-wastin' and I'm not getting any younger."

• • •

Friday, April 14

Dear Ian,

This letter should be accompanied by "The 1812 Overture" and fireworks exploding across the sky! Victory is mine! I am divorced and Slipway has been vanquished! I've even returned to my maiden name. I am Emily Rosenbloom.

I am thrilled with the outcome. Thanks to Gretchen Battle and a fair-minded, age-appropriate female judge—no bias suggested—I have been awarded enough money to reinvent myself. I feel as though I've done that several times already, but maybe this is what 21st-century life is about.

I am sending the biggest, most gorgeous bouquet of roses, tulips, and peonies to Gretchen. She deserves every petal. Then I'm either going to treat special people to dinners or throw a big party—I haven't decided which yet. You're in that category, so I owe you a delicious night out.

Then, I'll probably take a long nap and maybe treat myself to a day at a spa before I begin to pack up and move out. The house is going on the market immediately. Slipway is anxious to sell and "soar and live on the edge." Did I tell you about that declaration of independence? It was one of the last things he said to me as he scurried out the door. It reverberates in my brain. "I want to soar and live on the edge." When Gretchen questioned him in his deposition, she asked if that was an idea he got from his astrologer. Not exactly. He confessed he had read it in his horoscope in an American Airlines Magazine!

Good luck on soaring in Dallas!

While he soars and hovers on the edge, I'm going to rent a furnished apartment until I decide on my next move. That's as far as I've gotten. I'll keep you posted, I promise.

Ian, thank you again for your caring and support. You deserve a big bunch of flowers, too!

Fondly,
Emily (Rosenbloom—yay!)

• • •

Tuesday, April 18

Dear Emily Rosenbloom,

Congratulations!! I knew you could do it! I wish I were there to celebrate with you. I'll definitely take you up on your offer of a night on the town. Maybe we can light those fireworks to the accompaniment of "The 1812 Overture." The sky's the limit.

I'm delighted for you and eager to know what's next. It sounds as though you'll be busy for a while with your move. Is it easy to find a furnished apartment in your area?

I know you're probably anxious to move on, but they say it's wise to give yourself time and not make major decisions hastily. I sound like an old fart. Who are "they" and what do "they" know anyway? You follow your gut. It's been leading you well lately, hasn't it?

Trust yourself, Emily.

Fondly,
Your West Coast Fan

CHAPTER 47
—
THE LAST CHAPTER

I lie on the lumpy mattress in my furnished apartment, trying not to wonder who slept here last. I'm watching two crows on the branch of the elm tree, playing tug of war with a twig. It's been eight months since I tossed my keys back over my shoulder and buried my second marriage. After an interval of mourning, which included the benefit of weight loss, I've begun to really enjoy life after Slipway. I can go to foreign films. I can eat in bed, scattering toast crumbs onto the sheets. I can take off for a weekend at Tanglewood, sit on the lawn, and listen to Saint-Saens' Third Violin Concerto or James Taylor and his All-Star Band.

Yet, as I watch the wrestling crows, I wonder if this is it. Am I doomed to labor in a part-time job as exciting and limp as last week's lettuce? Will I always live in a furnished apartment in a town that feels stale? I continue to look for full-time work, reach out to friends, and collect vacation brochures, but my heart isn't in it. Enough of this ruminating. Time to act.

I roll out of bed, grab fresh clothes, and head for the shower. I've slathered my hair in shampoo that smells like lavender and am luxuriating in the ultra-warm shower spray when I hear the phone ring. I hesitate, wondering if I should jump out of the shower. No, this feels too good.

My machine will pick up the message. After receiving a couple of calls from strangers looking for Slipway, I've changed my message to: "You have reached 617-345-7881. I can't take your call. If you're looking for Slipway, you'll find him two-stepping with his crackerjack cowgirl somewhere in the Texas Panhandle."

My friends tell me this isn't wise. "After all," they say, "you don't want to let the Boston Strangler know you're living alone."

When I've dressed and finally managed to shape my recalcitrant curls into something resembling a hairstyle, I walk into the kitchen to see if I have a message. The light is flashing.

"Hi, Emily. It's Nancy Newman, your long-lost pal from college. I just heard you and your husband have split. I'd love to talk with you. Give me a call."

She's left a phone number with a familiar exchange. It takes me a minute to realize she must live in San Francisco now. My older son, Gabe, and his fiancée, Jocelyn moved out there after grad school in Chicago. I'd hoped they'd return to Boston and was so disappointed, but they have jobs with Apple and Google, the hottest tech companies on the planet. I've been out to visit them a couple of times and have fallen in love with San Francisco. On my first visit, I took scads of photos, mostly of Victorian houses and cypress trees. I was smitten. I've toyed with the idea of moving there, but I don't know anyone else in the area and don't want to risk becoming too dependent on family.

I punch in Nancy's number. She answers on the second ring.

"Expecting an important call, Missy?" I ask, teasing.

"Emily! I'd know that voice and attitude anywhere. How are you?"

"Better than I should be."

Nancy laughs. "After Emily's Folly?"

"Long story—my ill-fated marriage to Slipway, the two-timing viper. You've probably heard the ugly details from one of the gang."

"Kate filled me in. I'm sorry, friend."

"Thanks, but I'm better off, really. Pickled snake may be a delicacy somewhere but not in my yard."

"A drinker and a philanderer? Lucky you to be rid of him!"

"Sounds like you're speaking from recent experience."

"How did you guess? Ethan, the downwardly mobile Stanford graduate, who tends bar while he auditions for the role that will bring him stardom. Forget what you've heard about the joys of dating younger men. Sex was great, but it turns out he was like a flea, jumping on any bare leg!"

I giggle. "How old was he?"

"I dunno, 10 maybe?"

After my romp with the serpent in the Garden of Eden, who am I to judge?

"Emily, talking with you feels like old times. I miss you."

"Me, too," I sigh. "Since when are you out in San Francisco? Last I knew you were in Minneapolis, working at the Mayo Clinic."

"Good job. Bad climate. I'm not a winter girl. I hate having to take a pickax and blowtorch to break up ice on my steps. I came out to the Bay Area on vacation and never went back. I love this city, and I've got a job in social services at UC Medical Center, which brings me to the reason I called. I'd love it if you'd come visit me. I have an extra bedroom and you're welcome to stay as long as you like."

"Wow, that's quite a generous offer—so tempting. Let me think about it. Did you know my older son and his fiancée are out there? It would be great to see them, too."

"Absolutely. Come out anytime."

A week later, I wake with excitement at 3 a.m. I have been dreaming about San Francisco. In my dream, I'm not visiting. I'm living there in an apartment in one of those Victorians I love, high ceilings, lots of light—a fresh start. I sigh as I get out of bed and walk out to the living room, open the curtains to await early morning light, and sink onto the sturdy, brown rental couch that's built for durability, not comfort.

What would it be like to live in San Francisco—a beautiful city? Nothing familiar, but that's the problem. I'd be a stranger in a strange land.

A shifting air current ruffles the beige curtains. "Getting a bit melodramatic, aren't we? Stranger in a strange land? Wasn't that a sci-fi novel in the 60s?"

Dr. Rothman plumps a beige pillow and settles against it on the other end of the couch. He's wearing a beige shirt and slacks, so only his pale, dumpling face keeps him from disappearing into the background. His legs barely reach the floor.

Wait! What am I seeing? I usually hear Dr. Rothman's voice and sense his presence, but I haven't really seen his chubby self since we terminated therapy years ago and I hugged him goodbye at his office door.

"What are you doing here?"

"Don't I always show up when you need me?"

"Not in person! Not on my sofa. Not in a beige polyester shirt."

"What's wrong with it?"

"Please, you know what I mean. I can see you."

Dr. Rothman grins. "The occasion called for a dramatic gesture. You've been stuck in a rut for months and it looked as though you were about to dig that rut into a canyon."

"I've needed time to recover," I snap.

"But not wallow. I'd say time's up."

"I don't know what to do. I want to try something new and I've fantasized about moving to San Francisco since the first time I saw it."

"So, what's keeping you here?"

"I'm afraid. I'd have to make new friends, find a job, and learn to drive a stick shift on those hills. I once almost abandoned my son's Honda halfway up Telegraph Hill."

"Poor thing. And go to the San Francisco Symphony, the Asian Art Museum, Golden Gate Park, maybe a Giants game. Before we get all weepy, isn't that what you want? Besides, who's to say your move has to be permanent? If it doesn't work out, you can always come back."

"I keep going back and forth. I feel like I'm riding a teeter-totter and am about to lose my lunch."

"I know." Dr. Rothman hesitates, looking at his hands and then at me. "I don't mean this to be morbid, but if you were on your deathbed, would there be anything you'd regret not doing?"

I make a pot of coffee and try to wait until it's a decent hour in San Francisco. At 11 a.m., ET, I can't wait another minute. I call Nancy.

"Nance, about your invitation. When would your spare bedroom be available?"

• • •

Saturday, June 17

Dear Ian,

I've just made a life-altering decision and am about to embark on a major adventure. I'm moving to San Francisco in the early fall! I'm going to stay with my college roommate, Nancy Newman, who has an extra bedroom and is willing to put up with me while I job search and find my own place.

This isn't a decision made on a whim. I feel as though I've lived at least three lifetimes on the East Coast, and I've wanted to live in San Francisco since I first visited a couple of decades ago. Now's the time to try it out while I'm still young enough to get a job and make a new life. Besides, my older son and his fiancée are living there now and seem pretty settled on the West Coast. I don't know yet where my younger son will land.

It will be hard to leave my family and friends out here, but I'm hoping I'll lure them out for visits and will be able to travel back to the East Coast now and then.

Who knows if this will be permanent? I feel I have to give it a try.

I hope you and I can see each other from time to time. At least we won't be thousands of miles apart.

Fondly,
Emily

• • •

Thursday, June 22

Dear Emily,

Terrific news! You are a brave woman! I'm not sure I could pull up roots and make that kind of move at this point. I salute you for your spirit and applaud your decision, partly for selfish reasons.

I'd love to be able to visit back and forth, and it will be so much easier when you're out on this coast. Seattle and San Francisco are about two hours apart by air. I'd love to show you Seattle and I'd like to get to know San Francisco better. We'll have a good time in either city.

This is such good news! If there's any way I can help you with the move, please let me know.

I can't wait until you're out here.

Most fondly,
Ian

• • •

In October, before the leaves begin to fall, I load luggage, maps, and CDs into my trusty, rusty Toyota and am about to pull away from the curb when I feel a brisk breeze and hear a familiar wheeze.

"Wait!" Dr. Rothman slides through the passenger door and collapses into the seat beside me.

"Don't tell me you're coming with me!" I yelp.

"Just until we make it to the other side of the Rockies, and I can see you're still heading in the right direction."

We pull away from the curb and head West.

ABOUT THE AUTHOR

Elinor Gale has been a writer, observer of human nature, and lover of the English language since childhood. An inveterate eavesdropper, she has woven her curiosity about human behavior into her work as writing teacher, editor, and creator of humorous yet poignant fiction and poetry. Her essays, poetry, and articles have been published in print and online. Elinor moved to the Bay Area from New England 20 years ago. She lives in San Francisco with her partner and his chubby Burmese cat.

ACKNOWLEDGEMENTS

With deep appreciation to:

Gifted writing instructors Laurie Wagner, who taught me free flight in my writing, and Diane Frank, who helped me find my voice, inviting the poet in.

Mates in Diane Frank's fiction/memoir workshop, Claudia Bluhm, Elizabeth Kert, Bill Jones, and Thelma Swan Tucker, who motivated, challenged, and encouraged me.

All the other wonderful writers I've worked with in groups and classes, including Lynne Rappaport, Sue Barizon, Tice Swackhamer, Yvonne Lorvan, Laila Kramer, Kathie Evers, Pat Skala, L.J. Cranmer, Alice Lewis, Christie Allair, Deborah Crooks, and Elizabeth Gallagher.

Astute and helpful readers Lois Cosloy, Kent MacMaster, and Judy Wilson, who gave me invaluable feedback and encouragement. Sue Oliver, who helped me find the perfect language to describe my novel in 30 seconds or less.

Dedicated and skilled editor Cynthia Hanson, who helped me prepare my manuscript for publication with patience, perseverance, and good humor.

Final proofreaders, Lynne Rappaport, Genia Jones, Kent MacMaster, and Cynthia Hanson.

Artist and book designer Melanie Gendron.

Supportive and loving family and friends, who have always been in my corner, no matter what.

I thank you all!

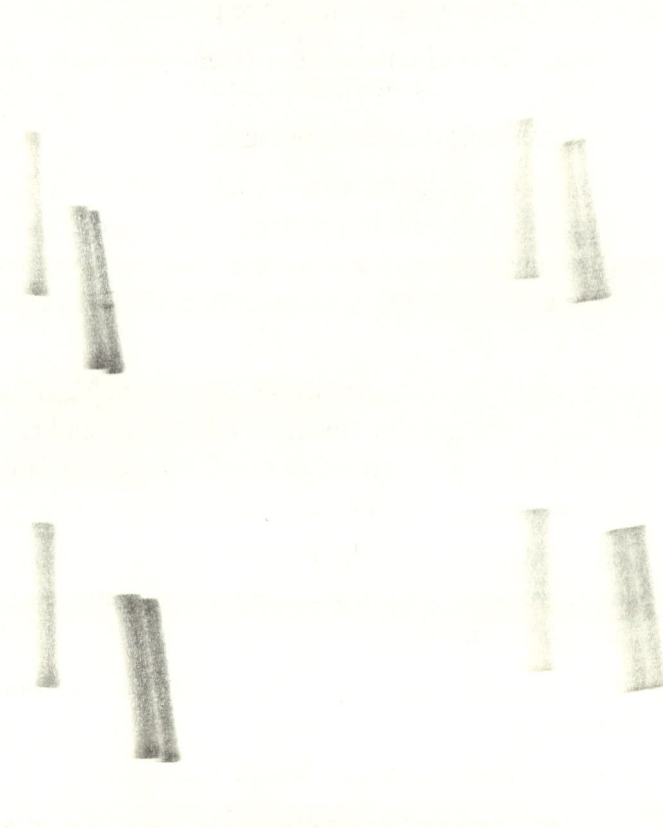

www.ingramcontent.com/pod-product-compliance
Lightning Source LLC
Chambersburg PA
CBHW022000010726
47494CB00003B/827